THE HAND HE DEALT

TANITH DAVENPORT

The Hand He Dealt
ISBN # 978-0-85715-735-5
©Copyright Tanith Davenport 2011
Cover Art by Posh Gosh ©Copyright 2011
Interior text design by Claire Siemaszkiewicz
Total-E-Bound Publishing

Published in 2011 by Total-E-Bound Publishing, Think Tank, Ruston Way, Lincoln, LN6 7FL, United Kingdom.

Manufactured in the USA.

THE HAND HE DEALT

Dedication

For Mark

Chapter One

A third red-backed card flipped over on the green baize. The ten of hearts.

"Twenty-four. Bust."

With a scowl, the man pushed his chips to the centre of the table and got up to leave.

"Too bad," Astra called after him. "Have a good night."

It was four in the morning and the casino was closing. Around the room, the croupiers were clearing their tables and preparing to leave. Astra's table was the first one closed—as the lights began to snap off she was already halfway to the door.

She passed another croupier, an attractive blonde, just unhooking her coat, her forehead smeared with blood, and she paused.

"Hey, Becky? What happened to you?"

The girl scowled. "Some jerk threw a glass at me. Think he just lost the expense account."

"Ugh. Men." Astra could taste the bitterness in her words. "They're all pricks."

The cold air hit her like a wall of ice. The skies were still pitch-dark. The night was clear, starlit, the edges of the full moon sharp. Streetlamps spilled pools of light across the sidewalk as Astra started the long walk home.

Thank God she didn't have an early lecture.

Across the street, shouts and raucous laughter filled the air as the door of a neon-fronted bar opened and a group of twenty-something men fell out. Astra's stomach twisted as a painful image forced its way into her mind.

Are you out tonight?

She dropped her head, fighting against the picture that haunted her. Oh God, she was beginning to hate this walk home. The surrounding dark engulfed her like a wave, weakening her, dragging her down.

Every time you do this, I lose another part of you, something I'm afraid to forget.

Her feet knew the way home as well as her mind did.

I can't remember the scent of your hair.

It was amazing how quickly the sidewalk was passing.

I can't remember the feeling of your breath on my neck.

It really wasn't such a long walk after all.

She broke into a run, one hand over her face, tears choking her. Astra stumbled up the main road through the campus and into the Omega Zeta sorority house. She dashed up the stairs to the first floor, dived into the bathroom and locked herself in a cubicle.

It was stupid to feel this way. Stupid. But the aching feeling of loss was rarely absent these days.

She had only herself to blame. She had been too intelligent, too arrogant, to believe she could lose herself in the intense gaze of a pair of blue eyes. Too clever to recognise her own weakness in the face of a cheeky smile.

Fuck. The door had opened. She wiped her face and stepped out of the cubicle, her carefully-crafted neutral expression dissolving when she saw the girl turning away from her reflection.

"Sash."

"Astra?" Sasha looked her up and down in concern. "Are you okay? What's…"

"Don't ask."

Sasha nodded slowly and turned back to the mirror with an assumed casualness.

"Oh — by the way. News."

"Oh, yeah?"

"It's Ash."

"Oh, yeah?"

"He knows."

Astra caught herself in the middle of a third "Oh yeah?" and stepped behind Sasha. Their eyes met in the mirror.

"What?"

"Ash knows."

Astra leant back against the row of sinks and ran her hand through her hair in shock.

"Ash… Fuck."

Chapter Two

January, two months earlier

"Hey. Whatcha working on?"

Sasha glanced up from the sofa where she was lying full length, notepad in hand.

Just entering the sorority house lounge was a tall, slim girl with a lever arch file pressed against her chest, her left hand wrapped around the neck of a Fender electric guitar. As she crossed the room, her gait had a lazy rhythm that suggested the beat of an inaudible song.

"Hey, Astra."

Astra dropped her file on the arm of the sofa and leaned over it to grin down at her friend. Catlike green eyes glinted in a heart-shaped face, framed by a mane of dark red, fire-streaked hair.

"That better be a party plan. Only three hours till they get here."

"It's a lab report, thank you." Sasha threw the notepad at Astra, who deflected it to the coffee table. "The party's ready to go. I had the girls doing the food all afternoon."

"Who did you rope in to *that*?"

"The usual. Liddy—Starla—Sveta. Aimee and Leonie picked up the drinks, everyone else was out at class. Did you get the absinthe?"

"It's in my room."

Astra threw herself backwards onto the neighbouring couch, leaving the file balanced precariously where it was and the electric guitar propped against the table.

"God, I'll be glad to cut loose tonight. I've been buried in coursework almost all fucking day."

"You don't have enough hours. Gaming Management my ass. Do you know how much lab time I put in?"

An uncontrollable giggle was Astra's response. Blonde, blue-eyed and rosy-cheeked, with a high-pitched voice and a substantial cleavage that constantly threatened to escape her shirt, Sasha looked more like one who put in more mirror time than lab time.

"It's your own fault, science geek."

"Vocational void."

Laughing, Sasha ducked as a pen flew over her head.

"When's your next shift, anyway?"

"Tomorrow night."

"Night shift again. You do nothing but flip cards and party—I don't know when you ever sleep. You live by starlight."

Astra arched her back like a cat and stretched. "You know me so well."

"Give me data entry any day." Sasha leaned over to pick up her notepad, beat the air with her fingertips, then gave up, too lazy to reach the table. "I see you've been jamming again."

"Yeah, Tori and I went down to the music centre for an hour." Astra stretched one hand out and idly plucked the strings of the Stratocaster. "There's nothing like a bit of Michelle Branch to ease the mind."

"And nothing like a party to ease the body."

"Ash coming tonight?" Astra asked, one eyebrow raised meaningfully. She had never known Sasha's boyfriend to miss a party. His own fraternity was renowned for having keggers that lasted all weekend.

"Yeah – Harry coming?" Sasha responded, equally pointedly.

"Oh yes. Repeatedly, with any luck."

"Yeah, well, if you two disappear upstairs, can you try and make it to your room this time? I'm still having therapy."

Astra's response was cut off by a sticky-sounding explosion from the kitchen, followed by a shriek of, "Oh *fuck!*" Sasha was on her feet and heading for the doorway at once.

"Was that tequila jelly?" Her voice carried as she crossed the hallway. "I told you *not* to do it in the microwave! Oh, for God's sake, the door's hanging off! Astra, I'll see you later, okay?"

Shaking with laughter, Astra stood up, collected her file and guitar and headed for the staircase, calling, "See ya!" as Sasha's outraged voice continued to rage in the kitchen.

Omega Zeta was one of the smaller sorority houses on campus, built in a modern style with a sweep of uneven steps leading to an elegant stone exterior. Decorated in clean creams and inviting golds, it gave the impression of being contemporary yet inexpensive, with deep red sofas in the lounge and a polished hardwood table in the white-tiled kitchen. Astra had chosen it partially for its charitable work with the homeless and partially for the sake of having a single bedroom, which was a rarity among the houses.

She made her way around the top floor of the house, one long corridor panelled with bedroom doors, running around a central bathroom. When she reached her room on the opposite side, she unlocked the door and went in.

She threw her file down on the double bed, then paused at the sink to check her hair, and winced. Straightening, definitely. She stepped over the guitar stand, crossed to the shelves along the far wall and moved aside one of her cheerleading trophies to retrieve the hair straighteners before scanning the room for her hairspray.

Ah, there it was. She threw herself across the bed and lifted the can from the bedside cabinet, knocking over a photo frame as she did so. She glanced at it as she picked it up, and smiled. It was her favourite family photo— herself in full cheer uniform, flanked by her older sister Emmy, who was smiling openly and holding up a stylised movie clapperboard; and her younger brother, Dashiell, wearing the uniform of a high school linebacker. On the wall in the background was a collection of posters which now covered her bedroom walls—mostly rock stars, interspersed regularly with shots of the Las Vegas Strip.

Party in three hours. Just enough time to get ready. She opened the wardrobe door and scanned the hangers for a particular blue-green dress with an asymmetric hemline— Harry's favourite.

Harry was a computer science student from Beta Phi. They had met six months previously, at the end of the last academic year, and had carried on a relationship over the summer, as her casino job and his bar job had required them both to remain in town. Harry had since quitted the bar job as his workload had increased, but somehow always had free time whenever he wanted it.

Harry. Just thinking his name made Astra grin. Though he claimed he couldn't see it, Harry was one of the most unconventionally attractive men on campus. Well, she thought so, anyway. He was tall—taller than her, at least—and slim, with a heart-shaped face, vivid blue eyes and dark hair that was always in a mess. Though he was her age, twenty-one, he looked younger than his years and had a swift, lithe way of moving that suggested somebody still in his teens. But what seduced the girls—what had seduced her, in fact—was his chameleonic range of expression. Looking serious he gave the impression he was thinking deep and meaningful thoughts, a widening of the eyes and he was vulnerable, his cheeky grin could light up a room, while his head-on gaze had an intensity that left girls weak in the knees.

He was also, of course, one of the most…adventurous…men she had ever met.

Astra hung the dress on the wardrobe door, then stripped off her clothes and wrapped herself in a towel ready to use the shower. She strained one ear towards the door to make sure Ash hadn't arrived early. The last thing she wanted was to run into him in the corridor.

Ash had made his presence felt at a start-of-year party in September. Six feet tall, slim and obviously athletic, he was clearly used to having an effect on women. His pointed face was framed by gelled-yet-floppy white-blond hair and punctuated by green eyes that were apparently supposed to knock girls dead on the spot. Astra had been unmoved by the fact he was on a football scholarship, although his choice of subject—geology—had come as something of a surprise. It had not, however, been a surprise to discover he was barely scraping by.

The manner of their meeting was something Sasha was unaware of, and Astra intended it to remain that way.

"Hey, Astra, what do you say we blow this place and you can blow me instead?"

Astra had initially pleaded 'taken', but had been pushed to reject him in earnest by his flat refusal to take no for an answer. He had picked up Sasha later at the same party and had flaunted his presence ever since, a fact that had not gone unnoticed by Harry, with whom Ash shared a mutual loathing. Ash despised Harry for his lack of obvious physicality, his English accent and his slight air of nerdiness—Harry despised Ash for his lack of brains, his excess of masculinity and his Stallone sneer. Seeing this, Astra and Sasha had dropped the idea of double-dating and made a point of keeping them apart whenever practical.

This was more difficult at parties, although not impossible.

* * * *

By ten, the party was in full swing.

In the lounge, a group of frat boys from Alpha Nu Mu were having a vodka shot contest. Liddy, one of the younger sorority members, was having tequila jelly eaten off her fingers by an enthusiastic jock. Techno music throbbed from the speakers. In the corner armchair, two people were squirming, one tickling the other into submission.

"Stop it, woman, you'll kill me…"

"Say it."

"All right, all right! You're the hottest girl in the room." Harry batted futilely at her hands as Astra raised an expectant eyebrow. "In the building. On the campus, all right? *Stop!*"

Astra collapsed in giggles, her face pressed to Harry's neck as he tried to look aggrieved.

"Get you a beer?"

"*Yes.* In a bottle. I'm too weak for a glass."

Standing up, Astra ruffled Harry's hair and smiled as he caught her wrist and kissed it. "I'll be back in a minute."

She made her way past chair after chair of wrestling couples into the hallway and across into the kitchen. The fridge, she knew, was fully stocked with enough beer to sink an ocean liner. As she reached inside for two bottles of Corona, she heard footsteps approaching behind her at a speed which suggested one person, and one person only.

She grabbed the bottles and spun around, slamming her back against the fridge door just as the person caught up with her.

"Ash."

Ash braced himself against the fridge door, a hand on either side of her head, thereby blocking her in. He fixed her with an intense stare, which she returned with interest.

"Astra."

After a short pause, Astra held up one of the bottles.

"Can I get you a beer?"

"If it comes with plenty of head. I hear you're good at that."

"What, coming with plenty of head? I hear you can't last two minutes."

Ash leaned closer to Astra, who took an involuntary breath at his proximity. He smiled.

"Hey, I'll return the favour."

"I'm taken." *You arrogant jerk.*

"So am I."

"She's my best friend."

"Seychelle won't mind."Astra snorted at his use of his nickname for Sasha—Sarah Michelle. "Trust me. She'd mind."

Ash leaned closer again. Astra, expecting this, arched unconcerned eyebrows. A smile was all he would get this time.

"I'm hotter than Harry."

Oh, he was hot. But still a jerk.

"And modest to match."

"I could tell you a few things about Harry."

And what was that supposed to mean? Astra paused briefly, but refused to give him the satisfaction of asking.

"I could tell you some better ones."

"You're a prick-tease."

"You're a prick."

Astra attempted to move his arm. When he held it firm, she slammed the bottle of beer into his chest and darted sideways, leaving the spluttering jock doubled over.

"Fucking tease," Ash spat behind her.

As Astra came into the hall, she saw Harry standing in the opposite doorway, features twisted in anger. Swiftly, she moved forward in time to block him.

"Leave it."

"One of these days," said Harry forcefully, "I'm going to slap him."

Astra rather doubted that, but kept her face straight. Harry was at least two inches shorter and considerably skinnier than Ash, who would have laughed for a week straight at the suggestion the computer geek could do him an injury.

Harry eyed the blond jock coolly for a moment, then pulled the bottle of beer out of Astra's hand and wrenched the top off, apparently deciding it was a safer outlet for his violent urges.

"Blond fuckwit."

"Oh, absolutely." Astra watched in some surprise as Harry downed the beer in one go. "Want this one, too?"

Harry looked at his watch. "Ah, hell. No, I'd better get off actually. I've got an early class." He pulled Astra over to the side, pressed her into the wall and kissed her. Astra responded by flicking her tongue into his mouth, running her hands up his spine and into his hair at the same time.

"Oh, stop…"

As he responded with desire, she ran her hands down to his hips and pressed them against her own.

Harry groaned as he came up for air. "Oh God, just you wait. I'll never get to sleep now."

"You'll find a way," Astra drawled, making a cocktail-shaker gesture with one hand.

Shaking his head, Harry disentangled himself. He started for the door. "I'll see you tomorrow, okay?"

"See you," Astra called, then turned and headed back into the lounge.

She had barely taken two steps before she was overtaken by Sasha, who stormed past her with the force of a tank.

"You all right there, Sash?"

"Ugh! That man!"

Ah. Right.

"What's he done?"

"He's stomping about in the kitchen like a bear with a sore ass. He's punched the carrot cake…"

Punched the…?

"…sprayed cold water all over me when he tried to wash his hand off, and he keeps asking me to suck his balls. I'm fed up. Where's the absinthe?"

Astra picked up a bottle from beside her ankle and handed it to Sasha. She turned to pick up a nearby empty glass, then paused as Sasha swigged straight from the bottle and offered it back.

"Where's Harry?"

"Gone home."

"Men." Sasha waited for Astra to finish drinking, then reclaimed the absinthe. "Ash is getting nothing tonight, I can tell you. I'm getting drunk."

"I think I'll join you."

* * * *

Midnight, and most of the rooms in Beta Phi were empty, their inhabitants out at one party or another. In his darkened room, Harry lay on the bed, dressed for sleep but wide awake and staring at the ceiling.

I should have told her. I should have.

He had meant to tell her for ages. Over and over it flitted into his mind, preventing him from drifting off.

She'll be so hurt. I can't do that.

Hell, he was confused enough without bringing her into it.

Why can't I just stop?

He couldn't tell Astra what was eating away at him. He was in love with her — he couldn't risk losing her, not for this.

Damn it, he was never going to fall asleep.

He was just about to roll off the bed and switch on his computer when there was a noise at the window. Raising himself off the pillow, he could just make out a shadow behind the curtain, struggling to lift up the sash.

What the…?

Before his brain had made contact with his body, the sash flew up and the figure crawled between the curtains onto the chest of drawers before sliding its feet down onto the floor. In the half-light he could make out a red glow around its hair.

"Astra?"

As the shape moved slowly, sinuously, across the room, the moonlight lit her from behind. Squinting, he became aware she was only wearing a satin vest and French knickers.

"Astra? Did you…?"

"Shhh," came the response as the figure mounted the bed, crawling catlike on all fours until she was level with his face. With a soft giggle, she rubbed her nose against his.

"Thought you might be still awake."

"Did you walk all the way from Omega Zeta like that?"

"Hell no." Astra sank down onto her elbows and nuzzled his neck, her body resting softly on top of his. "Took my clothes off on the fire escape before I came in."

Harry opened his mouth, but his voice caught and came out as a throaty moan. He laced his fingers into her hair, longing to kiss her.

"Might have to walk back like this though…"

"Oh God," Harry gasped, pulling her face down to his. As he kissed her, breathlessly, passionately, her hips rocked on top of his, brushing against the hardness he was now painfully aware of. He slid his hands to her buttocks, pressing her down against his crotch, aching to get some friction against her skin.

She ran her hand down his chest, over his stomach and down to his hip, then looked at him with an evil glint in her eye and slid down to where his boxer shorts were straining. With a soft moan, she wrapped one hand around his erection through the material and flicked her tongue across the head.

It was too soft for him to feel, but the moonlit outline was enough to make him gasp and buck his hips.

"Oh God, you... I..."

She hooked her hands on to his shorts and slowly slid them down his thighs, releasing him. Before he could catch his breath, she had the edge of his T-shirt in her hands, pushing it upwards, and he lifted off the bed to help her slip it over his shoulders. He pulled her back down on top of him and groaned at the feel of the satin lingerie sliding over his skin.

"I'm going to make you forget your name," she whispered, her breath tickling his ear.

Harry ran his hand down her back, over one satin-clad cheek, and came to a shuddering stop between her legs.

"You make me so wet," came the breathless voice as she nipped his earlobe, sliding one hand up to stroke his nipple.

"Oh, you bitch," Harry groaned, struggling to wrench off the French knickers as she continued to tease him with her fingers. "Please..."

She ran her other hand down and caressed his erection, slowly and tortuously.

"Got to be...inside you...please..."

Those French knickers were proving very difficult for his shaking fingers to shift, and all the while her fingertips were driving him crazy, her mouth trailing over his chest.

"So take me," she breathed against his hot skin before her lips closed over one of his nipples.

In that moment he came undone. He pushed her roughly upright, then ripped the vest off over her shoulders before catching hold of her waist and rolling her onto her back. He pulled off the satin knickers while her thighs were still in the air. Groaning through his teeth, he bore down on top of her, entering her even as he buried his head between her breasts.

"Oh yes, like that...there..." he heard her breathe. "Fuck me..."

Shuddering, he slid up to kiss her as he began to thrust, already knowing he wouldn't last very long. He dug his fingers into the mattress, struggling to hold back.

"Oh God, Harry...don't stop..."

Oh God, don't talk... I can't...

He pressed himself down on her, rubbing against her clitoris as she slid her hands down to squeeze his buttocks, biting his lip as her soft cries grew stronger in his ear.

"Oh God, yes...yes...I'm going to...to..."

Harry pressed his face into her neck, sweat dripping from his forehead as the pleasure threatened to overwhelm him.

"Oh fuck...Astra...I'm so close..."

"Oh...yes...I...*oh!*" Astra gave a high-pitched cry and threw back her head, writhing as her muscles clenched around him.

"Oh God, Astra...I...ohhh! Yes—"

His body thrashed as his orgasm slammed through him. She clung to him until the ecstasy subsided, both of them trembling in the aftermath and glistening with perspiration.

For a moment, the air remained heated and silent as they lay, sated and exhausted. Harry was the first to raise his head.

"You okay?"

"Yes."

He cupped her face in his hands and kissed her, over and over, as their breathing slowed.

"I love you," he whispered against her mouth. "Stay here tonight."

"I love you too," she whispered back. "My clothes are outside the window."

"You can get them a minute." He lay his head beside her neck, sleep threatening to overtake him. "I'm not done with you yet. If you like, I'll do the ice thing."

Astra snuggled down, drifting off to sleep, but with the stirring of him still inside her telling her it was going to be a long night.

Chapter Three

The following evening, Astra stood behind her blackjack table at the Fountain Casino, dealing out one of the many, many games she would deal that night.

The Gaming Management major was heavily vocational, focussing on work experience and requiring an internship in the final semester. Astra had worked the front desk in the attached hotel until she had turned twenty-one the previous year, then she had worked as a croupier for the first semester before being taken on for her internship. Since then she had been rotated through a number of areas, but always seemed to spend the most time on the casino floor.

The work had its drawbacks. Sore feet. Unflattering maroon uniform. Numb fingers reeking of cards, and cigarette smoke in her hair. But it was all worth it to work at the Fountain.

The Fountain Casino drew the eye from the first moment. A sweeping drive lined with underlit palm trees led to an elegant yet modern exterior, its every plane and curve edged with neon lights. Immediately inside stood an atrium with an underlit fountain, three jets of water rising high to splash into a large rectangular pool. The doors into the casino area remained open, ensuring the delicate rush of water could be heard from the farthest end of the casino floor.

Astra had fallen in love with the place at first sight.

She had already learnt the tricks of the trade. She knew about the weighting on the roulette wheel, she knew salt water did *not* make the fruit machines pay out—although she was beginning to wish the patrons also knew that—and she knew what to look for in a blackjack player, at times feeling pangs of pity for those who believed they could beat her at counting cards. The bar staff had come to learn the signals she made when she spotted a card-counter, and were trained to send a waiter over immediately. It was amazing how quickly, "Can I get you a drink, sir?" could throw off someone's count.

She shuffled the four decks of cards expertly as the hand ended. One man got up irritably and left, leaving three others around the table.

Two cards, and the man to her left gave a pointed, world-weary sigh. He had drawn a ten and a five.

"Hit me."

A jack. Bust.

"And you, sir?" Astra asked the man in front of her, who had seventeen in his hand.

"Stick."

Smart. Even if he had been playing on more than luck and experience, Astra would never have recommended playing fast and loose after a shuffle, particularly when, as in this case, he had gone all in.

"And you, sir?"

"Hit me."

She dealt a third card to the man to her right, leaving him with twenty-two. *Ooh, too bad.*

"Astra?" came a voice behind her as the hand was ending.

She turned to see one of the other croupiers, Ally, hovering at the corner of the table.

"I've been sent to relieve you. Brad wants to see you."

"Oh, okay," said Astra, looking at her watch. It was only ten minutes until the end of her shift anyway. She left Ally to take over the table and crossed to the manager's office.

The manager, Brad, a blond man with a lantern jaw and muscles that were straining his suit, was sitting behind his desk staring blankly at one of the security monitors, a biro hanging out of his mouth.

"You wanted to…"

Brad jumped, causing the pen to drop and bounce off the desk onto the floor.

"Oh! Yes, hello, Astra. Yes, I wanted to discuss your employment with us."

Astra cringed inwardly, trying to remember if she had inadvertently handed out too many chips to a customer. Another croupier had been fired the previous week for the same thing.

"I gather you will be finishing your degree this year?"

"Um—yes, that's right."

"Right. Well, as you're aware, we have a graduate management training programme, and we have been particularly impressed with your performance over these past months. You've avoided the unprofessional behaviour we often get from interns… No drunken photos on Facebook, for instance…"

Astra smiled innocently, inwardly thanking every deity who might be listening. A number of student croupiers had been fired over the course of the year for poorly-judged status updates and intoxicated photographs. Fortunately Omega Zeta had a policy of keeping such images to itself.

Brad reached for his pen but, as it was on the floor, his hand instead wandered about aimlessly on the desk, as if it wasn't under his control. "Well, yes...we were wondering if you would be interested in undertaking full-time management training after you graduate."

Astra paused for a moment to allow the butterflies in her stomach to settle.

All these nights of card-flipping and wheel-spinning, having shots of whisky thrown at her by customers who had lost all their money, watching people cavort in joy as the house paid out more money than she would ever see in a lifetime. Months of floorwork. Years — *years* — of a degree.

"Yes, I would be interested."

"Ah, good," said Brad, now leaning over the side of his chair to retrieve his biro. "I'll put your name down on the list...where the hell is it...? Anyway, I'll get the information for you later. I believe your shift is about to finish?" His chair wobbled dangerously as he extended his arm further. Astra thought this an appropriate moment to say goodbye and walk out.

Management. Management!

The walk to the front door passed in a blissful blur. Astra stepped out onto the darkened street and thrust her hands into her coat pockets. She gazed up at the stars as she began the walk home with an unusually jaunty gait. In her mellow mood, the usually lurid glare from the nearby bars and clubs seemed to bathe her in a peaceful, glowing haze.

Suddenly she paused mid-bounce as a familiar voice rang out in the distance.

That sounded like Harry.

She turned and scanned the other side of the street. A number of people were exiting bars, either to go home or to move on to clubs, but there was nobody she recognised.

Must be going mad.

"Pass my jacket, Harry," she faintly heard a male voice saying.

Another voice responded indistinctly, but it was unmistakably Harry's voice. It was coming from a group of men just leaving a club on the corner of a side-street. This time Astra caught a glimpse of him, talking and laughing as he threw a jacket to the other man. The sign over the door of the club showed two palm trees over a neon-outlined beach; flashing between the trees was the name *PINK*.

She raised an amused eyebrow as she turned to continue the walk home, not wanting to intrude on his night out. Harry visiting a strip club, as it clearly was with a name like 'Pink'? He had never been particularly demonstrative about his sexuality in front of his friends—all the lewd remarks about lap-dancers and 'juicy jugs' usually came from the more mouthy types, like Ash. It certainly would not have surprised her to see Ash coming out of a strip club—he rarely let an attractive girl pass without making some sneering comment.

She debated whether or not to mention it to Harry. They had arranged to meet for drinks the following night at a cocktail bar just off campus. She didn't have a problem with strip clubs or even lap-dancing clubs, provided there was no touching involved, but guys always seemed to expect girls to make a fuss. It was unlikely he would say anything about it without prompting.

With a mental shrug, Astra headed down towards the entrance to the campus, wondering if was worth making him suffer a bit.

* * * *

When Astra left her room at six-thirty the following evening, she was suffering considerably herself. Having got in at half past twelve, her sleep had then been disrupted by her next-door neighbour Leyla, who shared her opposite wall with Sasha. Apparently Ash had paid a visit.

"For God's sake!" *Bang.* "Will you two give it a rest?" *Bang.* "No! She does *not* want it again! Go to sleep!"

Until four in the morning. To make matters worse, Astra had had a nine o' clock lecture and been given a paper to prepare on transactional analysis for the following day, which made her seriously wonder if all university professors were sadists.

On her way down the stairs she passed Keely, Sasha's other neighbour, who looked about as good as she felt.

"Sleep any?"

Keely fixed her with a bleary-eyed glare.

"Sasha does chemistry, right?" she asked hollowly. "Think she can get hold of some fucking bromide?"

"I'll ask her," said Astra, hiding a smile behind her hair. Keely shook her head hopelessly and staggered up the stairs, tripping over the top one and nearly falling flat on her face.

As Astra reached the bottom of the stairs, she could hear Ash's brash tones floating out of the lounge doorway.

"And then that jerkwad Lenscher tried to tackle me, but he couldn't catch a fucking cold…"

"Hello, Ash," said Astra, leaning against the door frame. "Hi, Sash."

Sasha glanced up from where she was reading *The Devil Wears Prada*. "Oh, hi, Astra. Meeting Harry?"

"Yeah, we're going to Paradisa."

"Ooh, cocktails!"

There was an undeniable snort from the corner.

"Oh, shut up, Ash. You never take me out for cocktails."

"Be very glad I don't." Ash smirked, flicking a smug glance at Astra.

"Got something to say, Ash?"

"Oh hell no." Ash smiled at Astra's poorly hidden irritation. "Have fun with the — with Harry."

Flipping her hair over her shoulder, Astra stalked out, slamming the door behind her. God, he was a piece of work.

Paradisa was in the centre of town, a large modern building decorated inside to look like a fairy grotto. Tropical plants uplit with red gels surrounded the tables and fairy lights twinkled from the ceiling. A central fountain glowed blue and green as water splashed merrily into the stone basin. Astra paused in the doorway, squinting around in the dark in the hope of glimpsing Harry.

"Looking for someone?" said a voice behind her.

Astra turned around to see Harry, hair rendered even more untidy by the wind. She felt a sudden surge of happiness.

"Hi, Harry."

"There's a free table over there, I think," said Harry, gesturing towards the far corner.

They made their way over to the table and sat down. After a quick glance over the menu, Harry caught a passing waiter and ordered for them both before turning back to Astra, eyeing her with some concern.

"You look a bit tired."

Astra shook her head. "Oh, I'm all right. Ash and Sash were at it like rabbits all last night and kept everyone awake." She considered complaining about her professors, too, but decided not to. Harry probably had much worse to deal with in the computer department.

"Figures," said Harry, rolling his eyes.

To take his mind off Ash, Astra told him about her offer of management training. Harry was suitably impressed.

"Wish someone would offer *me* a job after uni."

"You're doing computer science. *Everyone*'s going to offer you a job after uni."

"I don't know about that," said Harry, running one hand through his hair and leaving it even messier than before. "They've got computer geeks coming out of their ears. And the wages are shit. I need to sell an algorithm to Microsoft or something, make myself a multi-millionaire."

Astra grinned wickedly. "I could quite like you as a multi-millionaire."

"I bet you could." Harry grinned back, leaning out of the way as the waiter set a tequila sunrise and White Lady on the table.

The conversation waned for a moment as they both drank, Astra imagining Harry as a rich techno-genius and thinking how Ash would seethe with envy. This thought apparently transmitted itself to Harry, as he spent the next ten minutes commenting on how he had seen Ash playing football earlier in the day and how he had been thrown off the field for stamping on another player's stomach. Astra nodded dutifully in all the right places, but felt a change of subject was necessary.

"Did I see you in town last night?"

Harry broke off in mid-sentence, his face taking on an adorably nervous cast.

"Er, you might have done... Where?"

"I was on my way back from the Fountain. You were coming out of..."

"Oh. Yes." Harry looked as though he would rather be anywhere but there. "That. I was..."

Astra hid a smile in her cocktail glass. It was really quite comical watching Harry blush and stutter. She let him mumble for a few minutes before interrupting.

"You know, it's all right, Harry. Guys do it all the time."

Harry froze with his mouth half-open.

"Really? You don't...mind?"

"It's hardly anything to be ashamed of." Astra adopted her most open-minded expression.

"Oh, thank fuck."

Harry slumped in his seat and rubbed his hand over his face, smiling in relief.

"I didn't think you'd...I mean, most women wouldn't..."

"I'm not most women."

"No. You're absolutely unbelievable. I honestly thought you'd kill me. I just...I was curious. Wanted to know what it might be like."

Astra smiled as he continued talking, relief obviously having loosened his tongue.

"I mean, I didn't, like...*do* anything... I wouldn't... I just, you know...wanted to know...still do, really..."

Harry's nervousness was starting to jar slightly. This didn't sound like someone having been to a strip club.

"Harry, you know...it's all right..."

"You haven't told anyone, have you?" Harry asked suddenly, eyes widening.

"No, I haven't." *Why does he care about that?*

"Oh, good. You know. Not everyone would be as understanding as you. I wouldn't want anyone to know I'd been going to gay bars..."

Going...to...

Harry was still talking, but the last two words were still ringing in Astra's ears. *Gay bars...gay bars...gay bars...*

Pink was a gay bar.

Harry was going to gay bars.

Harry was curious about...wanted to know about...was meeting other men at...

"Do you want another drink?"

The waiter was hovering around the table.

"Yes. Yes I do." Astra became aware her fingers had turned white around the glass. "Same again, please."

The rest of the evening went by in an aching haze. As they walked home from the bar, Harry's arm around her shoulders, Astra felt as though a cold quilt was wrapped around her body, leaving her devoid of all feeling. Before her eyes the garish neon sign flashed mockingly: *PINK. PINK. PINK.*

She had hoped Harry would leave her to walk the remaining few metres alone when they reached Beta Phi, but Harry would have none of it—his gentlemanly instincts had kicked in. On the front doorstep of Omega Zeta they kissed goodnight. Astra found herself holding on to him more tightly than usual, running her fingers over his slim shoulders, committing their shape to memory.

"Night," Harry whispered, giving her one last kiss on the nose. "Love you. You're amazing."

"Night," said Astra hoarsely, biting her lip to maintain the last vestiges of control.

They touched hands briefly as Harry moved backwards down the steps, smiling up at her, his eyes glinting in the lamplight. Then, with a last wave, he turned and Astra was left watching his fast-disappearing back.

* * * *

Her control held for as long as it took her to close the front door behind her. Teeth clamped down on her bottom lip, she made a headlong break for the stairs, praying no one would be around to see the tears already spilling down her cheeks.

She couldn't face anyone right now. She couldn't. The thought of trying to explain this to a sea of concerned faces was simply unbearable. And if Sasha had *him* round again—oh God.

I could tell you a few things about Harry. Oh God, oh God.

By a stroke of luck, the corridor was deserted. Astra hurtled around the corners, violently wrenched her key in the lock and fell through her bedroom door, kicking it shut behind her. The bed was too far away—her blind dive landed her on her knees, allowing her to bury her face in the quilt.

He was bisexual. Bi-curious, anyway. She could have lived with that. People had curiosities. But that he was acting on them, visiting gay bars, wanting to know what it was like—his reassurance he had done nothing, and wouldn't, meant little to her. If he was looking to satisfy his curiosity, it was only a matter of time.

Love you. You're amazing. Too damn right she was. She was amazed at her own idiocy.

Presumably he did still love her—she cursed herself as her heart involuntarily leapt at that thought—or he would have finished with her as soon as his secret was out. But now he thought he had a free pass to...

She pulled the quilt up around her ears to muffle her sobs.

And she couldn't end things herself. She just couldn't. She loved him, against all reason, all rationality.

Pulling her face out of the sodden mass of eiderdown, she struggled to picture their encounter in his room at Beta Phi. He had been *hers* then, she was sure of it. He hadn't been thinking of anyone else.

But as the images passed behind her eyes, there seemed to be something missing.

Harry's eyes falling shut with arousal...the sweat on his face as he struggled with her underwear...his shuddering breaths and his moans of excitement...

There was no emotion, no involvement. Nothing. It was as though it had happened to two different people.

I can't remember the taste of your sweat.

I can't remember the way your breath caught...

Someone was pounding on the door. She must have been overheard.

"Astra! Are you all right?"

Sasha.

"N—not now," Astra choked, feeling with one hand for the box of tissues on her bedside table.

"Astra, what...?"

"Not now!"

33

Astra's heart was beating painfully, in panic. No matter how hard she forced herself to remember, the memories refused to return.

I can't remember that catch in your throat…

She heard the door open behind her. Twisting around, she saw a concerned-looking Sasha, and behind her…

Oh, God, no!

But as her stinging eyes adjusted to the blaze of light in the doorway, she saw Ash's face and realised that, when she had expected to see a smirk, he was looking shocked.

"Tell y'tomorrow…"

"Is it Harry…?"

"Not fucking now!" With a sudden surge of energy, Astra wrenched herself off the floor and stormed to the door, feeling a dark gratification as Sasha jumped back in shock. "Leave me!" And she slammed the door and locked it, catching a final glimpse of Ash's stunned face over Sasha's shoulder as the light was extinguished.

Their footsteps retreated down the hallway.

Then, with slow, heavy steps, she moved back across the room. Her body felt numb and lifeless, and the mattress came up to meet her.

Chapter Four

The following morning Astra felt strong enough to discuss the previous evening's events with Sasha. Her non-appearance in the kitchen for breakfast had led Sasha to hammer on her bedroom door and demand to know what the hell was going on.

The explanation left Sasha's jaw an inch deep in the shag pile.

"He's...he's *what?* But how... Oh God!"

Astra was lying on her bed, staring at the ceiling. She saw little in Sasha's contribution that merited a response.

"So what did you do? Did you break up?"

Okay, that merited a response.

"No. We didn't." She glanced at Sasha, whose expression had gone from shocked to stunned. "He thinks it's all right."

"Why the hell would he think it's all right? I'd rip Ash's balls off if he said that to me."

"Ash would rip his own balls off before he went into a gay bar."

"Well, bypassing Ash's balls, why does he think it's all right?"

"Because I didn't *know* Pink was a gay bar. I thought it was a strip club. I could have lived with a strip club." Astra paused for a moment to mentally cuff herself around the head for her own stupidity. "And then he said 'gay bar', and I'd already told him it was fine. Now he thinks I'm the most tolerant woman on the planet."

"If you're going to let him do this, you *are* the most tolerant woman on the planet."

"I'm not." Astra stared out of the window, feeling her features twist into a glare. "I'm pathetic. I knew what I was supposed to do, but I couldn't fucking *do* it."

Dump him. Her stomach dropped at the very thought. *I can't. I can't.*

"Well, I suppose I can pretend to be okay with it if you can." Sasha shook her head, eyes wide and disbelieving. "But I think he's being an ass. He's screwing you around and he's not even sure about it."

Astra rolled her eyes at that. It sounded, to her, like a very accurate assessment.

"I'd better not tell Ash," Sasha mused. "He'd kick his ass."

"No, you're right, *don't* tell Ash. I told him I wouldn't tell anyone."

The thought of Ash having his snide little insinuations confirmed made Astra inwardly cringe. Ash, in all his rabid heterosexuality, would certainly have no problem with outing Harry in front of a large group of people.

"He knows you were upset. I'll just tell him you had a fight."

He'll probably figure it out anyway. "Yes. Good thinking."

Sasha looked at her watch and groaned. "I've got biochemistry in ten minutes. Will you be all right?"

"I'll be fine. I've got a seminar to get to anyway." The seminar in question wasn't for another hour, but Astra thought she might wander downstairs and find something to eat in the meantime.

"Okay. I'll see you later then."

"See you later."

Sasha got up off the floor and made her exit, leaving Astra to put on her shoes and make her way down to the kitchen.

On reaching the kitchen door, she involuntarily gagged. Maybe eating wasn't such a good idea yet. She turned and walked out of the front door, intending instead to pay a visit to the campus administration building and check her mail. It was around that time when bills made an appearance.

The administration building was in the opposite direction from Beta Phi, along the main road which led to the quadrangle at the centre of campus. On the expanse of grass, now rather brown and frostbitten, some diehard students were tossing a Frisbee, but for the most part the students were keeping to the road around the edges. Astra made her way along the right hand side to the modern block that extended ahead of her, keeping her eyes open in case the Frisbee flew her way.

The clerk behind the desk looked up from his computer as she entered, eyeing her with an air of utter disdain. Ignoring his obvious reluctance, Astra asked for her mail, at which he stood up with a great sigh and began to run his finger along the pigeonholes behind him.

"Mail for Astra Scott…Astra Scott… Ah, yes. There." A small bundle of letters wrapped in an elastic band hit the counter as the clerk flopped back into his seat. Shaking her head, Astra took them outside to read them.

One was her payslip, unsurprisingly. The second was an advertisement for car insurance — not owning a car, Astra dropped the paper straight into the nearest trash can. The third looked official, computer type behind a plastic window. Probably a bill. Astra sighed, slit the top and tipped it upside down.

FOR IMMEDIATE ATTENTION, black type demanded.

It was from her bank. Words collided — *late fees, penalty, collections agency.*

Her tuition fees had been taken out a day ahead of her pay cheque, and the payment had bounced.

Hand covering her face, Astra fought against tears.

* * * *

"What's that?"

Astra jumped sharply and turned, automatically shielding the paper against her chest.

"Ash!"

"What's that?" Ash repeated, reaching around and plucking the paper out of Astra's hand. He scanned the words, then looked at her with an expression of disbelief.

"This is it?"

You prick! "What more do you want?"

Ash eyed her coolly for a minute, then apparently decided it couldn't be all that bad if she was still able to give him lip. He grabbed her wrist.

"Come on."

Feeling as if her arm was coming out of its socket, Astra allowed herself to be dragged further down the road into the refectory building, where Ash shoved her bodily into a seat and marched over to the coffee machine. As with most things, he treated it with the same violence one might use on a punchbag, but came back carrying two steaming plastic cups.

"Here. Drink."

Astra blinked at this uncommon concern for her wellbeing.

"Uh, thanks." Picking up the cup, she was even more surprised to find it contained hot chocolate. She hadn't realised Ash had noticed she never drank coffee.

"So let's just get this straight," Ash said, his own cup halfway to his mouth. "Is this the first time it's happened?"

"Yes."

"Do you have enough to pay it off?"

"Yes."

"Good. Go down there today and talk to them. You'll be fine."

Astra took a mouthful of hot chocolate to avoid having to say anything. Ash was eyeing her with an expression she recognised, both indulgent and slightly insulting.

"Having a hard day?" was his next question.

Astra gave him a cool look. *You know exactly what kind of day I'm having, and if you give me the sympathetic head tilt I'll smack you in the mouth.*

"You know, I'm kind of surprised you care."

Ash arched an eyebrow, his coffee now sitting forgotten on the table. "Why wouldn't I care?"

"You don't exactly like me very much."

"What? Fuck off. Of course I like you."

"Oh yeah? A few days ago you called me a 'fucking tease'."

There was an uncomfortable pause before Ash spoke again.

"That would be because I *do* like you."

For a few moments silence descended on the table as both tried to avoid each other's eyes.

He likes me?

The idea that Ash might actually like her had never occurred to her. Ash was a jock. He dated girl after girl. He didn't like to be turned down. It was as simple as that.

Ash wasn't the type to *like* someone.

I should never have started this.

"Well, anyway," she said finally. "I have the afternoon off today. I'll go down to the bank and sort this out."

Ash nodded slowly, obviously appreciating the change in subject.

"When's your next shift?"

"Tonight. They always need me on Fridays."

"Need anyone to walk you down?"

Astra paused for a moment, wondering why tonight would be any more dangerous than any other night, before the realisation hit.

He thinks I walk down with Harry. And that I won't be tonight, because –

Ouch.

"No, I'll be fine. I'm working five till eleven tonight – it'll be daylight."

"What about coming back?"

Astra shook her head. "It's not that far. I'll get a cab if I'm worried."

Ash didn't look happy, but a glance at her watch told Astra she didn't have time to argue. "Shit. I've got a lecture in ten minutes. Better go."

"Okay. Just...look, if you're worried, call my cell, okay? Seriously." Ash pulled a pen from his coat pocket, wrote a number on a napkin and handed it to her. "I'll be with Seychelle tonight, so we can come and get you."

It was on the tip of Astra's tongue to ask why she shouldn't just call Sasha, but she stifled the impulse. It was good of him to offer. Standing up, she took the napkin and put it in her pocket. Ash nodded, as if to say he approved of her good sense.

As they parted outside the refectory, Astra's ponderings about Ash's sudden concern for her welfare were interrupted by the memory of his mutual antipathy with Harry, and the knowledge of what Harry would think of the situation. Her stomach twisted uncomfortably. Usually she told him everything.

No.

His current issues...he was probably going out again tonight...he had enough to worry about...it was better he didn't know.

She would be seeing him tomorrow night anyway. The Sigma Delta Theta sorority were holding a party which they had agreed to go to over a week ago, although she resolved to text him later to check he still wanted to go.

But it was odd to think that, after nearly breaking down on campus, she had ended up leaning on Ash.

* * * *

Rather than face the crowds in the refectory, Astra chose to take a bus into town and drop in to the Subway inside the shopping mall. Securely isolated in the middle of the crowd, she had time to retreat into her thoughts.

An image of herself walking back from the casino, alone, vulnerable, flashed into her head. It was immediately followed by one of herself walking with Ash, accompanied by a feeling of security.

Because he's a guy. Because I'm a girl on my own.

Astra bit into her sandwich, the ham and sharp mustard helping to counteract the sudden sour taste in her mouth.

Waking up at intervals the previous night, the same question had hung in her mind: *What do they have that I don't?* At the time, the answer had been obvious, but now —

They're stronger. They can fight. They grow taller, their shoulders are broader. Their voices are deeper. They command respect. They take charge.

And, of course, the obvious answer again.

They have dicks. They can fuck.

Her chest stung at the thought that immediately presented itself.

He said he wasn't.

Yet.

Her Pepsi seemed to curdle on her tongue. Before her eyes, unrolling as inexorably as a reel of film, an image formed of Harry lying face down on his bed, hands fisted in the quilt, toes curling, as a muscular figure lay moulded to his back, perfectly-formed buttocks thrusting over and over again.

He will. What can I do?

I can take charge. But I can't fuck him.

Finishing the last bite of her sandwich, she gathered up the waste paper and cup and dropped them into the bin on her way out of the door.

Half an hour remained before the next lecture. The door led straight into the mall—Astra automatically turned towards the front exit onto the street, then paused, wondering if it would be quicker to walk past the shops and exit at the back. Lost in thought, she looked back over her shoulder into the central section.

Then she saw it.

Her feet seemed to carry her of their own volition. She stopped in front of the window and her eyes slid over the display of lace-covered, beribboned mannequins, plastic breasts slipping out of black leather and red silk, before trailing further back towards the glowing sign which read OVER 18 ONLY.

She had visited this shop before with Harry. The box under her bed was filled with multi-coloured toys—toys that thrust, vibrated, throbbed. But there were other toys available, she knew.

Toys Harry had never suggested, but now...

Her jaw set firmly, fists clenched, Astra strode into the shop.

* * * *

Two hours later, and Astra stood in front of her bedroom mirror, holding in one hand the toy she had bought from Amy's Delights.

Rubber underwear was laced through her fingers, a small plastic remote control dangling below on the end of a long cord. And attached to the front—

Well.

It was a strap-on.

It was a strap-on dildo.

And it was *purple.*

A purple length of shiny plastic. A perfect simulacrum of a veined, circumcised penis, five inches long and of a thickness Astra considered average, just the right width to wrap a hand around.

She stared at her reflection for a long time, contemplating the dildo, before slowly drawing it back towards her body, holding it against her stomach.

No.

One foot through the straps, two feet…rubber caught against denim-clad legs, but after a moment's struggle the strap-on dildo was in place, and Astra's image stood before her, the purple dick jutting out in front like the hilt of a sword.

Slowly she rotated her hips, watching the dildo glide from side to side, before stopping abruptly with a giggle.

Shit. It looks like a fucking light sabre.

Watching herself in the mirror, she closed one hand around its length, giving it a tentative stroke.

Nothing. Unsurprisingly.

She tried it again, this time holding the remote control and flicking the switch. A sudden buzzing, accompanied by a muted vibration through her jeans, made her jolt sharply.

Interesting.

Flipping the switch again, she rocked her hips slowly, her eyes glazing. In her mind formed a picture of Harry's smooth back and bare buttocks, thighs parting to receive her, Harry's voice gasping, begging for *more, more, please, more…*

Oh.

The switch snapped off.

Astra eyed herself coolly, squaring her shoulders, her legs automatically widening into a masculine stance.

Chapter Five

Astra had never considered Sasha to be the mother-hen type, but by four-thirty she was beginning to realise her error.

"Look, I really think you need to get a cab. Anything could happen."

"Yes. I could get to work on time, for a start."

"You should have let Ash walk with you. He said he'd be happy to do it. I can call him now —"

"I'll be *fine*," Astra insisted through gritted teeth, struggling to force her way past Sasha, who was blocking the front door. It was extremely tempting to have Sasha call Ash just so she could tear him a new one for not keeping his fat mouth shut.

And equally tempting to just shove Sasha against the wall and...

Whoa.

Sasha's body was close, too close, her mouth just inches from Astra's, her breath tickling her face, and the aggressive stance Astra had seen in the mirror was forcing itself into her mind, urging her to press forward—

"Look," Sasha continued obliviously, "you've had a hard day; there's no need to act brave in front of me—*Harry!*"

Caught between Sasha and the door frame, Astra twisted around to see Harry standing in the road with a slightly bemused smile on his face. He raised his eyebrows playfully at the position the two girls were in.

"Having fun?"

"Oh, absolutely," said Astra, trying to fight the butterflies swirling in her stomach. "Sasha was just seeing me off to work, weren't you, Sash? She misses me when I'm not here."

"Are you going to ask him to walk with you or what?" Sasha hissed in her ear.

"Or what," Astra hissed back.

Sasha gave her a hard look for a moment, then turned back to Harry.

"Can you walk Astra to work, Harry? So I don't worry about her? Please?" She widened her eyes and treated Harry to an innocent smile which didn't fool Astra for a moment.

I don't know if she's trying to keep us together or make him feel guilty. But I don't like either.

"Don't worry, Sash," said Harry decisively, slipping an arm through Astra's as she reached him. "I'll get her there safely."

Astra rolled her eyes, but resigned herself to the situation. If anyone was going to walk her to work, she would much rather it was Harry, even a Harry with his current proclivities.

But it was a long walk to work, a long way to go with someone whose presence was causing such surges of feeling, such prickles in her skin, such nervous energy. Harry had his arm through hers, was stroking her arm with his other hand as he happily chattered about everything and nothing, and his sunny smile and his clear blue eyes and his messy hair were still as attractive as before, his slender figure was accentuated by his close-fitting jeans and his blue T-shirt, all his lines and curves —

—which he had sworn were only for her, no matter where he went in the evening.

But could she be sure of that? Would he tell her if he had done anything with anyone? He might never have told her in the first place if she hadn't caught him.

"Are we still going to that party tomorrow night?" Harry's voice broke into her thoughts.

"Oh. Yes, if you've not got other plans." *Please tell me you've not got other plans. Please.*

"No, no other plans. I'm looking forward to it."

Astra felt a sudden desperate urge to kiss him, but translated it into a heartfelt rub of his arm.

"So listen," said Harry, turning to face her as they rounded the last corner. "Are you sure you'll be safe walking home? I mean, I'm off out with a couple of the frat boys tonight, but I can always come back early."

Frat boys? That didn't sound like one of his Pink nights out. That sounded like a standard bar crawl. Astra kept her breathing steady, but felt her muscles relax in relief.

"No, no, it's not a problem. I'm finishing at eleven — you don't have to cut your night short. I'll get a cab if I'm worried."

The casino was gradually coming into view ahead. Still holding on to her arm, Harry broke into a run, nearly pulling Astra off her feet.

"Come on, slowpoke!"

Oh, it was impossible, just impossible not to love Harry, Astra thought as her feet pounded the pavement alongside him. And surely he was entitled to his thoughts, as long as they were shared with her.

The memory of herself in front of the mirror, the toy standing erect, made something low inside her tighten. Maybe she could suggest it to him later, just as a possibility.

Maybe.

As they reached the side door, Harry caught Astra in his arms, whirled her around and kissed her. Astra tangled her fingers in his dark hair and lost herself in the moment, her heart racing in her ears.

I love you, I love you, I love you.

Breathless, they broke the kiss, but remained in each other's arms.

"I'll see you tomorrow night, okay?" Harry whispered against her skin, his intense blue eyes locked with hers and a wicked smile playing around his lips. "If we get bored we can go outside and get a few grass stains."

"I've got the perfect green dress." *And the perfect purple toy – possibly.*

Laughing evilly, Harry stepped back to arm's length, still holding her fingertips.

"Call me if you need to. Seriously!"

"Okay!" Astra called back, mock-annoyed, as Harry's fingers left hers and she turned to go into the building.

She was damned if she was going to disrupt his night out. She would get a cab. Hell, she would walk before she would drag him away early.

It was turning into rather a nice evening.

* * * *

Walking through the red-carpeted interior of the Fountain Casino, beside gold pillars and beneath twinkling crystal chandeliers, Astra always lost herself in the atmosphere—both soothing and exciting at the same time. The smell of green baize and perfume and freshly-circulated air, the noise of chiming slot machines and clinking tokens and croupiers' voices over the splash, splash, splash of the fountain. Standing at her table, the room was in a constant state of movement, almost hypnotic, as suits and silks passed each other, shuffling from table to table, bathed in the dazzling blinking of the lights—

And yet once, between hands, Astra had stretched, lifted her eyes to the ceiling, and been mesmerised.

A dark, vaulted ceiling, studded with bulbs.

The velvety darkness had seemed to draw her in. Spellbound, Astra had caught her breath, the sounds of the room below dulling to a gentle hum, and she had been surrounded by twinkling stars, the blaze of the floor taking on the hazy glow of twilight.

It had been enough to make her feel like the only person on earth. Astra had wanted nothing else ever since.

It was a pity some people seemed determined to ruin it. Her thoughts darkened.

Ally had spoken to her before their shift, just as they had been leaving the staff room. Her low whisper had caused Astra's gut to twist.

"Management material. Yeah, *right*."

Astra had played deaf and retreated behind a mask of cheerful professionalism for the evening, secure in the knowledge that Ally had been assigned to a table as far away from her as was possible. She could ignore her all night with impunity.

But as she had been clearing her table, Ally had stepped into her space. Astra glanced casually over her shoulder.

"Hey."

Ally's smile was irritatingly smooth.

"I hear Brad's got Becky lined up to be a manager."

"Really?" Astra had responded coolly. It was certainly possible. Becky wasn't an intern, but was an able croupier and experienced on most of the tables.

"Yeah, really." Ally looked Astra straight in the face, eyes wide and innocent. "Don't know who else he had in mind, but she's sure to get it, don't you think?"

Astra kept her own eyes bright as images of flying fists skittered through her mind.

"Guess we'll find out soon enough."

Ally threw her another syrupy smile and danced away, leaving Astra grinding her teeth.

What a fucking nerve. If I get in, I swear I'm having her fired.

The words continued to ring in her head as she collected her coat and passed through the lobby. *She's sure to get it, don't you think? Don't you think?*

Well, don't you?

Fuck you.

She was still lost in thought as the clock struck eleven. Astra stepped out onto the chilly street and glanced left and right, contemplating whether or not to look for a cab.

The nearest cab rank was a few blocks away, further into town. It seemed pointless walking up there if it wasn't necessary. It was nowhere near closing time — most of the ranks would probably be empty now. With a shrug of her shoulders, Astra decided to walk. Harry didn't need to find out.

She was just passing under the first street light when she heard footsteps behind her. She turned, but saw nobody.

Okay. Now you're getting paranoid.

At the second street light, something scuffled behind her.

Astra stopped dead and span around. This time she saw a shadow flit into an alleyway a few feet away.

It's nothing, she told herself firmly. *You're acting like a stupid girl.* But she slipped her left hand into her purse and closed it around the pepper spray she kept there.

Third street light.

This time she heard nothing. Letting her breath out slowly, she stepped out of the pool of light.

It all happened so quickly.

Footsteps running up behind her. A hand gripped her right arm and forced her sharply around. Astra's brought her left hand quickly up in front of her, pressing down on the button on the canister, even as she wrenched her right arm away, a wild scream escaping her.

The figure in front of her was unclear, obscured by the darkness, recoiling from the cloud of pepper spray. Astra chose not to wait around for a closer look. She bolted across the road and into the side street that led into town, her terrified breath tearing her throat.

Harry. Someone. Anyone.

The streets were busier now — it would be easier to blend in. Panting, Astra dived into a nearby bus shelter to take stock of the situation.

She needed to get back to Omega Zeta. She could call Harry, but if he was in a bar or a club, he might not hear the phone. She could call Sasha or Ash, but neither of them had cars — they could only walk into town, which would take longer than she wanted. She could hail a cab — that was probably her best option. Struggling to control her breathing, she scanned the street to get her bearings. Which way was the rank?

— Who was that?

A familiar figure had stepped out of a doorway into a street at right-angles to the main road. It was poorly lit, the intermittent blinking of a neon sign its only illumination, but that unruly hair was unmistakeable.

Harry!

The figure turned in her direction, and for a moment Astra thought he had seen her. But as she moved forward, another man came out of the doorway and Harry slipped around a corner, out of view.

The other man followed.

Astra's feet carried her almost involuntarily across the road, bringing her to a halt at the entrance to the alleyway.

The alley was plunged into almost complete darkness. The flickering neon light to her right allowed her to see occasional outlines, but nothing more. She could see Harry — his hair, the slope of his nose, the curve of his lips — but the other man was bathed in shadow, offering only brief glimpses of a shock of hair and a square jaw. He was taller and bigger-built than Harry, broader across the shoulders and chest.

And then, as a haze of sickening dread began to settle over Astra's vision, the two outlines met in a kiss.

* * * *

Heart pounding crazily, her breath shrieking in her ears, Astra became aware of a distant voice as the sorority house thundered unsteadily into her dazed vision.

"Sasha? Sash! Get downstairs! She's here!"

From the Minnesotan accent, it was Liddy, up on the balcony that ran around the top floor of the building, serving as a fire escape.

Her knees were giving way, her throat hoarse, her breath hot. The front door flew open as she reached it and a hand dragged her inside.

"Astra! What happened? Are you all right?"

Barely able to speak, shaking from head to toe, Astra caught glimpses of two figures in the hallway and knew she had to get rid of Ash.

"Man...following...grabbed me..."

"Fuck," Sasha gasped.

Without a word, Ash hurled himself through the front door and out onto the road, in hot pursuit of someone he would never find.

Sasha slammed the door behind him and led Astra into the lounge, pushing her down onto a couch and picking up a bottle from the coffee table.

"Here. Drink some. You need it."

She held the bottle to Astra's lips. Astra tasted brandy and coughed.

"Did you see who it was?"

"No," Astra croaked, taking the bottle and drinking from it again. "Too dark. Pepper sprayed him—"

Coughing again, she let the bottle slide through her fingers and hit the floor with a thud.

Sasha sat down beside her and put her hand on Astra's shoulder.

"Did you run all the way here? You should have called us."

"No...I..." Astra took a deep breath to steady herself, but as an image of Harry floated into her mind, her eyes filled with tears. She covered her face.

"Oh, Astra! Don't! It's okay..."

"It's not okay. It's not."

Astra shook her head, her voice quavering.

"I ran into town...was going to get a cab..." She rubbed her hand over her face as her vision blurred, hot tears spilling over. "Then Harry came out of a bar...with another man..."

Sasha groaned. "Oh *no*."

"They went into a back street! I saw them...s — saw them *kissing*." She covered her mouth as her throat closed, unable to speak.

"Oh God. Oh, Astra, I'm so sorry."

"I couldn't say it in front of Ash..." Astra took another gulp from the bottle, her fingers shaking. "Couldn't..."

Sasha slid closer and put her arm around Astra's shoulders.

"It's okay. We won't tell him."

"H — he won't find anyone. I lost the guy back at the casino..."

"Then he'll be back soon, and I won't say anything to him."

Astra leaned against Sasha's shoulder, fighting to control her tears.

"*Why?* He was so nice earlier. Why did he have to...?"

Silently, Sasha squeezed her tighter.

For a long moment, neither spoke, Astra's breathing slowly returning to normal.

Then Sasha's voice broke the silence.

"Are—are you sure it was a serious thing? I mean, couldn't it just have been, like…"

She pulled back to look Astra in the eye. Astra turned to meet her gaze.

"Like…well…that?"

Before Astra could say or do anything, Sasha had leant forward and kissed her.

Astra froze as Sasha's lips moved over hers, then felt her own hand tightening on Sasha's back, pulling her forward. Their tongues gently touched.

"Can't see anyone."

The front door banged open, startling them apart. Ash stood in the lounge doorway, chest heaving, breathless.

"He must have run off when Liddy shouted," Sasha suggested with remarkable composure.

"Must have," Astra agreed.

Ash crossed the room and put his hand on Sasha's shoulder, looking from one of them to the other.

"I'll leave you to it, shall I, Seychelle?" he asked finally.

"Yeah, probably best."

"You," Ash continued, turning to Astra. "Stay safe."

"I will."

Ash leaned in to kiss Sasha, then left, giving her shoulder a brief squeeze in parting. Sasha got up to lock the front door behind him, Astra joining her.

"Head up?" Sasha asked quietly, looking at Astra over her shoulder.

"Yeah."

They made their way up the stairs and around the first-floor corridor to Astra's bedroom. As Astra unlocked and opened the door, she turned to see Sasha waiting behind her, eyes fixed on hers.

A brief image flashed through her mind: herself in front of the mirror, the swaying weight between her legs, and a button under her thumb.

Fuck it.

The door slammed shut behind them.

Sasha's skin was smooth, her kisses passionate. Astra's calves hit the edge of the bed; falling backwards, she felt the soft support of the mattress, and then Sasha's warm weight tumbled over her and it was all too much.

She slid her hands under Sasha's shirt. At her touch, Sasha moaned, fingers clutching convulsively at Astra's hips, and in a sudden instant of blinding mutual excitement they were tearing at each other's clothes, desperate to feel skin on skin.

It was — *different.*

Softer. Warmer. More delicate; more curves. Hands settling in different places, finding new spots to catch and hold.

And a strange twisting heat in her stomach, something slightly...wrong.

And yet right, a voice in Astra's head noted as, with a swift movement, she rolled them over and started a slow slide down Sasha's naked body.

Definitely right.

Chapter Six

When morning dawned, Astra was pleasantly interested — although not surprised — to find herself not alone in the bed.

Sasha had still been there when she had woken up four hours ago, and it was highly unlikely she would have bothered to get up and dress at five in the morning. Even the average one-night-stand usually stayed the whole night, after all.

But then, how likely was it she and Sasha would have...

What was the word? ...'experimented'?

To Astra's mind, experimentation was what you did when you weren't sure what something was like. And certainly last night had been a new experience for both of them.

At first.

At eleven-thirty it could have been considered an experiment. But there was no excuse for their having reassessed the situation at two, or again when they had woken at five.

So not just experimentation, then.

And yet...

Thinking of Harry still inspired that same sparkling rush of feeling, if a little embittered by the memory of his actions the previous night. Looking at Sasha left her with feelings of warm friendship, possibly with an added twist of excitement. This didn't strike her as the start of a new relationship, or even as the start of a fling.

Friends with benefits, then?

Possibly.

Nice and non-committal, something which suggested fun rather than messy emotional entanglement. Astra felt she had enough emotional trauma in her life at the moment without adding more.

Still, it would probably be best not to mention this to Ash or Harry.

The more she thought about it, the more an uncomfortable image presented itself—Harry feeling free to share details about his boyfriends, while expecting her to be equally forthcoming. The thought was unbearable. Harry's private life might be an unarguable fact, but it was one she would much rather ignore.

And Ash...

True, Ash had been nice yesterday.

But Ash's primary interest would always be himself, and if it suited him to taunt Harry with his girlfriend's personal activities, he would do it. And if he chose to throw a fit of jealous rage in front of all their friends and sorority sisters, thereby exposing them to any amount of ridicule, innuendo and disgust, he wouldn't hesitate for one moment.

So no. Best not to mention it to Ash or Harry.

The sheets stirred beside her and Sasha's blonde, dishevelled head rolled on the pillow, coming to rest against Astra's shoulder. Blue eyes fluttered open and came to light on Astra's face, a warm smile kinking Sasha's mouth in recognition.

"Hi, *hermosa*."

"Hi, *guapa*."

"What time is it?"

"About nine. And it's Saturday, so we don't have to get up if we don't want."

"Ah, good." Sasha stretched out under the sheets, catching hold of the headboard at the same time. "I'm not seeing Ash until the party tonight—he's playing football again. Is sir coming tonight?"

"Doubt it. He'll be with me at the party."

Sasha gave her a wry look, which Astra returned with interest.

"You don't plan on, like, telling him what you saw..."

"No, I don't. I just don't want to know any more. And I don't plan on telling him about this either."

"I didn't think you would, somehow. I won't be telling Ash. He'd go crazy."

Astra paused, a wicked little smile crossing her face.

"Speaking of driving Ash crazy..."

"What?"

"About the party tonight..."

An equally evil grin crossed Sasha's face as Astra whispered in her ear.

* * * *

Sigma Delta Theta was right on the edge of campus, a grey stone building in the Gothic style, at least twice the size of the other Greek houses. Astra knew it fairly well, as two of her friends from Gaming Management lived there. Unlike Omega Zeta, most of the rooms were doubles, making Sigma a considerably larger sorority than theirs. It also had a reputation for riotous saturnalia that usually resulted in at least one person waking up in a dumpster.

The party was just getting started when the blonde and the redhead approached the house. Lights blazed from the large front windows, casting long shadows behind the numerous students as they crossed the driveway. As Astra pushed open the front door, a wave of pulsing rock music drenched them and filled the still night air, along with the strong aroma of chicken wings and ribs and the heady scent of alcohol.

"Astra!"

As Sasha entered the house behind her and moved into the kitchen to get drinks, Astra was embraced by a smaller girl with short black hair and a formidable, Army-cadet appearance that mismatched terribly with her girlishly enthusiastic welcome. She was dressed in a red halterneck and boot-cut trousers, and wore a gold stud in her right nostril.

"Hi, Jayla." Astra hugged her back.

"God, aren't you glad it's the weekend? That regulations class nearly killed me. You want a rib?" Jayla picked up two ribs from a platter on a table in the hallway and offered one.

"Thanks." Astra took it, glancing around for familiar faces. "Anyone here yet?"

"Nicole's in the lounge getting smashed — oh, and your Harry's in there too." Jayla gave Astra a knowing smile which vanished as something else came to mind. "He looks like he's going to slap someone. Uh, that guy from Alpha Nu Mu—Ashley Drake?"

So Ash was here too. Good. Nevertheless, Astra thought it prudent to grab Sasha and get into the lounge as quickly as possible, before punches were thrown. She looked over her shoulder, saw Sasha behind her carrying two glasses of punch, and gestured towards the lounge with her head. Sasha nodded.

Astra leading, they made their way into the lounge to find Harry sitting in one of the armchairs and Ash leaning casually on the mantelpiece. They were glaring at each other.

Harry looked up as Astra entered, flushing guiltily. He swallowed as his eyes travelled down from her laughing, cat-like green eyes, over her sleeveless green cheongsam, and down her smooth, bare legs to the glittering green sandals with straps that twisted round her ankles. God, she was hot.

And he didn't deserve her. She had no idea.

He had never intended things to go as far as they had. The risqué thrill of going to gay bars had been enough for him for some time. But then Marcus had come up to him at the bar and offered to buy him a drink, and one thing had led to another.

They hadn't gone home together, but the events in that alleyway had been some of the most erotic of his life.

That jawline…those shoulders…that kiss. *Oh fuck.*

But Astra…

Entering the room behind her was a smaller, slighter figure in a deep blue skirt and sequinned boob tube. Sasha Brereton. She leaned against Astra's shoulder, handed her a glass of punch and whispered something in her ear.

Astra laughed softly and whispered back, her lips brushing Sasha's neck. Harry found himself breaking out into a sweat.

There was always something about two girls together, even when he hadn't been confused about his own sexuality.

Astra turned away from Sasha and caught Harry's eye. Her face lit up in a warm, wicked smile which made his stomach twist as she approached him.

"Hi, Harry," she purred, leaning over the arm of the chair to kiss him. Harry jerked his hand to the back of her neck as she met his mouth with hers, tangling his fingers in her hair.

There was an audible snort from the other side of the room.

"Lost your tissues?" Sasha commented caustically from her position alongside Ash, who responded with a glare.

Astra twisted on the spot and fell backwards into the chair, landing across Harry's lap. Slinging an arm around his neck, she treated Ash to a dazzling smile which was met with a sneer.

"Were you all right last night?" Harry whispered, leaning in towards Astra's ear.

"Oh, *yes*. Very much so," Astra whispered back.

"No strange men?"

"Maybe a couple of over-familiar men." Astra stretched herself out like a cat, wiggling her hips against Harry's crotch. "But nothing you need worry about, honey."

As the smooth curves of her buttocks shifted against him, Harry found himself shivering, wondering if he could persuade her...

If we get bored we can go outside and get a few grass stains.

Oh God. He glanced breathlessly down at the short green dress she was wearing and became painfully aware of his own excitement, now thankfully hidden beneath her — *oh fuck!* — beneath her ass, which was still shifting as she chatted to that damn idiot McLaine behind her, shifting and twisting and rubbing against him…

Oh, you wait. You bloody wait.

* * * *

By the time the clock struck eleven, the alcohol was flowing freely and the partygoers were revelling, although the atmosphere in one part of the lounge was somewhat frosty.

Earlier in the evening, Astra had picked up a bar of chocolate from a passing tray and eaten it rather more seductively than was necessary. Apparently unable to draw his eyes from the sight of her tongue flickering over the head of the chocolate, Ash had involuntarily crushed his full can of beer, spraying the contents violently over Sasha's outfit. The ensuing argument had lasted fifteen minutes, only ceasing when one of the Sigma girls had offered Sasha a towel.

Ash and Sasha were still standing in front of the fireplace, Sasha stony-faced with arms folded while Ash leaned nonchalantly against the mantelpiece, staring off into the distance. Astra was now lying back across Harry's lap, ignoring the slightly agonised expression on his face, demonstrating her lack of gag reflex to McLaine, a brawny football player with blond hair and a pug nose. She was craning her neck back and sliding a cylindrical ice lolly into her throat, leaving only the stick visible.

"Mmm...so you see it's really not that hard...is it, Harry?"

"Harder than it looks," Harry muttered, fingers clenching on the arms of the chair. It was bad enough having Astra wiggle her hips on top of his aching hardness without her showing off her deep-throating ability to all and sundry.

Astra glanced across the room at Sasha and Ash, still fluttering her mouth over the ice lolly. Sasha was looking irritated, standing with her arms strategically placed to try and hide the beer stains on her outfit. Ash, on the other hand, was staring at her, mouth slightly open, with an expression of extreme lust.

Hmm. Maybe time for the second phase of the plan.

"Here, McLaine, have that." She handed the lolly over her shoulder to the startled McLaine and rolled off Harry's lap, giving him only seconds to grab a cushion and jam it over his groin.

A Diana Ross album was currently playing—the song just starting was *I'm Coming Out*. Astra shook her head, pressed a few buttons and *Chain Reaction* began belting out of the speakers. Catching her eye, Sasha understood immediately and stepped away from the mantelpiece.

The two girls met in the middle of the room, locked eyes, and began to dance.

Astra had the satisfaction of seeing both Harry's and Ash's jaws drop almost simultaneously. Most other male eyes were on them as well. She and Sasha had agreed that morning the two of them dancing together would drive both Ash and Harry crazy. And, as their bodies passed close to each other, as Sasha slid behind Astra and rested her hands on her hips, as Astra turned to face her and brushed against her from forehead to knees, it was becoming abundantly clear they had been right.

Halfway through the first chorus, Harry finished adjusting himself through his trouser pocket, stood up abruptly and marched out of the room, pausing only to lean into Astra's ear and whisper, "Meet me out back."

"Okay," Astra whispered back, her eyes glinting wickedly. Had Harry chosen to remain, she would have directed her attention at him for the second verse, but as he had left, she was safe to join Sasha in directing it at Ash.

Both girls, following the rhythm of the music, moved to face Ash as Ash backed slightly against the mantelpiece; Astra to his right, Sasha to his left, each stood astride his leg and pressed a hand to his chest, eyes fixed intently on his rather startled face.

Ash jolted in shock as she ran both hands down his chest, softly caressing the defined muscles of his stomach.

Sasha ran her hand back up and fanned the fingers across his chest. Astra slid hers down over his thigh, casting her eyes down to watch. A sharp intake of breath at her ear made her snap her gaze back up to immediately meet Ash's green eyes, looking at her with a passionate intensity which was unexpected.

He wants me.

Sasha glided away to taunt one of the football players on the other side of the room, seductively undulating her body in front of him. Ash's attention, however, was focussed entirely on Astra, now twisting sinuously to rest with her back against his chest, bringing one hand up to caress his neck.

He wants me. He's not thinking about men. All he sees is me.

She slid down his body, hips swaying. *Does he go to watch pole dancers? I bet he does.*

"Fuck…" she heard him say breathlessly.

As she rose, her body brushing against him, he caught her hips in his hands and pressed her against his crotch. Astra arched her back, feeling heat and hardness and pulsing against her cheeks as she ground her hips against him.

"Oh *fuck*… please…"

He was shaking, his voice unsteady, his breathing short and hot against her neck. Astra darted a glance at Sasha, who was still gyrating in front of the wide-eyed, slack-jawed football player, and turned in Ash's hands to face him, resting one hand on his shoulder. The song was entering its final chorus.

"Astra…" Ash dropped his head to look at her, their faces almost close enough to kiss. His face was flushed, glistening with sweat.

She trailed her hand down his chest, over his stomach and — *do I dare?* — palmed his erection for a moment before running down to his thigh.

The music was loud enough to cover Ash's groan.

"*Oh*, I — oh, *God*, yes…"

Astra twisted in front of him and struck a pose against him as the music hit its final beats.

The next song, *Why Do Fools Fall In Love*, began almost immediately. Sasha broke away from her football player and turned back to look at Astra, who was still shielding Ash, still resting her right hand on his thigh. She smiled back at Sasha, uncomfortably conscious of dampness under her hand.

"I think they enjoyed that, don't you?" Sasha commented cheerfully, apparently unaware of Ash's condition.

"Mmm," Astra agreed, casually wiping her hand on her dress. "We must do that again some time."

"*Fucking* hell," muttered a voice behind her, too quietly for anyone else to hear.

"Anyway, I'd better go find Harry," Astra continued, thinking it was time for a sharp exit. "He said to meet him out back."

"Ooh, lucky you." Sasha looked up at Ash, who had regained his composure enough to assume a casual sneer. "Do you want another drink, Ash?"

"If you're getting it," Ash responded coolly. "I'll be back down in a minute."

"Oh, okay."

Ash pushed Astra out of the way and strode, apparently rather uncomfortably, towards the door into the hallway.

"Looks like *someone* enjoyed it, anyway." Sasha grinned. "Think I know what *he'll* be doing."

"Yeah, me too," Astra agreed, privately thanking God Sasha had been engaged with the other boy. Tormenting Ash was one thing—making him climax was quite another. Gesturing towards the door, she mouthed, 'Harry' and made her way out into the back corridor, which led to a door into the garden.

The back wall had no windows, so the garden was only slightly lit by the residue of the blazing light from the sides of the building. Astra slitted her eyes and scanned the darkness for human-shaped shadows, but saw nothing.

"You."

A figure wrapped its arms around her from behind, its messy hair tickling her cheek as it buried its face in her neck. Astra gasped, reaching behind to touch the smooth, hot flesh through his shirt.

"You kept me waiting so *long*..."

"Hey, I couldn't leave in the middle of the floor show."

"Oh, God," Harry groaned, softly biting her earlobe. "What you did to me — you have *no* idea..." He ran his hands down the silk dress, moulding it to her curves. "You know it drives me crazy when you tease..."

Astra's eyes glinted momentarily. God, it was all too much.

She had just driven *Ash* crazy, just finished teasing him so much he came in his trousers in the middle of a crowded room, and she was still on fire. It was time for her to get something back.

"Oh, you wait, Harry," she purred, twisting in his arms and pushing him back against the wall. Harry moaned as she kissed him, undoing the buttons on his shirt and running her fingers across the bare skin on his chest.

"Oh, *yes*..."

Her fingertips brushed against his nipples, caressing them into points, as her mouth latched onto the weak spot just below his ear. Harry's hips jerked forward and he thrust against her, desperate for some friction.

"God, *please*... don't tease me... I can't..."

She ran her hands over his stomach and toyed with the button on his jeans. Harry groaned through his teeth, gripping her hips and crushing them against his.

"Astra, *please!*"

With a strength born of desperation, he span them both around on the spot and pressed Astra back against the stone, frantically pushing his hands under her skirt to get her underwear out of the way. Finding little more than wispy silk, he tore them off with a shaking hand and flung them aside, while he kept his other hand in place to find her wetness — *and smoothness, dear God, she's shaved* — and probe and tease and stroke and glide...

"Ohhh, God!" Astra groaned, pulling him against her and burying her face in his neck. "Right there..."

... his skin was so soft, and he tasted so sweet, and his fingers — God his fingers! — felt so *good*, and she had been so excited already, and this was *Harry*, whom she loved beyond all reason, and *oh fuck* he was unfastening his jeans with his other hand...

Trailing her lips from his neck to his mouth, she dropped her hands to his waist and swiftly helped him pull his jeans down to his knees before taking him in her hand, gripping him and working him, harder, faster, as he used his other hand to dip and swirl and tease and —

Harry groaned into her mouth and knocked her hand away.

"Fuck... don't, I'll come..."

He jerked his hands to her hips. Astra cried out in protest before he pushed forward and entered her, slowly at first, then thrusting sharply as her leg hooked around his thigh.

"Oh, *God*, yeah," he breathed, forcing himself to wait while he fought for control. "So good..."

Astra groaned impatiently and sharply tightened her leg's grip around him, causing him to thrust forward. "Fuck me *now!*"

"Oh, *Jesus!*"

As his hips slammed against her, Harry couldn't hold on any longer. He supported her leg with one hand while with the other he gripped her hip as he surged forward, thrusting and thrusting and *thrusting* while she clung to his shoulders and her cries echoed in his ear. He was already close, struggling to stave off his orgasm but gasping for breath as pleasure built up, muscles tightening, stomach tingling, *oh God not yet, not yet, just another few seconds, ohfucksoclose...*

Astra arched against him, crushing her body against his as he thrust, digging her fingers into his back as the tingling and pulsing and throbbing grew stronger. She was right on the edge, *fuck* it felt good, and then she was clutching at his hair and *ohgodrightnow*, she was *there* and she was screaming her pleasure in his ear and convulsing around him.

"Oh, God!" Harry gasped as her muscles contracted around him. "Oh, yes!"

Oh, yes!

When the haze had cleared, Harry and Astra found themselves slumped on the damp grass, still pressed against the wall.

"Didn't get any grass stains," Harry mumbled against her neck.

Astra shifted and felt the wall against her skin.

"No, but I think I've ripped the back of this fucking dress."

"Shit. Sorry."

"Oh, don't worry. I've got plenty."

"I didn't hurt you, did I?"

"No, I don't think so."

Harry slowly pulled out of her and stood up, tucking himself back into his jeans with one hand while he helped Astra up with the other. Astra turned around to check the back of her dress, which had several rips in the back and another over her right buttock.

"Any blood?"

Harry leaned closer to examine the skin through the rips, for slightly longer than necessary.

"No. All perfect." He bent and kissed her through the lowest tear.

"Thank you. But I don't know how I'm going to get back across campus like this."

"Wait here. I'll get my coat." Harry headed through the back door and returned a few minutes later with a long leather coat over one arm. "Here, this should cover everything. I'll walk you back."

"You can stop over if you want." Astra smiled up at him winningly.

"Now there's an offer I can't refuse." Harry helped her into the coat, then turned her to face him and reached into the inside pocket. When he withdrew his hand, he was clutching a bottle of Jim Beam.

"You come prepared, don't you?"

"Would you expect anything less?" Harry grinned, unscrewing the cap and dropping it into the coat pocket.

Hand in hand, they made their way around the outside of the sorority house and started the walk back to Omega Zeta.

* * * *

By the time Astra and Harry reached the sorority house, they were both quite cataclysmically drunk.

The stairs proved rather more complicated than usual, but they managed to conquer them by way of crawling up on their hands and knees. However, on reaching the first floor Astra decided now would be a good time to visit the bathroom. She handed the coat and her room key to

Harry, who had taken the opportunity to urinate behind a bush on their way in, and left him to stagger down the corridor while she fell through the bathroom door and into a cubicle.

She had intended to leave on the opposite side, thereby reducing the walk to her bedroom, but intoxication led her to leave through the door she had used on her way in. Faced again with the staircase, she paused and turned around to regain her bearings.

"Astra."

The low, breathless voice behind her had an immediate sobering effect, although not a complete one. Astra froze.

"Ash."

Ash's voice had now taken on a strained quality.

"Oh *fuck*... please don't tell me you're commando under that..."

Astra became conscious of cold air through the rip over her right buttock, and remembered with a blush Harry had torn off her underwear and left it in the garden at Sigma Delta Theta. She turned to face Ash, thinking it was probably safer.

Ash was standing at the bend of the corridor, flushed and slightly unsteady on his feet, breathing hard and staring at her with a drunken intensity. Astra took a step backwards, ready to flee if necessary.

"You staying over with Sash?"

"Don't you fucking... oh, you tease..."

Ash closed the gap between them in three strides. Astra turned to run, but found her arm in a vise-like grip.

His eyes still burned into her, but the anger she had expected to see had been replaced by desire and what looked like desperation.

"You drove me fucking insane tonight. Sitting there sucking that chocolate, deep-throating that *thing*, and all I can think about is your mouth on my dick. And then you dance like that with Seychelle, you grind up on me like that...oh, God...you get me so hot I can't see straight, you get me off in front of all those people...and then you go outside and fuck that—"

He broke off, breathing heavily.

"He doesn't deserve you. I swear, he doesn't deserve you."

Ash was starting to get into this a little too much for Astra's liking.

"Ash, you're drunk. Let me go."

With a hazy yet predatory grin, Ash redoubled his grip on her arm as Astra attempted to pull it free.

"Oh, no you don't. Get back here. You don't get to go just *yet*."

And with that last word, Ash yanked her towards him, catching and twisting her shoulders to pull her back flush against his chest. One arm pinned across her stomach, the other sweeping her hair to one side, he dropped his mouth to her neck and *bit*.

Unable to fight back, Astra threw her head back against his shoulder, conscious the world was spinning. Ash's mouth was sucking at the tender skin, his crotch pressed up against her bottom, and the heat between them was starting to send tingles along her spine as it rested against his chest, and he was *hard*, and it was easier not to struggle, and maybe she didn't want to...

Ash's grip loosened a little and Astra tensed, waiting for an opportunity to break free.

I did not just enjoy that. I didn't.

"Fuck..." Ash moaned, his breath ragged. "I *want*..."

Astra snaked her hand behind her, ready to punch him in the groin, only for Ash to abruptly release his hold and push her softly away. Weak with relief, Astra caught hold of the bathroom door handle to steady herself and darted a glance over her shoulder to see what he was doing.

Ash was standing straight, watching her with a twist to his mouth, but looking oddly defeated.

Not wanting to dwell on this too long, Astra wrenched open the door and lurched through the bathroom, diving out of the other side and through her own bedroom door, locking it behind her as she fell back against it.

"Well, hello," murmured Harry's voice from the bed.

"Well, hello," Astra murmured back, taking deep breaths to steady herself. "You should see what you've done to my neck."

Chapter Seven

Astra's life was becoming complicated.

The end of her final year was looming, coursework deadlines beckoned, and her internship at the Fountain took precedence over everything. Yet, over the weeks that followed the party at Sigma Delta Theta, she found her life had become busier and more confusing than any reasonable person would wish.

Like with Sasha.

It was rather difficult to find time to spend together. Sasha spent a remarkable amount of time in lectures, seminars and lab sessions. Astra herself had little contact time but far more coursework, and was still spending three evenings a week working at the casino. It left little time for stolen moments, even discounting their social life and the obvious male influences on their calendars.

And finding a place to be alone was virtually impossible.

Their sorority sisters, who would so happily have left them alone with their boyfriends, were a constant presence when they were alone with each other. And, of course, while spending the night in each other's rooms was always a possibility, it was necessary to keep as quiet as possible to avoid waking their next-door neighbours.

Sasha was considerably more imaginative than Astra had realised. She had a collection of toys that included a triple-headed Rampant Rabbit and a number of items which suggested either she or Ash had a strong dominant streak.

More importantly, she had taken to the strap-on dildo like a duck to water, even going so far as to suggest wearing it herself once or twice—although Astra had found she didn't much care for that. Still, Sasha seemed relaxed about always being on the bottom.

And she was prepared to do the ice thing.

It was good to have at least one relationship which was straightforward, if unorthodox. Astra often caught herself wondering why her other relationship was so stressful.

Harry was still a constant fixture. Their relationship remained as passionate as ever and Astra told herself this was surely proof of his heterosexuality, although little else seemed to exist in their relationship. Buoyed up by her apparent acceptance and his so far unspecified manoeuvrings in the gay scene, he had begun to express himself more *exuberantly* than before. In fact, it appeared he had decided to embrace his inner gay stereotype.

"You look... great," Astra had said supportively the first time he had turned up at her door wearing spray-on white trousers, glitter make-up and with his hair gelled into a fin. There was actually something attractive about Harry's feminine side—she found herself watching him, her hips automatically falling into the swaggering pose she had seen in the mirror. However, she couldn't help thinking this was making her look either needy or delusional.

She had mentioned this to him casually one afternoon while sitting on his bed. The daylight was streaming through the windows, spilling across minimalistically bare white walls. In the blaze of light her spirits were lifted, spurring her forward.

"Do you think it looks a bit weird, us going out places with you dressed like you were last night?"

Harry looked over his shoulder from his squatting position on the other side of the room, where he was plugging in his computer.

"No. Why, do you?"

"Well, I did hear someone behind me say 'hag' when you started dancing to the Weather Girls."

"Ah, right."

Harry straightened up and stretched, hooking his thumbs into the belt loops of his black jeans and rolling his shoulders under his grey T-shirt, before crossing the room and throwing himself down on the bed beside her.

"Well, I'll tone it down a bit if you like, but it *is* what I wear most nights when I go out. I didn't want to hide it from you."

Astra raised an elegant eyebrow at his rather sweet attack of morality, given what else she knew he was hiding.

"Anyway, it should be pretty obvious I'm *not* gay. We spent five simultaneous songs making out under the mirror ball."

Astra felt it was even more unlikely a genuinely gay man would have had the response Harry had just had to her mouthing him through his jeans. Nevertheless, this was skirting the real issue.

"Have you worked out what you actually *are* yet? I mean, are you bi or what?"

Harry paused for a moment, looking uncomfortable.

"I'm...not sure. I'm not *gay*. I definitely like girls. And I love *you*. But I'm not really sure how I feel about men. I mean, it's kind of exciting when..."

He trailed off uncertainly.

"When you disappear off with them into alleys?"

Harry nearly broke his neck turning to look at her.

"When I...*what?!*"

Astra was almost as surprised as him, having spoken without thinking, but it was impossible to leave the subject hanging at this point.

"I saw you. Couple of months back. You went off down an alleyway with this tall guy and kissed him."

Harry stared at her for a moment, then slumped back against the headboard, shaking his head in disbelief.

"You saw... Shit."

Silence fell between them.

As the tension increased, Astra's stomach twisted painfully, her hands and knees trembling. It was impossible to know what was going through Harry's head as he stared, stunned, off into space.

She should never have brought this up. She should have ignored it. It was easier that way. Now she had ruined everything.

Shit.

Breaking his reverie, Harry turned to look at her.

"Why didn't you tell me?"

"Didn't want to talk about it." Astra heard her voice come out tense, strained.

"I...I'm sorry."

Astra flicked her eyes at him, not trusting herself to speak. She saw Harry wince, an expression of contrition on his face.

"No, I really am… I should have told you. I didn't mean to lie—"

Astra was embarrassed to find herself on the verge of tears. She bit her lip and looked away, but from his look of horror, Harry had already noticed.

"Oh God, don't cry. I'm so sorry—I just, I wanted to know what it was like—I didn't want to hurt you, I had no idea you'd seen me. I thought, you know, it didn't count, with men—I mean, I'm not having sex with them, I would never do that to you." Harry pulled her against him and wrapped his arms around her, pressing his face into her hair.

Astra paused, struggling with her emotions, before an image of Sasha forced its way into her mind.

Who am I kidding? I'm no better than him.

The words came out in a rush.

"Maybe we should date other people."

Harry pulled back and stared at her.

"What? Do—" His voice faltered. "Are you breaking up with me?"

"No! No. I just think—" Astra stopped to clear her throat and rearrange her thoughts. "Then you can date men and not feel bad, and I can date other people too."

Harry continued to stare at her, his face working. Mentally Astra categorised the emotions in his eyes. Desire to experiment versus jealousy over his girlfriend.

Desire won.

"All right."

The reluctance radiated from every angle of Harry's tense body, but his face had relaxed slightly, and Astra sensed relief.

"Fine."

For a moment they sat in silence, Astra wondering how Sasha would feel about being considered a 'date'.

It didn't sound right to her.

But Harry was going to date men anyway, whatever happened, no matter how much the thought made her stomach clench.

And she could stop feeling guilty.

"I'll promise you this," said Harry finally, drawing Astra's legs over his and holding her in his lap. "If you want to know anything about what I'm doing, ask, and I'll tell you. For me, it's just experimentation, but I don't want you to bottle it up. Just ask me."

Enfolded in the familiar warmth of his arms, Astra thought she would have agreed to anything.

"Okay."

"There's no-one else I want. Only you." Harry held her gaze for a second, then kissed her. "And on that note..." He kissed her again, shifting his weight so as to manoeuvre her onto her back. "I think I owe you something. All the blood..." He rolled on top of her, supporting himself on his elbows as he rocked his hardness against her. "...has gone back where it belongs, and since I'm going to enjoy this, I'll just have to make you come twice to make up."

"Well," Astra sighed resignedly, "if you insist."

* * * *

Regardless of the situation with Harry, the situation with Ash was becoming untenable.

Immediately after the party, Astra had elected to feign memory loss. This plan of action had served her well on the Sunday morning, when she had run into Ash and Sasha having breakfast in the kitchen. Judging by Ash's look of slightly hungover confusion, he had been expecting awkwardness at the very least, possibly even physical retribution. It was really quite amusing to watch his attempt to process her cheerful greetings and airy flitting around the kitchen, all the while trying to surreptitiously spot the bruise on her neck, which Astra had covered with a heavy layer of makeup.

Following this incident, Ash had adopted the same attitude of casual indifference. His relationship with Sasha didn't seem to have suffered. They were still as vocal as ever, regardless of whether they were on good terms or bad, to such a degree that anyone walking past Sasha's bedroom could gauge the situation and decide if one should knock or run for cover.

"Look, just because you're in a filthy mood—"

"I wouldn't *be* in this mood if you didn't wake me up at crazy hours—"

"So don't invite me over when I have training and you can sleep in."

On other occasions, the conversation would be running much more smoothly.

"Oh yeah, right there, yeah, *oh God yeah*, I'm going to— *ohfuck*—don't stop, don't stop—oh fuck I'm gonna *ah!* gonna *oh sweet Jesus!*"

Quite chatty, that Ash, when he wanted to be.

Astra had relaxed after a few days. Maybe Ash had shocked himself with the violence of his reaction. Surely she could now be in his presence with impunity. Her own reaction to him was something that could be easily dismissed.

Or suppressed.

Unfortunately, this state of ease had evaporated a few days previously.

Having spent an hour in Sasha's bedroom, Sasha had been feeling far too lazy to move and had sent Astra over to Ash's room to pick up her cell phone, which she had left behind the day before. Never having been further than the bathroom in the Alpha Nu Mu house, Astra had been relying solely on Sasha's directions and had knocked on Ash's bedroom door with some trepidation, not convinced she wasn't about to disturb some unknown frat boy in the middle of something embarrassing.

The strained, breathless response had been surprising, but uniquely Ash.

"Fuck off, Conley, I'm busy!"

Astra blinked.

"Um…it's not Conley, it's Astra."

There was a sharp intake of breath, followed by a gasp and a scrambling noise.

"Um, hold on…"

More scrambling. Something soft-sounding hit something else with a thud and then there was the sound of a wardrobe door opening.

"Look, I can come back later, I'm just here to get…"

"No, it's okay, I'll be right with you, hang on…"

There was the sound of a coat-hanger rattling, then three steps and the door flew open to reveal Ash, flushed and sweating, wearing half-buttoned jeans and an unbuttoned shirt.

For an eternal moment, neither said anything. It was only when a door slammed further down the corridor that Astra realised she had been staring unashamedly at Ash's chest. Snapping her eyes up in embarrassment, she immediately met Ash's gaze.

He apparently had been too busy staring at her to notice.

"Uh, Sash said she left her cell behind…"

"What? Oh." Ash shook his head to clear it. "Yeah, she did. I'll get it." He turned away from the door, then paused and turned back as Astra stayed in the doorway. "Uh, come in if you want."

"Oh, thanks."

Closing the door behind her, Astra took a moment to fully take in the room as Ash rummaged through a cabinet beside the bed. It was a fairly typical fraternity room—the walls were plastered with rock music posters, while the floor was littered with discarded shoes and pizza boxes. Against one wall, surrounded by junk, was an electric guitar in a stand.

"I didn't know you played the guitar."

Ash straightened up, holding Sasha's cell phone. "Oh, that. Yeah, a bit. Here, catch."

He threw the phone to Astra, who caught it one-handed.

"Thanks. Mind if I…?" She gestured towards the guitar. "I play a bit."

Ash raised intrigued eyebrows. "Go for it."

With a private smile, Astra picked up the instrument and gave it a test strum to make sure it was in tune. She had fourteen years of lessons under her belt, which was apparently more than the incredulous Ash gave her credit for. Hooking the strap over her shoulder, she steadied the guitar and broke into the first few bars of a Michelle Branch track.

"I've been driving for an hour…"

"Who sings that?"

"Michelle Branch."

Ash shook his head in exasperation, disentangled her from the strap and climbed up onto the bed, arranging himself with his back against the headboard and the guitar in his lap. "You are not using my guitar to play that crap. Watch and learn."

With an inward shrug, Astra sat down in a nearby swivel chair and waited while Ash adjusted one of the strings. As she shifted, trying to get comfortable, one of the wheels caught in something on the floor. Astra twisted round to look.

A green T-shirt lay on the carpet behind the chair.

Astra reached down and touched the fabric, intending to release the wheel, before realising the shirt was warm and spattered with—oh *God*. Her hand snapped back and automatically wiped itself on her jeans.

So that's why it took him so long to open the fucking door.

Ash's attention was, fortunately, still on the guitar. Astra eyed him slyly. It was interesting to think about where those hands had been a few minutes earlier.

"Ready?"

"Um, yeah."

"Good."

Ash struck up the opening chords of *Sweet Child O' Mine*.

"She's got a smile that it seems to me…"

Shit, he's good!

Ash had a surprisingly deep, controlled rock voice—a little rough, a little unpolished in places, yet with a raw darkness that struck some inner chord. Astra found herself leaning forward in her seat, losing herself in the music as Ash's fingers moved over the strings.

It had always been a favourite song of hers. That was obviously why she was staring at the man who played it so well.

Why her hazy eyes slid from his skilled fingers to the soft, white-blond hair that fell over the pale skin on his face, to his green eyes as they focussed on the guitar, to his expression of concentration, to the bare skin on his chest, to the way his legs splayed over the quilt and the flash of blond that showed in the gaps where his jeans were still half-buttoned...

"Where do we go now..."

Blushing, Astra jolted out of her reverie, hoping against hope Ash hadn't noticed her eyes lingering on his crotch.

Ash slowly raised his eyes to meet hers as he finished the final chords, one eyebrow raised knowingly.

Whether he had noticed or not, he was obviously aware of the effect it had had on her. Possibly not aware of the effect *he* had had on her.

"You're really good," Astra croaked hoarsely, before coughing.

Ash arched his eyebrow again. "So they tell me."

A heated silence fell between them, Astra surreptitiously wrestling for control, conscious of Ash's determination to retain it.

She won.

"Well, I'd better get back..." She held up the cell phone. "Sash'll be wanting this."

Ash's expression cleared immediately.

"Course she will."

He picked up the guitar by the neck as he swung his legs off the bed and crossed to hold the door open for her. Being Ash, he held it open with his back, thereby blocking half of the doorway.

"Thanks," said Astra, sidling awkwardly through the gap. Her arm caught the edge of his shirt and flipped it further open, briefly revealing his nipple.

"Don't mention it."

"See you later."

"Hope so."

"Bye, now."

"Bye."

It wasn't until she was out of the building and down the street that Astra felt safe from having that green gaze on her.

Clearly, while Ash had regained control over himself, he had devised a new plan of attack. One that seemed to actually *work*.

And equally clearly, her own response was not something that could be easily pushed aside.

What with a confused Harry and a seductive Ash, Astra was beginning to wonder if sticking with Sasha might not be the easiest alternative.

* * * *

Day after day, night after night, Astra found herself sitting alone on her bed, or staring out of the window, or standing in front of the mirror, asking herself the same question over and over again.

What is this?

There was no emotion at the image of Sasha. Friendship. Affection. But her heart seemed untouchable, unobtainable, shielded behind glass.

She conjured up a memory of Sasha and herself together, and felt a brief flicker of something, something that tugged at the stomach — exciting, yet evanescent.

Fleeting.

Until, one day, she parted her thighs further and lowered her chin, eyeing herself with a confident, almost aggressive stare, her hips falling into a cocky thrust.

The surge of excitement left her gasping, clutching at the sink as her knees buckled, and although the answer immediately echoed in her mind, her heart shrank from it.

The second time Astra tried it, she hung her guitar around her neck.

Yes.

The masculinity of the pose made her body tense, made her skin flush and her nerves thrill as her back arched involuntarily, trembling with desire.

It only required one more thing.

The strap-on dildo.

Standing in front of the mirror, swaggering, the purple phallus rising proud, Astra looked herself straight in the eye and flicked the button into the *on* position.

A few minutes later she dropped to her knees, shuddering and panting as the final throb of pleasure hit her.

What is this? What the hell is this?

* * * *

For the few weeks immediately following the attack, Astra had taken a taxi to work and back, apart from the few occasions when she had been escorted by her friend Nicole's boyfriend Chip. Chip was what Nicole liked to describe as a 'card-carrying emo kid'. Walking down the road with him, his black hair falling over his scowling face and barely revealing his darting, charcoal-rimmed eyes, had students and passers-by alike sliding nervously out of the way. *Uh-oh. Don't get involved.*

It would have made more sense, of course, to ask Harry to escort her. In fact, it would have made sense for her to tell him what had happened. But she couldn't.

Initially it had been an instinctive reaction.

She hadn't wanted to discuss any of the events of that night with him, she had wanted only to force them to the back of her mind. Later, she had reasoned that to tell him would create more problems than it solved. He would want to know why she hadn't called him, which could only convincingly be answered by admitting what she had seen.

However, now she had told him that, she found time had erected a barrier.

And, quite frankly, she didn't want to discuss that night again.

Nothing had happened in weeks. She no longer felt in any danger, and the taxis were eating away at her salary, so walking home had seemed the best option. But while walking home, alone in the dark, all she could do was think of what Harry was probably doing.

Most of the time she could push it to the back of her mind—cloud it with thoughts of Sasha, or Ash, or work. But it was always there, pulsing beneath the surface. And at night, alone on the street, so close to those bars where she had seen the things she had seen, she was powerless against it.

She was losing Harry.

When they were together, he still felt like he was hers. But he was out nearly every night in the bars. Whatever he said, when this feeling overwhelmed her Astra was unable to believe he wasn't having sex with the men he picked up.

And even if he wasn't, it was only a technicality. Closing her eyes left Astra bombarded with images that left her breathless with pain. Harry rutting against another man in a dark alley, Harry climaxing in the hands or the mouth of a stranger, Harry on his knees, sucking on another man's shaft, swallowing, or pulling back to have his face bathed in—

Too much.

In the past he had been *hers* every minute of every day. But now... now when she thought of him, the intimacy was lost. She fought to remember, was afraid to forget, but it was slipping away all the time.

I can't remember the way your lips felt.

I can't remember the taste of your skin.

Sex between them was as passionate as ever. Astra threw herself into it, desperate to experience again all those details she was losing. But within a day of each encounter, the memory would fade, leaving only an echo.

Often, the walk home would turn into a hopeless, awkward run—she would fall into the sorority house with one hand over her face and hide in the bathroom until the tears had finished falling, when she would wash her face and step out to face the world as if nothing was wrong.

Things *were* wrong, and they were getting worse every day.

And it was on one of these hopeless, tear-stained nights that Sasha cornered her in the toilets and uttered those words that Astra had dreaded.

"Ash knows."

Chapter Eight

"Ash... Fuck."

Sasha said nothing, but Astra heard her exhale tensely.

"Shit." Astra shook her head. "I can't..."

Sasha shrugged helplessly.

"How does he know? We were careful."

"Apparently he was planning to sneak through my bedroom window one night last week." Sasha leant back against the bank of sinks. "He came up the fire escape and saw us in my room."

"Christ."

The two girls stared straight ahead for a silent moment, each lost in her own thoughts.

After the silence had stretched out for a long time, Astra spoke.

"So what did he say?"

"Well, he asked how long it had been going on..." Sasha shifted uncomfortably. "Asked what we did together, you know...it's always been a fantasy of his..."

"It's a fantasy of just about every guy on the planet." The bile rose in Astra's throat. "Except Harry, of course."

Sasha eyed her sardonically.

"Sorry, ignore me," Astra muttered. "What's he going to do about it?"

"You're not going to like it."

"He's going to tell Harry. Right?"

"No."

No?

Astra sagged against the sinks. "He's going to tell everyone else, then…"

Sasha shook her head with a mirthless laugh. "Oh God, no."

"What then?"

There was an uncomfortable pause. Astra eyed Sasha as she twisted her fingers together awkwardly, her gaze skittering all over the floor.

"Sash? What?"

Sasha took a deep breath, turned to Astra and held her in place by the shoulders, looking her straight in the eyes.

"He wants to join in."

* * * *

The following morning, Astra and Sasha met in Sasha's room to finish the conversation of the previous night, which Astra had unceremoniously cut short by storming out of the bathroom and going to bed.

Ash wanted to join in.

It shouldn't have been a surprise. If any man was going to fantasise about a threesome with two girls, it was Ash, in all his defiant heterosexuality. And if any man was going to fantasise about sex with his girlfriend and Astra, it was definitely Ash. He had been wanting to possess her ever since she had turned him down.

And Astra had taunted him.

She had held him at bay, but had flirted with him, had danced with Sasha purely to drive him crazy, had deliberately touched him in a way that was decidedly inappropriate for the boyfriend of her best friend.

And she knew, too, that his feelings for her were stronger than she had initially imagined.

He had admitted that he liked her.

He had responded to her, at the party, in a way which had suggested more than just lust.

Oh fuck, please… Astra…

And his response to her, after the party, had been more violent, more passionate, than she had expected.

You make me so hot I can't see straight.

She had known he wanted her, and she had used that to her advantage.

So it was no surprise he chose to press his own advantage now he had one.

If she refused this, he would tell everyone else.

If she agreed to this, she would break Harry's heart. Dating another men in the abstract — or even Sasha in the concrete — was one thing, but sleeping with Ash?

It was an impossible situation.

* * * *

"Ash wants to join in."

"Yes."

"I'm not sure about this."

"I know you're not."

"How do you feel about it?" This was Sasha's boyfriend, after all. If Astra didn't like sharing Harry with men, surely Sasha wouldn't like sharing Ash with another woman.

Sasha dropped her eyes and smiled coyly. "I've always fancied it, actually."

"*Really?*"

"Yes, really! I like sex with him and I like fooling around with you, so both of you together..." Sasha's eyes rolled back into her head in exaggerated ecstasy.

"You little slut," Astra laughed, whacking her over the head with the pillow.

"Hey!" Sasha picked up a giant teddy bear from beside the bed and hit Astra back. Astra pressed back against the bear with the pillow. The two wrestled for a moment before Sasha fell back onto the mattress and allowed a triumphant Astra to pin her arms.

"Hello there," Sasha said playfully, winking at her dishevelled friend from her supine position.

"Hello there, my little submissive friend."

"Only with you." Sasha's eyes twinkled. "When I'm with Ash, I'm his dominatrix."

Astra stilled.

"You're his..."

"Oh yes." Sasha sat up, bringing herself flush against Astra, who was straddling her hips. She leaned in and whispered, letting her breath ghost across Astra's lips. "He *loves* being dominated."

Okay. That *really* shouldn't have sent tingles through Astra's stomach.

"You like that, don't you? I knew you were a closet dom."

Astra paused to steady her voice. "Well, I didn't know he was a closet sub."

"Oh, you have *no* idea. I bet you thought all that shit under the bed was used on me, didn't you? Fuck that." Sasha giggled cheekily at the look on Astra's face. "I can tell you everything he likes. I can tell you how to drive him *wild*. He likes to throw his weight around with you, doesn't he? Just think what we could do to him if we double-team him."

"Stop it, you." This was *not* turning Astra on.

"Oh, you do like that, don't you," Sasha teased. "You liked getting him all worked up at Sigma. You got him off, didn't you? I could tell by the way he was acting all night. You made him cream himself."

"From what I've heard," Astra retorted, struggling to regain control of the conversation, "that's nothing new. He's not known for his staying power."

"Oh, well..." Sasha screwed up her face dismissively. "That all goes back to a little incident with a girl on Liddy's course. It was before I met him. I gather he hadn't had it in a while and she had a Brazilian, so he got a bit carried away. Are we looking a little jealous here?"

"No, we are *not*." Astra hastily straightened her face.

"Of course we aren't. Anyway, don't worry. He can last, and I know a few tricks if he can't. Which we may need, since you have a Hollywood. Assuming you agree to it, of course." Sasha peeked up at Astra through her eyelashes. "I bet we could make him do the ice thing."

"I'll think about it, my little sub." Using her full body weight, Astra bore down on Sasha so the two of them fell back onto the bed. "What do you think you're playing at, honey, getting me all excited?"

"Oh, you know what? I think we need to do this the other way, since you find it *soooo* hard to believe I can dominate." Sasha rolled them over, reaching over the side of the bed for the strap-on. "I think *you* need to bottom for a change. Just lie back and relax, baby, and I'll relieve you of all that excess excitement."

"I haven't agreed to this yet, you know."

"I know. Do let me know when you do. If you do. You know what I mean."

"Stop babbling, sweetie."

"Of course, honey. Knees up."

* * * *

Over the course of the next few days, Astra turned her dilemma over and over in her head.

She was forced to pay attention during lectures, not wishing to explain to anyone she was considering a threesome with her best friend and an admittedly sexy athlete with a reputation for a short fuse, but the remaining time was spent on autopilot as she wrestled with her conscience.

She could reconcile her experimentation with Sasha as being equal to Harry's experimentation with other men. Even if he was, in fact, having sex with them, which he had fervently denied. But sex with Ash was a different matter entirely.

Harry hated Ash.

Hated him.

Of course, it wouldn't be dating. It would be a threesome. Dating suggested she was emotionally involved—a threesome would just be sex. More experimentation.

But did Harry see it that way?

This was the point which always twisted the knife.

While Harry might not be emotionally involved with any one man, the fact remained he was slipping away, and this was a betrayal far greater than simple sex with others. He was disappearing into his own world, despite his assurances he was still hers.

And in his absence, Sasha and Ash seemed much more attractive.

Oh God, Ash was attractive.

He was an arrogant jerk who had been hitting on her for months. He was an idiot jock whose brains were almost entirely in his trousers. He was the perfectly toned, green-eyed possessor of a remarkable rock voice and skilled guitarist's fingers, and from what she had accidentally seen, he was definitely a natural blond...

And apparently he was a closet sub. The idea of him at the mercy of herself and Sasha was frankly intoxicating.

Oh fuck, please... Astra...

Could she really do this?

Memories of that party at Sigma kept flitting back into her head. He had looked at her with a passionate intensity she had only ever seen in Harry, and these days it was never clear what was really in Harry's head. But it had been clear what had been in Ash's head during that dance, when he had been flushed and shaking and desperate under her hands...

And it had been equally clear during that incident upstairs, when he had caught her knickerless in that green dress and had marked her neck.

You make me so hot I can't see straight.

Maybe she could do this. Maybe she could let Sasha tell her what Ash liked… That sounded good. Exciting, even. Maybe this really was just experimentation…

All I can think of is your mouth on my dick.

No. Hold on.

She couldn't do that.

It was a minor point, and a ridiculous scruple given what she was considering, but she couldn't do that. She and Sasha had done many things together, but they had a mutual agreement to save that only for their boyfriends — fingers and vibrators worked just as well. Ash would probably be very pissed off, but too damn bad. She wasn't giving him head.

And she wasn't taking it from him, either. Whether that would be an issue was open to question. Just because Harry liked it, if enthusiasm and frequency were anything to go by, didn't mean Ash did.

Maybe it was one of Sasha's dom tricks to sit on his face. This image, coming to mind as it did while she was at work, caused her to erupt in giggles which she was forced to hurriedly cough over. It simply wasn't done to fall about in hysterics at the blackjack table, particularly when a rather peeved-looking man on her left had just lost a fortune on two queens.

Especially when she was in line for a management role.

Clearing her table at the end of the evening, Astra deliberately kept her head low as she sensed Ally's presence behind her.

What's she going to say this time?

Her spine tensed, but instead of words, there was a sudden *thud* as a glass of orange juice bounced across the table in front of her, knocking over a pile of chips and drenching several cards before Astra could move them.

"Oops," a little voice giggled in her ear. Astra span around and glared, but Ally had already disappeared from view.

Damn it.

Why can't I just stand up to her? Why do I let her walk all over me?

She was going to be management. She would be over people who might resent her, people who might refuse to respect her authority.

People like Ally.

And Brad would expect her to deal with it. Hell, if she couldn't contain one idiot Valley Girl, he might pass her over altogether. No point showing off her skills as croupier and keeping her Facebook clean if she buckled in the face of resistance from her co-workers.

I have to take charge. I have to find a way.

The mantra repeated in her head as she swiftly cleaned up the mess, as she treated Brad to a carefree smile as he passed, carefully concealing the stain with one hand, as she caught up her coat and made for the door, deliberately keeping a straight face as she passed Ally in the corridor.

As she stepped outside, she was briefly conscious of a presence to her left before something moved, fast, *fast*…

Pain. Something hard, heavy, struck her with force. Stars swirling… spinning… world tipping sideways…

Cold, hard concrete rising to meet her.

* * * *

Something cool and soft pressed against her cheek, supporting her body.

Slowly, Astra opened her eyes, squinting in the light.

She immediately winced as a throbbing pain pounded through her head. God, it was agony. Pressing one clammy hand to her face, she succumbed to a bout of dry-retching as nausea rose in her throat.

A figure in blue entered the room hurriedly and pressed a bowl under her face just before Astra vomited explosively.

"It's alright. You have a concussion. Try not to move."

As Astra's eyes focussed, she recognised the blue as part of a nurse's uniform.

"What...? Where...?"

"Don't talk," said the nurse unnecessarily as Astra lost control of her stomach again. "You're in the emergency ward. You were brought in two hours ago by your manager. The police are waiting outside for when you feel stronger. They'd like a statement."

"A statement?" Astra croaked dizzily, raising her head from the bowl. Oops, bad idea. "What hap...? Ugh..."

"You were hit by a bicycle outside the Fountain Casino. Your colleague Allison overheard the accident and called the ambulance."

Astra had a sudden, clear vision of the street outside the casino, of a fast moving shape at her side, and then violent pain and blackness. *Hit by a bike.*

"You're very lucky you weren't more badly hurt." The nurse gestured towards Astra's left temple. "As it is, you may have some scarring, although the wounds have been sutured, and you will have to remain in bed for a few days to recover from the concussion. I'm afraid we can't let you leave without an escort. The police have telephoned your family, but I gather they live in Michigan, so they found the number of a Harry Delfino on your cell phone. Your manager indicated he was your partner?"

"Yes. Is he coming?"

"I believe the officer left a message on his voicemail. His phone was switched off." After watching Astra for a moment to see if any more eruptions were forthcoming, the nurse removed the bowl and moved towards the door. "Get some rest, Miss Scott. I'll send the officer in when you're ready. If you need anything, press the buzzer on the table."

"Thank you."

As the door closed, Astra lay back and stared at the ceiling, struggling to ignore the pain in her head and wondering if any painkillers were on the way. Probably they would have to wait for her nausea to settle.

Harry's phone was switched off.

Harry almost *never* switched his phone off. She had been woken up by it enough times to know it was always on, all day and all night. He only switched it off when he was in class or didn't want to be interrupted.

And he wasn't likely to be in class at four in the morning.

Astra bit her lip, fighting the sickening ache threatening to overtake her.

He's with another man.

Though other explanations flitted through her head, they were forced out by that hopeless realisation. *He's with another man.* And though Astra drifted in and out of sleep, though she spent half an hour in a singularly useless interview with a coolly clinical police officer, though the hours passed, Harry remained out of contact, and when morning broke, it became clear Harry would not come.

* * * *

Standing in front of the mirror, his shirt half-buttoned, his hair unkempt, Harry paused to look at his reflection.

What is this?

He loved Astra. He really did. But the thought of a smooth, muscular chest, of narrow masculine hips and firm buttocks, snatched the breath from his lungs and left him shivering.

Returning last night, he had been racked with guilt.

Tonight he was dressing to go out again.

It was dangerous, it was wrenching, and the degree of *need* was terrifying, and yet it was impossible to resist.

Exciting, erotic and somehow *right*.

Why do I do this? Why do I risk what I have?

Astra was love. This was...lust.

Could I ever fall in love with a man? No.

The eyes of his reflection seemed to flash with sudden knowledge — the embodiment of his guilt, framed in a silver square of spite.

Harry finished dressing, ran a hand through his hair, and turned his back on it.

Chapter Nine

After Astra checked her watch for the three hundredth time and saw it was now nine in the morning, she decided it would be safe to find someone else to escort her home.

Clearly Harry was far too *busy*.

"No cell phone calls," Nurse Hardbrook said firmly upon seeing the phone in Astra's hand. "We have an office phone. *I* will make the call," she added, stepping forward as Astra attempted to get out of bed. Finding herself weak-kneed and with her head swimming in the nurse's arms, Astra was forced to agree.

The first number they tried was Sasha's. Unfortunately, Nurse Hardbrook was back in less than a minute.

"Her phone was switched off. Is there another number I could try?"

Sasha did switch her phone off overnight, so presumably she was still asleep. Astra considered Jayla and Nicole for a moment, then changed her mind. If Sasha was still in bed, Ash was probably alongside her, and he might have left his phone on.

"Try her boyfriend. His name's Ash."

Nurse Hardbrook nodded, flicked through the numbers in the cell phone's memory, and left the room.

She was back in five minutes, looking a little dazed.

"He's on his way."

Astra wondered where the dazed expression had come from. Things all became clear, however, when the voices of Ash and Sasha floated down the corridor half an hour later.

"I can't fucking *believe* that fucking prick couldn't be bothered to come down and get her!"

"I know! If I catch him I'll murder him."

The door flew open as Ash's voice rose.

"If I find out he was out partying while she was in here with a fucking *head injury* I'll knock his teeth out. That little *cunt* – "

"Morning, Ash," Astra said hastily from the bed.

Ash, halfway through the door, was suddenly pushed aside by Sasha, who dashed into the room and froze stiff at the sight of Astra.

"Oh God, what happened to you?"

She ran forward a few steps, then pressed one hand to her mouth and burst into tears.

"Holy crap," Ash said coolly, crossing the room to put his arm around her. "Shouldn't Astra be the one crying here?"

Sasha nodded, but buried her face in her hands and began taking deep, shuddering breaths. Nurse Hardbrook took the opportunity to step forward and address herself to Ash, who looked the nearest of the two of them to being in control of the situation.

"She'll be unsteady on her feet for a while, so I don't want her walking home, Mr…?"

"Um, Drake," said Ash, obviously unused to being Mr anything.

"You can call a cab from the telephone in reception. And she'll need complete bed rest for the next two days, is that clear?"

"Perfectly clear." Ash darted a glittering glance at Astra. "If I have any say in the matter, she won't leave her bed."

Astra rolled her eyes. If there was one positive thing about this, it was that it gave her more time to think. There was no way either Ash or Sasha could persuade her into anything when she was concussed.

She sat up and threw her legs over the side of the bed, lowering herself slowly to the floor. Sasha and Ash moved forward to support her as her head promptly span and she staggered, clutching the bed with both hands.

"Seychelle, run on ahead and call a cab," Ash ordered.

Sasha looked at him for a moment, then nodded. Together they manoeuvred Astra out of the private ward and into the corridor, then Ash slid his arm tightly round Astra's waist while Sasha detached herself. Casting a final glance at Ash, she turned and set off at an awkward run down the corridor.

Ash smiled down at Astra, whose head had dropped onto his shoulder, before gathering her up in his arms as though she weighed less than a football.

"You're enjoying this, aren't you?" Astra murmured, jolting in his arms as he strode down the corridor.

"Let's just say there's something about rescuing a helpless woman."

"I suppose I can't argue with that. I can't even walk." Astra lowered her head back to his shoulder, finding it hurt too much to support it. "I hope I didn't get you out of bed."

"I wasn't in bed. I was just out of the shower. Seychelle crashed at mine last night."

Astra obediently allowed images of Ash stepping out of the shower to float around in her mind.

"Anyway, what the hell happened to you last night? All we were told was that you were concussed."

Astra sighed and quickly went over the story again.

"Dizzy bitch." Ash shook his head as if in disbelief at her inability to take care of herself. "First you get mugged and then hit by a bike. From now on, I'm walking you back. I don't care how late you finish."

"I might see if I can get on earlier shifts." *Ones without Ally on them*, Astra finished silently.

Ash tightened his arm around her as they rounded a corner.

"By the way…"

Astra flicked her eyes upwards and groaned inwardly at the determined expression on his face. This could only mean trouble.

"Mind if I ask where Delfino has been in all this?"

Oh yes. Definitely trouble.

"He didn't pick up his phone."

Ash rolled his eyes. "And we all know why."

"I have no idea why," Astra mumbled, knowing perfectly well neither of them believed it.

"I know he went out last night," was Ash's relentless response, "because a couple of the guys from my floor went with him, and they're both out and proud. I don't know where he is this morning, but it doesn't take a genius."

Which you're not, said Astra's brain automatically, taking revenge for those invading thoughts of Ash in the shower.

"I'm not surprised you've been, uh…" Ash paused, eyes narrowing in thought. "Looking in other places for your entertainment."

So he had finally got to that, had he? Astra had been wondering how long it would take.

"Well, if he's allowed to experiment, I don't see why I can't."

"Hey, I'm not against it. I'm all for experimentation."

I bet you are.

Ash was silent for a moment as they continued down the corridor, his muscles tense, obviously working up the courage to ask the question Astra was already expecting. They had rounded the last bend before he spoke again.

"Did…uh…did Sasha say anything to you?"

Astra raised one eyebrow, out of sight against his shoulder.

"She did say something, yes, but it might be better coming from you. I really think you need to give it to me slowly so I can take it all in."

Ash stopped dead and looked at her.

"Thanks. Thanks for that. All the blood needs to be in my muscles, okay? Don't say things like that when you're all vulnerable in my arms."

"Well, it's just that it's a really big thing for me to take all at once…"

"Shut up."

"I'm sorry, I'm just making it harder."

"One more word. Just one."

Astra giggled and snuggled into his shoulder. Ash eyed her for a moment, then set off walking again with a slightly uncomfortable gait.

As they reached the reception area, Sasha appeared in the doorway waving at them frantically.

"Out here! They said they'd be here in ten minutes, and it's nearly been ten."

"I'm not standing around holding her like this," said Ash firmly, lowering Astra's feet to the ground. "If it's not here yet, she needs to sit down."

"Oh, hold on, this might be it…" Sasha's attention had been drawn by a cab that had just drawn up outside. "Hold her up, I'll be right back."

She disappeared through the sliding doors, reappearing a few moments later.

"Yeah, this is it."

Astra turned towards the door, took one step and dropped like a rock. Ash caught her around the waist and manoeuvred her the short distance through the doors and out to the cab, where Sasha was holding the rear door open, fussing like a mother hen.

Who needed Harry, anyway?

* * * *

Astra might have decided she had no need of Harry, but apparently Harry thought differently.

She had been lying on her bed, having flatly refused to actually go to bed, all day. It was now three o'clock in the afternoon and Sasha was discussing dinner options with Ash, having been out earlier in the day and bought sandwiches for lunch. Ash, not being the washing-up type, was pressing her to order pizza.

In the middle of this debate, her cell phone rang.

"I'll get that," said Sasha, reaching down to Astra's purse and retrieving the phone. Scanning the screen before flipping it open, an expression of disgust crossed her face.

"It's him." She batted Astra's hand away and flipped the phone open to answer it. "Hello, Astra's phone? Oh, hello Harry. It's Sasha."

Astra cringed.

"Yes, she's right here, but she can't come to the phone right now. She's concussed." She paused, smiling airily as she held the phone away from her ear, Harry's frantic shouting clearly audible through the speaker. "Since last night. Didn't you hear? I'm sure the hospital rang you. Oh, they did? And you didn't pick up the message until now? What on earth were you doing?"

Astra darted a glance at Ash as Sasha cheerfully held the screaming phone out again. Ash arched an eyebrow at her, obviously enjoying this just as much as Sasha was.

"No, the hospital says she'll be fine in a couple of days if she stays in bed. She will have to go back to have the stitches out, though. Yes, stitches. Might be a little scarring, but that's what happens when you get hit by a bike."

There was another burst of desperate shouting from the speaker.

"She's here with us at the moment. Don't worry, Ash and I have it covered. Well, you can come over if you want. Okay, bye bye." Sasha closed the phone and dropped it casually back into Astra's purse, almost purring in satisfaction.

"Did we have fun?" Astra asked dryly.

"We did," Sasha responded calmly. "And don't look at me like that. He deserved everything he got there."

Astra opened her mouth, then closed it again, remembering how she had felt when Harry had failed to turn up at the hospital.

"Exactly. Now, judging by that conversation, he'll be here in two seconds flat, so Ash and I will get lost while he's here — yes we *will*, Ash," she added as Ash opened his mouth indignantly, "and you can text us if you want us to order dinner in. In the meantime, we'll think of a few ways to keep you occupied while you're languishing in bed."

"I bet you will," said Astra without thinking.

Sasha stifled a giggle and leaned in to whisper in Astra's ear. "Not that, you pervert. Not yet, anyway."

"Well," Astra whispered back, shielding her mouth with her hand, "you could always distract me by telling me what he likes."

Sasha's eyes flickered, understanding immediately.

"Made a decision?"

"I'm leaning towards one."

"If you two are saying dirty things to each other," said Ash, with a playful smile, "feel free to speak up."

Ash being playful? Astra found herself leaning even further towards that decision, wrong as it felt.

Sasha straightened up, but before she could say anything, they heard rapidly approaching footsteps thundering down the corridor. With a supportive squeeze of Astra's shoulder, Sasha took Ash's arm and led him reluctantly over to the door, resting her other hand on the handle.

Someone screeched to a halt outside the door and hammered on it violently.

"Astra!"

Sasha calmly opened the door to let Harry stumble through it, pulling up abruptly as he nearly collided with Ash. Ash straightened up to his full height, scowling down at him.

"We were just leaving," Sasha said hurriedly. She scampered out of the doorway, sharply jerking Ash's arm to force him to follow. The door slammed shut behind them, leaving Astra and Harry alone in the room.

Astra looked up at Harry uncertainly.

"I—"

Her halting sentence was abruptly broken off when Harry cleared the few steps between them and flung himself on top of her, wrapping himself around her with scant regard for her injuries

"Ow! Mind the head!"

"Oh shit, sorry—" Harry tightened his grip, if anything, as he buried his head in her shoulder. Astra slid her arms around him and returned his hug. It was easier than talking.

After a few minutes, Harry raised his head and reached up to push her hair aside, revealing the stitches. He winced visibly, looking away. Astra was startled to see his eyes were red and glistening.

"Harry?"

"I'm an arse." Harry dropped his head, refusing to look at her.

Look, I don't want to know if you were with someone else, okay? Astra thought, willing him to understand. *Don't tell me. I'll live.*

"I'm a complete arse," Harry repeated, shaking his head. "I only switched my phone on fifteen minutes ago, you know? And the first thing I got was a message saying you'd been in an accident and taken to hospital at two o'clock in the morning, and can I come and get you." He covered his face with his hand. "You were in there with a bloody head injury, and I left you there on your own all night."

"Look, Harry…"

Harry pushed her hair aside again, forcing himself to look at the stitches.

"God. And you might be scarred…"

"It's not your fault I got hurt," said Astra firmly.

"It's my fault you had to call Sasha to get you home."

Astra decided not to mention it was actually Ash she had needed to call.

"I should have left my phone on. I could have come and got you. You needed me." Harry sank back down and laid his head on her chest. "You deserve to know why."

"No, I don't." *I don't want to know why. I already know why.*

"Yes, you do," Harry insisted, looking up at her. "I—"

"You were out last night and you hooked up with a man, right?"

In the silence that followed, Astra forlornly hoped Harry would deny it. *Tell me you weren't. Say you switched it off to charge it. Anything.* But it was obvious from the desolate look in Harry's eyes, from the guilty cast of his face, that he would not. Her heart sank.

"I didn't…" Harry started hopelessly. "I didn't sleep with him…"

Shit. She had known this already, and yet the knowledge was a stab to the gut.

"Right."

"I'm sorry."

"Yeah." Astra heard her voice come out sounding flat. Broken.

Harry laid his head back down on her chest, avoiding her gaze.

"I stayed at his apartment last night. We didn't—we didn't have sex. We just—sort of—messed around a bit."

"Messed around a bit." Her voice was sounding bleaker by the minute.

"Gavemeablowjob," was mumbled into her breast.

Astra took a deep breath, willing herself to be still.

"And you...?"

There was an awkward pause.

"Suckedhimoff."

Everything inside Astra went numb.

"Look at me if you're going to say things like that."

"Oh, God!" Harry moaned, throwing his arms around her again and holding her so tightly it was painful. "I'm sorry..."

Astra closed her eyes. She was so tired of seeing images of Harry's sexual exploits in her head, tired of wondering what was going on during the evenings they weren't together, tired of his guilty confessions which served to ease his mind while burdening hers.

If she could just push the other half of his life aside and forget it existed, if she could enjoy the time spent with him—but Harry wouldn't have that. He had to admit it, had to tell her what he believed she had a right to know, even when she would give anything not to hear it.

He had let another man suck on him. He had come in another man's mouth. And he had sucked another man off and made him come in *his* mouth.

"I'm really sorry..."

And he was still talking about it.

"I know it's wrong," Harry whimpered, burying his head in her neck. "I knew it was wrong last night... but he was just so... it was just so *hot*."

"It must have been," said Astra caustically, "if it lasted up until three o'clock today."

Harry's body froze, then went limp.

"We—I didn't get to sleep until seven o'clock this morning, and I didn't wake up until two. And then I had to get a taxi back here, and I didn't switch my phone on until I got back to my room." His shoulders heaved. "And then I got that message."

Oh God. They were back to that again.

I can't do this anymore.

" —what?"

Harry had lifted his head and was staring at her, mouth open, and Astra realised she had spoken out loud.

Well, it was as good an opening as any.

"I said, I can't do this anymore. We need to break up."

"*No!*"

Astra took a deep breath and struggled to arrange her thoughts as Harry broke into a stream of panicked babbling.

"I thought we agreed we'd date other people."

"I know, I just can't listen to —"

"Well, I won't tell you!"

"Look, Harry—" *You may say I can date, but you won't want me with Ash.*

"Astra, *no.*"

Harry fixed his gaze on hers with red-eyed determination.

"Please. You can date who you like. You can tell me anything or nothing, I don't mind. I won't tell you anything if you don't want me to. Just...please."

Why is he so desperate for this?

Astra sighed, which Harry apparently took as an acceptance.

"And I'll look after you until you're better. How long do you have to stay in bed?"

Somehow she couldn't muster up the strength to fight any longer.

"Two days. You can work shifts with A—Sasha." Best not to mention Ash, given Harry considered him to be a testosterone-enhanced idiot.

"Good. She should take good care of you." Harry gave her a watery smile. "What were your plans for dinner?"

"Don't know. I think Sash was going to order something."

"I'll get that. She can come in on it if she wants."

Astra picked up her cell phone to text Sasha, mentally envisaging Ash's irritation at this change of plans. Well, it would give her time to think.

In Ash's presence, *it* seemed a good idea.

The effect of Harry's presence remained to be seen.

* * * *

During the two days that followed, Astra's allegiance swayed according to which nurse was attending her.

Harry was an attentive assistant. Besides the first evening, when he ordered pizza for herself and Sasha, he spent three hours with her on the afternoon of the second day, bringing large amounts of food and a rather entertaining tongue which Astra briefly forgot had been wrapped around the penis of another man.

When Harry was with her, the idea of a threesome seemed more of a betrayal—although, rather worryingly, no less exciting.

When Harry left and Sasha took over, Astra became aware she had already forgotten the way his tongue felt on her skin, and suddenly the idea of a threesome was impossible to keep out of her head.

"Tell me. Tell me what he likes."

Sasha leant down to the tray of sweet-and-sour chicken balls, which was sitting on the floor next to a pile of her clothes. She dipped one in the sauce before bringing it up to her mouth, dripping sauce across Astra's bare stomach.

"Oh, sorry. I'll get that for you."

She bent her head and ran her tongue along the trail of sauce, flicking her tongue into Astra's navel.

"Back to the point, you fucking tease." *God almighty.* Astra twisted distractedly and tightened her hand in Sasha's hair.

"That was the point. That's one thing he likes."

"Licking food off?"

"Not necessarily. Licking *here*. It drives him crazy." Sasha dipped her tongue into Astra's navel again, running it around the edge.

"Je-sus…"

"Even more crazy than that." Sasha sat back up and bit into the battered chicken.

"Right. Got it." Astra surreptitiously dug one hand into the duvet in an attempt to regain her composure. "What else?"

"What else. Well, as I said, he's kind of a sub. Actually, he's a lot of a sub. He likes being tied up, held down, anything like that. And he's got *really* sensitive nipples.

Touch them when he's tied down and—" Sasha blew her fringe up in the air and rolled her eyes expressively.

"Yeah?"

"Yeah. Which is why he's going to love us taking him together. One of us teasing his nipples while the other strokes him off or has her fingers up his ass…"

"Has her what up his what?"

Astra sat bolt upright at this point, coming face to face with Sasha's piece of chicken. This was certainly a direction she hadn't expected the conversation to take. For someone like Ash to admit to liking something like that—well, it defied belief. Even Harry hadn't suggested that—yet, at least. Had he mentioned it, she could have offered to—

With a jerk of her head, she rejected the thought and returned her attention to Sasha, who wore the smug expression of an all-knowing entity.

"Oh yes. I'm not sure how he discovered his prostate, although I suspect it was when he watched *Road Trip*. But he does like that. Stick your fingers up there to make him scream, give him a rim job to make him melt. Never fails."

"Oh, God."

"Is this getting to you, honey?"

"Maybe a little." All this talk about Ash's weaknesses and hot spots was following Astra's blood and going directly south.

"Let me get that for you." Sasha slid a hand between them and set up a slow, caressing pace with one finger. "Okay, where was I? He likes getting blow jobs, obviously…"

"I'm not doing that," said Astra firmly, struggling to keep enough blood in her brain. She had decided to hang onto what few scruples she had left, despite Harry's betrayal.

"Well, that's up to you—I think he'll be a bit disappointed though, since he's apparently heard you're good at that."

"I am good at that. Doesn't mean he's getting any." Falling back onto the bed, Astra ran her hand up the inside of Sasha's thigh, bypassing the outer curves of flesh to press her fingers to the softness within.

Sasha moaned and stroked Astra more firmly.

"Anyway...he also really gets off on eating women out..."

"He's not doing that either..."

"You might change your mind about that. He's good—he has this thing he does with his tongue." Sasha's eyes widened as she threw her head back, possibly to demonstrate Ash's prowess with his tongue, but Astra thought more likely in response to her prowess with her fingers.

"He's good?"

"All round. He's v—very good. Not a—ohh—bad size, either."

"Oohh...big, is he?" Astra had assumed someone with Ash's swagger was either spectacularly well endowed or making up for his shortcomings.

"Not stupidly so...oh, God...just about right."

"No, I don't like too big either—hurts—oh *fuck*...don't stop..."

"Can—can we finish this discussion later?"

"Oh, yes."

Astra was almost convinced this was a good idea, but made a point of never making decisions while she was incapable of thinking straight.

* * * *

The decision remained unmade the following day, when Astra called the casino to discuss her shift times.

The under-manager, Sylvia, made sympathetic clucking noises and claimed to fully understand, but refused to make any decisions about her shift work without the manager being present. If Astra would come in during the evening shift to speak with Brad, she was sure something could be arranged.

On hearing this, Sasha insisted someone walk her there and back.

"I don't need anyone to walk me anywhere."

"You've been mugged and run over. I'm not letting you go on your own."

Astra had fixed Sasha with an incredulous look. "How many muggers can *you* face down?"

This issue had been easily resolved by way of a quick phone call to Ash, who responded with such alacrity Astra wondered if he had been waiting for this moment all day. Ash and Astra had walked down to the casino at eight that evening, Astra attempting to make conversation while Ash scanned the streets as though he expected her to be shot. As they passed through the floor area of the Fountain, dodging around the tables, Astra caught herself wondering if he was going to sweep the place for bugs.

"Okay, I'll just stop into Brad's office. I won't be long."

"Okay, I'll wait out here."

Brad had raised elegant eyebrows at the sight of a scowling blond leaning against the wall outside his office, but had chosen not to comment until after their discussion of shifts.

"I'll move you onto the three-till-nine shift. In the meantime, take a leave of absence. I don't want to see you for another two weeks." Smile, wink.

When Astra surfaced fifteen minutes later, it was to find Ash with his hands buried in the pockets of his long leather coat, staring off into the distance with his trademarked 'cool' expression.

"All done."

"Great. Let's go then." Ash pushed himself off the wall, took her hand and set off across the room, Astra stumbling behind him, trying to keep her arm in its socket.

The streets were dark and damp as they walked home, lit only by flickering streetlamps. Despite this, Ash seemed to view it as less fraught with danger. At least, Astra inferred as much by the fact he seemed to have relaxed a little. He was even willing to talk beyond the one-word answers she had got on the previous journey.

"So I don't have to go in for two weeks, and then I can do three till nine on the days I don't have lectures."

"Good. I'm still walking you back, though."

"I wasn't objecting to that." Astra smiled up at him. "I quite like the company."

Ash glanced down at her with his usual cool expression, but then his mouth twitched and his eyes glowed as a warm smile lit up his face. He shook his head in disbelief and turned back to face ahead.

"What?" Astra nudged him.

"You. You're turning me into a fucking sap." Ash lowered his head, still grinning. If Astra didn't know better, she would have said he was embarrassed.

"Oh, is Mr Supercool Ash Drake going soft in his old age?"

"Shut up."

"It's not before time. We need to loosen you up."

"Shu—*ah!*" Ash jerked as Astra, on the spur of the moment, lunged at him to tickle his ribs. "God, get off me—*ah*—you..." Struggling not to laugh, he squirmed away as Astra's fingers continued their torture.

"You love it."

"Oh God—"

"Go on, give it up."

"Get off, you—" Ash managed to catch hold of her hands and wrestle her back against the damp wall, breathless and laughing. "I think you need a good spanking."

Astra's eyes widened and glinted briefly as she felt a sudden stab of desire, the rough brick pressing into her skin through her shirt.

"I think *you'd* enjoy that more."

Ash's eyes darkened as he held her wrists against the wall, his breath quickening.

"I—you—"

Recognising her advantage, Astra arched her body towards him. Her hips pressed against his, rendering them both fully aware of his growing arousal.

Ash gasped. "*God.* Don't—"

"Looks like I was wrong," Astra teased. "Doesn't feel like you're going soft."

"Oh fuck," Ash moaned, dropping her wrists to catch her hips and grind himself against her. "Not out here..."

Astra stifled a gasp as his erection dragged against her stomach.

"No, you're right. Sash isn't here."

In his priapic state, Ash took a moment to catch her meaning. Astra watched him, waiting, until his eyes widened and his mouth fell open, momentarily speechless.

"Does — does that mean you want — "

Astra smiled meaningfully up at him, enjoying the stunned look of helpless desire on his face.

"Ohgod."

And now I'm in control.

"But not tonight. If we're going to do this, we're going to do it properly." Astra's hair stirred as she moved, catching, serving as a reminder. "And I want these stitches out first."

"Uh, sure... Whatever you like..." From the look on Ash's face, he would have agreed to anything at that moment.

"Shall we get back, then?"

Ash was still staring at her with a glazed expression.

"Ash?"

"Huh?"

"Shall we get back?"

"Oh — yes." Ash shook his head to clear it. "Get back."

Astra sidled out from the wall and they started walking back to Omega Zeta in silence, Ash still glassy-eyed and flushed.

It would be about two weeks until her stitches were out. That would give her time to discuss things with Sasha and establish exactly what was going to happen. If they were going to do this, really going to do this, then they were going to do it properly.

And, damn it, Ash would *not* be in charge.

If he wanted in, she could accept that. But she was damned if he was going to start giving his orders as though he was directing a porn movie or, God forbid, pimping them out for his pleasure.

* * * *

Upon reaching Omega Zeta, Astra was rather surprised when Ash followed her inside. *He's probably going to drop in on Sasha*, she told herself. It was therefore a greater surprise when, rather than saying goodbye at her bedroom door, Ash stepped in after her and closed the door behind him.

The lights were out, the only visible light coming from the window, casting shadows across the room. They stared at each other for a moment through the darkness.

"Ash, I *said…*"

"I know what you said." Ash fixed her with a look. "I know you didn't want to do it. Is this because of what that asshole did to you?"

Astra eyed him dangerously for a moment, then turned away from him to scowl at the wall.

Yes, partially. But no, not entirely. And I'm not going to tell you, anyway.

Ash crossed to stand behind her, resting one hand on the wall so his arm blocked her on her right.

"Look, I don't care why you said yes, okay?"

Then why did you ask? Astra thought furiously.

"He's treating you like shit, Astra. You deserve better than that. Even if you don't want that from me —"

"You're dating Sasha." The words came out fiercely.

Ash was silent for a moment.

"You won't regret agreeing to it. I won't let you."

His voice was shaking, and Astra caught at it. Here was a way for her to regain control. Her voice dropped to a low purr.

"Oh? Are you saying you're…good?"

Ash let his breath out slowly and unsteadily.

"Yeah. I'm good."

Astra deliberately lowered her voice further, adding a sultry lilt.

"I've heard you're *very* good."

This time she heard his throat catch sharply.

"I am. I will be."

"And you can last?"

"Of course I can last!" Ash still sounded breathless, but his voice was now tinged with something between passion and anger. "That happened *once* and that bitch told everyone. I hadn't had any in weeks and she got me all worked up. Anyway, do you know how long it had been since I'd been with someone who waxed?"

"Well, if you can't handle a Brazilian, I don't know how you're going to handle me. I'm one better."

For a brief moment there were only gasps and stammering noises from behind her.

"Ssssshit."

Astra raised a satisfied eyebrow and smiled to herself as Ash recovered his scattered wits.

"I can last," Ash said finally with determination. "I can last as long as you want. Hours, if you like."

Astra turned on the spot and looked him straight in the eye, smiling teasingly at Ash's strained expression. Leaning in close, she whispered to him challengingly.

"Not with us, you won't. We'll make you see *stars*."

As Ash gasped with desire, Astra stepped away from him and opened the door, gesturing for him to leave. She hid a smirk as Ash walked uncomfortably out into the corridor and turned to meet her eyes once more while the door remained open.

Astra winked at him before closing the door in his face and locking it.

You'll last? We'll see.

* * * *

I wasn't there.

The image tormented him — a bicycle frame flashing in the moonlight, Astra falling onto the cold pavement, blood spattering her face — and Harry dropped his head into his hands, fingers clutching at his hair.

She was hurting, alone, bleeding, and I wasn't there.

Another image, one of Astra lying alone in a shadowy hospital ward, the row of sutures standing out on her temple.

She was left alone all night and I was —

Harry's fingers dug further, clawing at his scalp.

Sitting there, alone in his room with no light but moonlight, it was impossible to stop the memories flooding back — memories of himself in the bar that night, of Marcus's persistence, gradually overriding his determination until finally, finally he had been unable to say no.

And he had switched off his phone, and then he had — they had —

Oh God.

He would stop going out, he told himself firmly. He would pay attention to Astra from now on. He would sit with her, and hold her, and stay with her, and make up for his neglect until he had earned her forgiveness.

A final image of Marcus flashed through his mind, and Harry shuddered.

Chapter Ten

Two weeks later, Astra and Sasha stood in Sasha's bedroom, adding the finishing touches to their outfits for the party that night.

Leaning closer to the mirror, Astra pushed aside a lock of hair to reveal a diagonal scar on her temple, now barely visible under a layer of makeup. The stitches had been removed the previous morning.

"Can you see it?"

"No," Sasha responded briefly, glancing over. "Only if I really look."

Astra let her hair fall forward again. Her reflection looked back at her with wide eyes, bottom lip caught between her teeth.

Why had she agreed to this again?

She hadn't discussed the threesome idea with Ash since that night. As she hadn't needed to be walked to and from the casino, the only times she had been with Ash had been in Sasha's presence, and from the looks she had caught

Sasha throwing him, he had been told not to mention it again. Instead, Sasha had raised the subject one morning in bed.

"Ash said you changed your mind."

Wondering exactly how much Ash had said, Astra could only answer, "Yes."

"Okay." Sasha had reached under the bed and pulled out her diary. "Then let's make plans."

Ultimately they had agreed the best chance for privacy was to coordinate their little 'event' to coincide with a public party downstairs. Sasha's neighbours on either side, Leyla and Keely, had never been known to come upstairs early, since Leyla had a boyfriend who refused to sleep in a sorority house and Keely was an exhibitionist who preferred to have sex anywhere but the bedroom. They were unlikely to be around to hear what was going on, provided the three of them were able to slip away discreetly.

Sasha, as the resident social secretary, had planned the party, and to make it even more entertaining, she had made it a theme night. Now, as she adjusted her school tie, Astra glared at herself in the mirror. *I look like a whore.*

"Are you sure Harry won't be coming tonight?"

Astra shook her head, casually avoiding Sasha's gaze in the mirror. "He said he was out with the guys tonight."

"The guys or the *guys?*"

"I have no idea and I don't want to know. Is Ash getting dressed up for this too?"

"Oh yes." Sasha gave Astra a naughty look as she adjusted her hair-ribbons. "That's why I chose 'Naughty Schoolgirls and Schoolboys' as the theme. I think he has a public school fetish."

"Oh really? Does he like you to cane him?"

"I haven't actually tried that, although I don't think he'd say no to a good spanking. But there was this one time when we were right in the middle of things and he shouted out *Oh, sir!*" Sasha dropped into a credible public-schoolboy English accent for the last two words. "I was quite surprised he could manage the accent at that point, but anyway..."

"...Oh my."

"Oh, I know. Let's see if we can get him to say it again."

Astra nodded slowly, letting out her breath in one long rush.

"Are we ready, anyway? We should be getting down there."

"I'm ready." Astra took one last look in the mirror, running her eye over all the details — the red lipstick and black eyeliner, the loose tie over the low-cut blouse, the skimpy pleated skirt and the white socks under black Mary Janes.

She was as ready as she was ever going to be.

Sasha nodded at her own reflection, the same except for the blonde bunches — Astra had refused to wear her hair up — and the freckles she had added on her cheeks with the eyebrow pencil. "Yeah, I am, too. Let's go."

"Right." Astra took a deep breath, then turned back to Sasha uncertainly. "He does know I'm not going down on him, right?"

"Yes."

"And he's not going down on me."

"Yes."

"He's not going to turn up wearing Buzz Lightyear boxers, is he?"

"Oh, for fuck's sake!" Sasha exclaimed, giving Astra's shoulder an exasperated whack. "No, he isn't. He never wears underwear when he thinks he's getting some."

She extended one arm dramatically towards the door, wearing an expression that brooked no arguments. Astra hesitated for a moment before turning to leave, only to find a hand descending softly onto her arm.

"Look, I know you're nervous, but don't worry. It'll be okay."

Astra took another deep breath and nodded. "Yeah, I know."

She straightened her face and put on her best 'party' expression as they left Sasha's bedroom, hoping and praying Sasha was right.

It'll be okay.

* * * *

Sasha had been right about one thing, at least. Ash had dressed up for the occasion. He was leaning casually against the wall, hands buried in his pockets, dressed in a pair of loose black trousers and a black V-necked sweater over a white shirt and red tie.

Not all of the boys in the room had made the effort to dress the part, but every one of the girls had. The effect was astonishing. Schoolgirls floated through the lounge and kitchen in short skirts, with naked legs, flicking their be-ribboned hair, casting saucily innocent grins at the hapless frat boys in attendance, dozens of eyes helplessly snagging on one pretty girl after another.

Ash, of course, was in his element.

In fact, he seemed to be intent on proving himself as the resident sex machine. Standing next to him, Astra noticed girl after girl looking at him on their way past, sometimes with desire, sometimes adoration, and occasionally with the steely glare of one who detested herself for a former indiscretion. It was little wonder Ash was at his most arrogant and obnoxious. He was continually leaning in to comment on the last girl who had walked by.

"That's Denise — picked her up last year at a party. She sucked me off in the bathroom."

"That was Kelly — bent her over the fountain out back of Beta Phi one time."

"Can't remember her name, but last May I finger-blasted her in a cupboard."

"You know, Ash," said Astra finally, "I think I've got the message now. Before you met Sash you were up to your ass in pussy."

Ash shrugged airily, smiling as if to say *Well, if you say so.*

"Although I don't know what you got out of finger-blasting whatserface, unless you've missed a point in the description."

"Oh, that's easy. I was doing this for the rest of the night."

Ash brought his right hand up to his face and rubbed his nose with his first two fingers.

"Lovely," said Astra dryly. "I had to ask."

Sasha leaned across Ash and caught Astra's sleeve.

"Want to dance?"

The arrogant smirk on Ash's face suddenly disappeared.

"I'd love to," said Astra sweetly, following Sasha out into the middle of the room.

The song just starting was *The Most Beautiful Girl In The World.* As Astra and Sasha circled each other, eyes locked and lips kinked knowingly, the floor began to fill with slow-dancing couples, as well as a few girls who had apparently had the same idea. Astra leaned closer to Sasha as their bodies undulated slowly to the music, whispering in her ear.

"Is he watching?"

"He is. Remember what I — ?"

"Oh yes."

Ash was watching them, biting his lip intently. Astra smiled and glided forward to brush against Sasha's hip. She saw Ash flush, remembering what Sasha had mentioned during their planning.

"He wants us to start by dancing for him. Like we did at Sigma. Only when we're alone, he wants us to go further. He wants us to undress each other a bit and touch each other more. It's become a fantasy for him."

"Isn't that going to get him too excited?"

"That's the point, really. We haven't done it in over a week so he's already dying for it. He wants to get off quickly so he can recover and last for the next one."

"Right, so..."

"Yeah. And then he wants us to dance up on him like we did and..."

While Astra had no problem with this idea, she had felt as though she should object on principle — Ash trying to direct things, exactly as she hadn't wanted.

However, on the one hand, Ash was in a position to blackmail her if he wanted to, although the feeling in her gut told her otherwise. On another hand, it was interesting to discover their little party trick had become a jerk-off fantasy for him. And on a third hand, it made sense for Ash to get himself off quickly so he could rally for a second, longer go.

And to think Ash of the 'I can last ages' expected to be brought off so quickly — well, it quite made her head spin.

* * * *

"For God's *sake*, you two…" Ash hissed at them as Astra and Sasha stepped off the makeshift dancefloor for a brief interlude.

Astra picked up a shot of Goldschlager from a nearby table and stared at it dreamily, watching the sparks of gold circle.

"Problems, Ash?"

"Um, *yes*. You've been doing that now for an hour and a half."

"Why," said Sasha cheerfully from his other side, "anyone would think you weren't enjoying it."

Astra raised her shot glass, noting the way Ash's eyes had drifted to her mouth. He winced visibly as her lips softly caressed the rim.

"Can we *please* go upstairs now?" he begged in a strained voice. "I'm dying here."

Astra glanced briefly at Sasha, who raised her eyebrows in a silent query. Downing the shot, Astra nodded once and pushed herself away from the wall.

"Just heading up to the bathroom," she said in a slightly louder voice, for the benefit of anyone who was listening.

"Okay," Sasha replied agreeably.

The stairwell was empty, the corridor deserted. Behind Sasha's bedroom door, she paced the floor restlessly, taking deep breaths and tugging at her hair.

It would be all right. He would probably want to watch her and Sasha for the most part. She could focus on Sasha and forget he was there.

Except their opening act wouldn't allow her to forget he was there—and there was a side of her that flared and clenched at the thought...

She froze suddenly.

Footsteps.

Cracking the door open slightly, she squinted through the gap and recognised the two figures approaching from the end of the corridor. As there were no other footsteps to be heard, she judged it safe to open the door.

Sasha was walking alongside him, one hand on his left shoulder and the other on his wrist, leading a trembling Ash almost as if he was walking to his doom. As the bedroom door opened, Ash lifted his eyes and immediately met her gaze.

God.

Astra flushed at the raw emotion in his face. He looked more vulnerable than she had ever seen him, his eyes wide, his lips bitten, reddened and moist. Rather than walking to his doom, he now looked as though he was walking into paradise.

Astra stepped back as Sasha guided Ash into the room, closing the door behind her and locking it. She gently moved him over to the side of the room, pressing him against the wall as she leaned in to whisper over his mouth.

"Now," she breathed, "I believe you wanted to watch?"

Ash let out a slow, shuddering breath as Astra picked up the remote for the CD player, moving towards the bed as Sasha stepped back to join her. *Play.*

The opening bars and slow, sultry beat of *Freak Me* pulsed through the room, the music melting in the air as Astra turned to Sasha, hips already catching the rhythm, and began to dance.

It was surprisingly easy to do this with Sasha. Away from the eyes of the other party guests, they were free to touch and move in the way they had always wanted to, could lose their inhibitions without fear. If Astra's leg slid between Sasha's thighs, if Sasha pressed forward and bucked against her, arching her back to offer her breasts up to be caressed, there was no-one to complain they were going too far. If Sasha's blouse came unbuttoned and Astra's mouth trailed kisses down the soft skin of her neck, there was nothing to stop them. If Sasha's hands teased at the hem of Astra's skirt and slid underneath, that was their prerogative entirely. And as the rising tension overwhelmed them, as they kissed passionately and pressed against each other, hands roaming everywhere, Astra could faintly hear Ash's voice in the background, breathlessly moaning "Oh, *fuck*..."

"God, this is hot," Astra breathed into Sasha's ear as the song changed to the throbbing beat of *Get Me Off.*

"I know," Sasha gasped back. "Let's get him."

Breaking away from each other, they turned to fix intense stares on Ash, who whimpered and quailed against the wall.

Let's get him.

The moment they reached him, Sasha ran her hands over his chest and up to his throat, while Astra slid her hands over his stomach and down over his hips to squeeze his buttocks.

Assailed from both sides, Ash bit his lip and moaned.

"Oh, God..."

Remembering his reaction the last time, Astra twisted in front of him and swayed down his body, taking care to grind against him on the way back up. As before, Ash's caught her hips in his hands and pressed her back against his crotch, urgently crushing his hardness into her skin.

Sasha's breathy giggle sounded behind her, and Astra had a brief impression of her friend lifting one knee and bucking against Ash's left hip. At the same time, Ash snaked a hand behind her neck and began moving it in a way that suggested he was undoing his shirt, which had become untucked at some point, the sweater lying a few feet away.

"Ohh…"

Astra turned back to face him and let her hands wander up Ash's inner thighs, watching his eyes flutter closed in anticipation as they slowly rose higher, his breath hitching, higher, until she closed one hand over the now very obvious bulge.

Ash's hips jerked and he threw his head back, groaning through his teeth.

"*Oh!* Oh, fuck!"

Sasha finished unbuttoning his shirt and pulled it open, baring Ash's defined, smooth chest and flat stomach. Astra caught her eye and they leant forward in unison to press open-mouthed kisses to his still-soft nipples, Astra tugging and squeezing at his erection.

The music swelled and pulsed in the background as Ash arched away from the wall, his mouth opening in a silent cry before giving way to ragged gasping. His body jolted as Astra hollowed her cheeks over the soft protrusion, flicking her tongue across the tip as his muscles tensed and he thrust into her hand.

"Oh God…*please*…so good, so fucking good…"

He shuddered, lifting his head from the wall to look down at them. Astra raised her eyes to meet his, humming gently around the hardening flesh, watching him struggle for control as she met his thrusts with her hand.

"Anything you want, baby?" Sasha murmured against his chest.

Ash groaned deeply and shook his sweat-drenched hair off his face.

"Kiss me...both of you..."

Without a moment's pause, Sasha slid her mouth over Ash's skin up to his cheek. Astra chose to follow at a slower pace, following their lead. Did he mean Sasha and then her, or both at the same time? How did three people kiss simultaneously, anyway?

Ash seemed to know what he was doing. Astra felt his arm snake around her waist, pulling both her and Sasha closer, as Sasha found his mouth first and attacked it with full force. For a few moments she focussed on biting and sucking his neck, testing to see if he had the same weak spot Harry had just below his ear. Then, with a breathless groan, Ash tore his mouth away from Sasha's and turned towards Astra.

Before she had time even to think, Astra had moved forward and captured his mouth with her own, sliding her other hand around the back of his neck.

Oh fuck!

Ash's was battling her tongue with his own, cupping his hand against the back of her head, pressing her closer as he devoured her mouth, driven more by passion than technique, but it didn't matter because it was hot and intense and dear *God* this was never going to end, it couldn't, it couldn't...

Another arm slid around her waist and Astra became aware of a second pair of soft lips connecting with her own. She turned to give Sasha more access to Ash's mouth, parting her lips further, and became lost in a tangle of tongues, softness and wetness, unconsciously grinding her hips against Ash's thigh.

Ash's slipped his hand downwards and gave her bottom a protective squeeze. Astra's eyes shot open in surprise and immediately met Sasha's equally wide gaze, suggesting she was not the only one who had been goosed.

"Ooh, I think *we* need to take charge now, don't you?"

Astra's eyes glinted wickedly. "Let's step this up."

Twisting one hand behind her, she grabbed Ash's wrist and slammed it against the wall alongside his head. As Ash's shocked gaze snapped round to hers, Sasha followed suit with his other hand, leaving him pinned to the wall.

Sash hadn't been lying about Ash's submissive side. On finding himself restrained, even though he could very easily have freed himself from their grip, Ash broke into a stream of incoherent babbling.

"Oh fuck yeah, oh *fuck*, please, please, oh God, so good, so good…"

His wild rambling increased as Astra undid his trousers and dipped her hand inside, running over the wiry hair to stroke his erection skin-on-skin.

"Oh, oh, oh *fuck!* Yes!"

Sasha slid her hand over his chest and began to toy with his nipples, meeting Astra's eyes as the two of them worked to reduce him to a quivering wreck.

Astra arched an eyebrow at her, hoping her meaning was clear.

Not stupidly big, Sasha? Really? Just who is stupidly big, then?

Harry would have turned green. Three extra inches. *Three.*

Ash's eyes were screwed closed under their onslaught, a fact which filled Astra with relief. He would probably have preened about the expression on her face.

"Oh, please — I need — I need —"

Still holding his wrist against the wall, Astra worked her hand on Ash's pulsing shaft, sliding his foreskin up over the head and teasing the slit with her thumb before twisting back down, over and over as Ash's gasps turned into broken moans, his hips jerking involuntarily.

"Oh God, I'm..." Ash threw his head back and thrashed helplessly against the wall, sweat plastering his hair to his forehead. "Oh, I'm close... God, I'm so *close...*"

Astra caught Sasha's eye.

"Get his hand."

Sasha moved away from Ash's nipple and caught his right wrist. Now freed, Astra switched hands on Ash's erection and plunged her other hand into his trousers to cup his testicles, running two fingers along his perineum as Ash's knees buckled.

"F — *fuck!*"

Astra felt him wince and tense as he struggled to stay upright.

"Oh God, I'm almost there...harder, *please!*"

Keeping her eyes on his flushed face, Astra worked her hand on him faster, pressing her body against him almost involuntarily as Ash's voice broke a pitch higher.

"Oh f — yes — oh, *yes* — I'm — *OHH!*"

Sasha released his hands and Ash crushed them both against him as he convulsed, sobbing and spurting his hot release all over Astra's hand.

For a moment, nobody moved.

Then Ash fell back against the wall, gasping for breath, and Astra buried her face against his sweaty neck, breathing the scent of him and becoming aware her own need was reaching a peak of almost painful urgency.

"Give me that," she heard Sasha whisper, and felt a hand on her wrist. Letting Ash's rapidly softening penis slip from her fingers, Astra lifted her hand as Sasha drew it up to her face and flicked her tongue out, licking a clean line across the palm.

Oh. Good idea.

Astra leaned closer and sucked one finger into her mouth, hearing Ash's breath hiss as she and Sasha shared her hand like a gourmet treat, the sour and salty taste spreading across her tongue.

Well, it's not like I went down on him, is it?

"I want you *now*," she heard herself whisper in Sasha's ear as the last few drops were licked away.

"So take me," Sasha whispered back.

Catching her shoulders, Astra gently steered Sasha backwards towards the bed, kicking off her shoes along the way. As the backs of Sasha's knees nudged against the mattress, Sasha wrapped her arms around Astra and kissed her passionately, falling back to roll them both on top of the quilt.

They faintly heard a thud as Ash slid down the wall to land on the floor. Despite this, they forgot about Ash entirely a few moments later as they wrestled with each other's clothes, tearing off shirts and skirts with wild abandon.

Astra had worried it would be too distracting to do this with an audience. She had always inwardly cringed when an over-enthusiastic lover had asked her to touch herself.

Her own pleasure, Sasha's pleasure — those were of paramount importance. Not an entertaining show.

Does he want this done pretty, or does he want it done right?

However, as Astra surfaced from sucking Sasha's neck to look over her shoulder, Sasha being occupied with teasing her nipples at the time, she became conscious of laboured breathing from the other side of the room, accompanied by a familiar *squicksquicksquick* sound which suggested Ash had recovered quickly and was enjoying the view.

I know a view he'd enjoy, said an evil little voice in her head.

"Sash…"

"Mmm?" Sasha hummed against Astra's breast, driving all thought from her mind as Astra's eyes rolled.

"Uh…"

This time Sasha detached herself. "Yeah?"

"Flip over."

Sasha arched elegant eyebrows, then pulled Astra up to face her, hooking one leg around her waist and rolling them over. Astra immediately raised herself up on all fours and heard a rather high-pitched "eep" from the wall.

Oh yes. He does like that.

She ran her hand down over Sasha's thigh and entered her with two fingers, stroking her thumb softly across her clitoris as Sasha's hand slid up to mirror her movements. As the pressure started to build, Astra threw her head back and felt Sasha's body rise to press flush against hers, clutching at each other's backs with their free hands, gasping in their mounting pleasure.

"Oh, God…"

"So good…"

"Don't stop…"

There was a scrambling noise from the other end of the room. Astra became dimly aware of unsteady footsteps and then a dipping of the mattress as Ash mounted the bed behind them.

"Let me," Astra heard him moan softly. "Please..."

Without moving her hand, Sasha wriggled backwards and rose up on her knees, shuffling sideways to leave an expanse of empty mattress.

"Here, Ash. Get on your back."

Astra opened her eyes as Ash crawled past her and found her gaze hopelessly fixed on his naked bottom. Instinctively, her hand flew out and dealt him a slap on his right cheek.

Sasha giggled softly in her ear as Ash paused mid-crawl to cast a sardonic look over his shoulder. Astra met his eye unashamedly.

Oh, shut up. It's so soft and round and fucking cute. Anyone would want to slap your ass.

For a moment Ash held her gaze, smirking, one eyebrow raised, then he rolled over onto his back and sprawled on the bed in an undeniable 'take-me' pose, his erection lying against his stomach and leaving glistening trails in the surrounding blond fuzz.

God, he was just *gorgeous*.

Astra became vaguely aware of Sasha's breath on her ear, dragging her away from a wonderful fantasy where she could stare at Ash's smooth, perfect body without anyone interfering. She briefly considered slapping her for the interruption, but decided against it.

"You ride him. I'll take his face."

Ah. Yes.

This was something she and Sasha had agreed on, it seeming inevitable in the face of Astra's refusal to allow oral sex. If they were both to take on Ash at the same time, one would have to be at the head end; process of elimination, therefore, suggested Astra would be the one to be penetrated. Astra had been slightly concerned at her own lack of concern about this, but not concerned enough to make an issue of it.

She crawled over to Ash's supine body, straddled his hips and took hold of his shaft around the base, running a nervous eye over it as Ash shuddered and groaned. The thought of taking something that *long* inside her was frankly terrifying. The last time she had slept with someone that well-endowed, it had been an awkward and painful experience. It had almost been a relief when he had finished prematurely after two minutes of thrusting.

Best to do this quickly. Astra moved forward, centred her body over her hand and, taking a deep breath, slid herself onto Ash in one swift motion.

Oh Christ!

Stalling for time as tender inner muscles protested, she reached out to help Sasha keep her balance as Sasha moved to hover astride Ash's face. The two held eye contact as Sasha steadied herself, holding onto Astra's hands.

And then Ash brought his hands up to pull Sasha's hips down, his knees rising to support Astra's back, and the spell broke.

Sasha's head was thrown back, her gasping cries escaping towards the ceiling. Ash slid his hands up to caress her breasts before moving to catch Astra's waist as his hips jerked rhythmically. Astra pressed her hands on Sasha's thighs for support as she rocked with Ash's thrusts, the pace increasing, becoming more frantic as Sasha's moans ate away at their composure.

Ash's groans were muffled—he was losing all control, moving more desperately as Astra crashed against him with every thrust. Sasha gripped Astra's shoulders and kissed her violently before her body caved and she let out a scream. Astra held on to her as she stiffened and swayed, then Sasha's eyes flicked open, sated and dazed, and Astra's head dropped back as her friend threw herself against her, hands roaming everywhere as she heard Ash's now-clear voice moaning "Oh God, please, I *can't…*"

And then Astra was coming, and Ash was coming, and the three of them slumped in a breathless, sweaty heap on the bed.

* * * *

Several minutes later, flushed and trembling, the exhausted trio lay side by side in companionable silence.

Conversation was beyond them.

Astra stared up at the ceiling, her mind churning. Not only had she just had sex with another man—with *Ash*, in fact—but she had done so with an ease which seemed to belong to someone else.

Oh, she had been nervous. But that had been more due to his unexpected length and girth than anything else. Once she had got past that, it had been surprisingly easy.

Uncomfortably so.

Sasha was saying something about going to sleep now. Without a word, Astra shuffled backwards onto the pillow and kicked the covers downwards to allow herself to slide under them. Ash, on her left, was silently doing the same.

They slipped under the duvet and pulled it up to their chins, staring fixedly upwards and avoiding each other's eyes.

She was a whore.

She was Ash's whore.

She had been unfaithf —

She didn't care.

Sasha rolled over onto her right-hand side. Automatically, Astra turned and spooned against her. A moment later, she felt Ash's body press against her back, his arm wrapping around her stomach.

Harry was out somewhere, picking up men in a stifling club or an alleyway in the cold night air.

She was here, in this room, between the bodies of her best friend and her — and Ash, who was snuggled against her, holding her protectively.

As Astra began to drift off into sleep, she was dimly aware she had never felt more secure in her life.

Chapter Eleven

At ten-thirty in the morning, Astra peeped out into the deserted corridor, listened, then bolted for her own bedroom before anyone had time to hear her.

God, she thought as she stood in front of the mirror, her dishevelled reflection staring back at her with smeared make-up and half-buttoned blouse. *I look a total wreck.*

Throwing the clothes on her bedroom floor, she washed hastily in the sink before grabbing the nearest outfit from her wardrobe and wrestling it on. Sasha had offered to cook breakfast for the three of them, and Astra's stomach was rumbling ominously at the thought. Sasha was a surprisingly awkward cook for one so organised, but she was known for her amazing fry-ups.

Her hair was a freshly-fucked mess. Astra ran her fingers through it, unkinking the tangles, smoothing out the waves, before stilling her hand as a light breeze ruffled the tips.

The window was wide open.

Astra automatically crossed to close it, all the while thinking as furiously as her slightly fogged brain would allow.

She *never* left the window open at night.

Even on nights when it didn't rain, the cold night air was never something she wanted in her bedroom. Besides, the overnight noise and carousing that took place on the streets of the campus was enough to wake the dead most nights. Leaving a window open would have been insanity, even on—*especially* on—a night when the room would be empty.

Shaking her head in confusion, Astra locked the door behind her and made her way downstairs to the kitchen, where she found Sasha frying eggs amidst the delicious smell of bacon and sausages under the grill. Ash was sitting at the table, staring into space, a glass of orange juice sitting untouched in front of him.

"Hey," Astra said cheerfully, pulling out a chair next to Ash, who jolted out of his dream at the sound of her voice.

"Hey," Sasha responded, attacking the frying pan with a spatula. "I've allowed one egg each and two of everything else, if that's OK."

"That's great. Anyone else up?"

"Yeah, Sveta's in the lounge. I think she crashed there — she looks like hell on a stick. Aimee came in the door a few minutes ago, so I'm guessing she went back to Alpha with whatsisnuts last night. Not sure about anyone else, but you *really* don't want to see the state of the lounge—the place is covered in jelly and spilt drinks and someone's thrown up in the fireplace."

"Oh, God."

"Yeah." Sasha started to serve the food out onto plates. "Apparently someone had sex on the fire escape too. They left the condom outside our window."

"Oh, lovely," said Astra, wrinkling her nose in distaste. "Maybe that's who got my window open."

"Got your window open?"

Ash's question hung in the air as Sasha put the plates of food down on the table, along with two more glasses of juice. Astra chose to dive into her breakfast rather than talk; she was ravenous and Ash could wait, but as she lifted her second forkload, he caught her wrist in his hand, insistent.

"I said, what do you mean, got your window open?"

Astra sighed.

"My window was open when I went in just now. I'm sure I didn't do it—I never do." Shaking his hand off, she took another bite of bacon as Ash and Sasha shared a concerned look.

"You know, Astra," said Sasha, placing one hand supportively on her arm, "maybe we should stay in your room tonight. All three of us. Then, if anything happens, you're not on your own."

Astra considered this for a moment. The thought of having Ash there to protect her was rather comforting, in fact, though Harry was unlikely to see it that way.

Not that she could have blamed him for that, hypocritical as it might have been.

The mention of condoms and the thought of Harry reminded Astra of something slightly more worrying.

"Speaking of condoms—"

"Yes, I know," said Sasha immediately. "I forgot as well."

"We don't use them," said Ash brusquely. The look on his face dared anyone to suggest he might have any kind of disease.

"Neither do we," said Astra coolly. "We stopped months ago. I'm on the pill."

"So am I." Sasha smiled in relief. "We should be fine then."

"Well...yes."

It was on the tip of Astra's tongue to point out that, while Ash and Sasha had been monogamous for months, Harry could very well have been sleeping with the men he picked up. His denials had long since worn to the point of transparency.

Maybe I should start using condoms with Harry. An image formed in her mind of herself suggesting this to him and she inwardly winced. Astra stabbed her fork into a sausage, forcing her mind onto other things.

"I need to get down to the computer cluster after this. I have a report to write up on my internship."

"Good point," said Sasha through a mouthful of food, flicking egg at Ash as she gestured with her fork. "I have a lab report to finish and an essay on gel electrophoresis. I'll come with you."

"Okay. What about you, Ash?"

Ash finished wiping egg off his cheek. "Yeah, I'll join you. My supervisor's been on my ass all week."

"Lucky him."

"Bite me."

"You wish."

"Children," Sasha interrupted in her best 'maternal' voice. "Play nicely and eat your breakfast, or you won't get any dessert later."

Astra glanced at Ash, who raised his eyebrows as if to say *Guess that told us.*

Flashing him a smile, Astra dug in to her breakfast again, thinking that for the morning after a threesome that had been rattling around in her head for weeks, this wasn't too bad at all.

* * * *

The computer cluster was relatively deserted when the three of them arrived, which was unsurprising for a Sunday morning. Astra headed for a workstation next to the window, Sasha taking the one beside her. As the next one along was already occupied by a girl with blue hair playing online poker, Ash was forced to move to the next row.

After logging in, Astra plugged in her flash drive and fired up the word-processor, signing in to her email account and Yahoo Messenger at the same time. Glancing to her left, she caught a brief glimpse of the opening paragraph of Sasha's half-finished essay and winced. She and Sasha had an ongoing agreement never to ask for details about each other's work. This agreement, Astra had decided, was also to be extended to Ash, after she had made the mistake of asking him about the subject of his senior project en route to the cluster. Astra had caught something about glaciation and hanging valleys before she had lost the will to live.

Opening up the report she had been working on, Astra pulled her notes out of her bag and started to type. Alongside her, Sasha was doing the same thing.

Ding!

A chat window had popped up on her screen.

"Who's that?" Sasha asked, pausing in her typing.

Astra squinted at the screen name, which was 'sexynerd'.

"Harry."

"Tell him you're busy fisting Ash."

There was a painful-sounding cough from the row behind.

"I'll bear that in mind. Thanks."

Astra turned her attention to the IM.

Hey babe! How ya doin'?

"Babe", indeed. Astra rolled her eyes.

Hi honey. Hungover?

Not really. Only had a few last night. How was the party?

Astra breathed an inward sigh of relief this conversation was taking place via IM. It was much easier to lie online.

Pretty good. Didn't get too drunk.

Anything good happen? was the response.

I hear someone fucked on the fire escape. There. That should divert him. *How was your night?*

There was an unusually long pause before the next message popped up.

He just left.

Ah. Right.

Astra leant back in her chair and considered the best way to respond to this.

She had no idea if Harry had actually slept with this man or if they had just 'messed around', as he put it. He would probably tell the truth if she asked, most likely with much guilt and self-flagellation.

And yet somehow…

There was a slight ache somewhere close to her heart, but nothing more.

You're supposed to feel hurt, her mind accused. *You should be heartbroken.*

And she should, she should have felt hurt, although she knew she had no right to—they had agreed to this, and regardless, his betrayal could be no worse than hers. But the picture the words conjured seemed detached. Unemotional.

I should care, and yet I don't. It shouldn't feel normal, and yet it does.

The barrier had been breached, and there was nothing but a slight sting, suffocated by numbness. Staring blankly into space, Astra started at the sudden ding from the PC.

Astra? Still there?

* * * *

Sitting on the swivel chair in front of the computer in his bedroom, Harry leant forward, his forehead wrinkling in concern.

Redstarlight is composing a response, the message at the bottom of the chat window assured him.

Above, his last two messages hung in the air.

He just left.

Astra? Still there?

Shit.

He'd finally pushed her too far.

He had been wondering how far he could take this without breaking the already fragile trust they still shared. Astra had accepted, even approved, his experimentation so far, had turned a blind eye to his frantic fumblings in dark alleys and his mutual blowjobs at other men's apartments, but now, at last, he had reached her limit. In those three words she had recognised his guilt and he had broken her heart.

Oh, God.

Slowly Harry's head sank towards the desk, his eyes falling closed as images of Astra flashed through his mind. Astra huddled in a chair in the computer cluster, wrestling with her composure, finally covering her pain in a cold mask as she typed the words that would end their relationship for good.

Ding.

Miserably, Harry raised his eyes to the screen.

Did you fuck him?

His heart dropped. This was it.

Yes.

He had promised her over and over he wouldn't sleep with any of them. Now Astra would know him for the weak-willed jerk he was, and he would lose her —

Did you top or bottom?

Harry sat bolt upright in surprise. This was unexpected.

I topped.

Not that he was sure if he *was* a top, but the guy had been willing to bottom for him, and he hadn't been able to resist —

Did you use a condom?

A fair question.

Yes.

The next response was startling in its matter-of-factness.

Okay. If you're going to start doing that, we should use condoms too. I'd like to be safe.

Oh, God.

Harry stared at the screen, jaw hanging slackly, barely able to believe it.

Astra was okay with it.

Astra had *forgiven* him.

Oh God, he had the best girlfriend in the world. He really did. Astra understood him, understood all this experimentation was outside their relationship, and still wanted him, even after —

Still there?

Harry hurriedly returned his hands to the keyboard.

Yes. You're right, we can do that. I can't believe you're so understanding!

Oh, that's just me. ;) All for experimentation.

Harry shook his head, a ridiculously goofy grin splitting his face.

You're incredible. I love you.

I love you too. Better get back to my dissertation.

Sure. See you later.

Redstarlight has signed out of Yahoo Messenger.

Harry fell back in his seat, limp with relief. He hadn't lost her. Astra had accepted him — Astra was still his.

Thank God.

* * * *

"Hey, Astra?"

"Yeah?"

Closing the chat window, Astra turned to face her friend, who was gesturing towards her monitor. The image of an elaborately-decorated restaurant filled the screen, under an ornate heading that read 'Thai Lotus'.

"You like Thai food, don't you?"

"Yeah, it's my favourite."

"Ever been to this place?"

Astra leaned across to look at the screen. She recognised the restaurant as one she had walked past a number of times, but never actually visited—Harry could occasionally be talked into Thai food but, after a nasty experience with a red curry, was more interested in pizza.

"No. Looks nice, though."

"Fancy going tonight, the three of us? I could really go for some sticky rice."

"Oh God, yeah." Astra's eyes momentarily glazed over at the mention of her favourite Thai dish. "I'd love that."

Sasha twisted around to catch Ash's eye.

"Did you hear that, Ash? Thai Lotus tonight with Astra?"

"I heard," was the dry response. Astra turned in her seat to face him.

"I didn't know you liked Thai food, Ash."

Ash arched one eyebrow coolly.

"There's a lot you don't know about me…yet."

Ooh.

Astra held his gaze, stubbornly refusing to look away from Ash's wickedly suggestive smile, while a persistent little voice at the back of her mind nagged that this was a dangerous, and slightly disloyal, thing to do in front of Sasha. Ash was, after all, her best friend's boyfriend. She would do well to remember that.

And, damn it, so would he.

* * * *

After several glasses of wine, Astra was still able to remember the strict boundaries she had set for her relationship with Ash, but was beginning to lose any inclination to care.

Thai Lotus was a popular restaurant, with a refined yet friendly, atmosphere. Its cavernous interior was richly decorated in gold and silver. The tables were adorned with dancing tea-lights and set out around a blue-lit waterfall, water-lilies floating in its basin. Traditional Thai music played softly in the background as girls in cheongsams flitted airily around the room, pouring more wine, offering to bring more, or suggesting items from the menu. For Astra, it was like something out of a dream.

The dreamlike haze had been encouraged by Sasha, who had called for their second bottle of wine after their waitress had refilled their glasses for the fourth time. Ash, already on his third bottle of Chang, was in slightly better control, but still unable to hide the fact he was looking a little glazed himself.

It was probably just as well.

Sitting at a table some distance away, but still within earshot, were a group of frat boys they had all recognised as being Beta Phi, talking at the tops of their voices about the 'screamer' who lived on their corridor. Confronted with Sasha's look of concern and Ash's steely glare, Astra had confirmed their suspicions.

"He did *what?*"

"Oh, that's fucking it. I'm kicking his ass."

"Look, seriously, you two," said Astra in exasperation. "If I don't care, I don't see why you should."

Sasha gave her a searching look.

"How can you *not* care?"

Astra shrugged, leaning back in her seat.

"I don't know. I just don't. Maybe I've been expecting it."

Sasha eyed her for a moment, then glanced to her left and flipped Ash's tie from where it was hanging in his coconut jelly. With this motion, Astra relaxed, assuming the subject was closed.

"I think we need to do something for you tonight."

Astra stilled at this.

"Oh really? Like what, and why?"

"Well, you've just discovered your boyfriend is a slut..."

You shoulda seen him trying to sneak his little fucktoy out this morning! Like he hasn't been bringing them back for weeks!

Yeah, but I reckon last night was the first time he fucked one. They kept me awake all fucking night. "Oh yeah, baby, give it to me hard!"

Astra shuddered. Oh yes, she *had* just discovered Harry was a slut.

"...and since last night was mainly for sir, I think tonight should be just for you." Sasha flicked her eyes saucily sideways, smiling at the look of naked hunger on Ash's face. "Don't you think so, Ash?"

Ash swallowed, dragging his eyes back towards her with a visible effort.

"Uh, yeah...sure..."

"Tell you what," Sasha continued mischievously, "we can do the ice thing."

Astra's stomach flipped.

"I could – um – go for that, yeah..."

"Okay, you win." Ash threw his serviette down on his dessert plate and waved at one of the waiters. "I keep hearing you two talking about the ice thing, I've even heard *Delfino* talking about the ice thing, and I have no fucking clue what you're talking about. Let's get the bill and get out of here. You can tell me what it is on the way home."

Sasha threw her cash down on the table, stood up and began making her way between the tables to the bathroom.

"Are you even sure you'd want to do it?" Astra asked casually, watching Ash's face as she dug around in her purse for her money.

The look Ash turned on her sent fire along her nerves.

"Oh, I'm sure I'll want to do it. Are you sure you want me to?"

Astra arched one eyebrow, challenging him.

"Because you *know* I'll do it better than anyone else."

"Oh yeah?" *Fuck. I am* not *breathless.*

"Yeah." Ash held her gaze, smiling in that predatory way that made Astra's skin tingle. "I told you I was good. I didn't get to prove it last night, but I will."

"No. Last night I proved *I* was good. And you liked it."

The grin on Ash's lips was overtaken by a look of restrained desire. He swallowed again.

"Didn't you?" Astra slid her high-heeled shoe along the inside of his calf, watching the strain in his face as her toe glided higher and higher. "When I had one hand on your balls and the other twisting on your —"

"God, yeah," Ash croaked, dropping helplessly back into his seat. A delighted laugh bubbled in Astra's throat.

"I told you we'd make you see stars."

Ash's glazed, desirous expression froze in place as the waitress reappeared at their table, check in hand. Astra swiftly withdrew her foot and counted out a handful of notes, smiling sweetly at Ash's discomfort.

"Are we done?" came Sasha's voice from behind the waitress.

"We are," Astra replied airily, standing up and shrugging her coat on.

"Are you ready, Ash?" Sasha asked.

Ash threw his cash down and stood up. Astra noticed him slide some change back into his pocket and adjust himself in his trousers at the same time.

"Ready as I'll ever be."

The walk home from Thai Lotus was short but slow. After stopping twice to allow Astra to catch up, Ash turned around, marched back to her, and hoisted her up in his arms, giving her a look that dared her to protest.

"Shut up, you. I am not walking at a fucking snail's pace just because you're wearing pretty little heels."

Feeling the cool air wash over her aching feet as they hung over Ash's arm, Astra chose not to suggest just taking her shoes off. She was supremely drunk, after all. Surely a ride home in Ash's arms couldn't hurt. She giggled as Ash set off walking again, her head swaying dizzily as she leant back over his forearm.

"Get up here, you drunken bitch," Ash muttered, jerking his right arm so Astra's head flew up and landed on his shoulder.

"Oh, you big, strong man, you."

"Ignore him," Sasha said, leaning round Astra's feet to grin at her. "Every man likes to have a helpless woman in his arms."

Astra smiled naughtily, remembering the last time Ash had carried her in his arms and how he had been left walking with a limp. From the look Ash darted at her under his blond fringe, he remembered it as well.

"And Ash *especially* likes to have y—"

"Ice thing," Ash interrupted.

"All right, all right." Sasha threw Ash a knowing look, leaving Astra feeling briefly confused. "It's reeeeaaally not that complicated."

As the trio reached the edge of the campus, Sasha's voice carried in the still night air, louder than usual, echoing off the nearby buildings. Astra buried her head in Ash's neck, swinging her feet as the alcohol slowly began to settle in her system.

It had been an accidental discovery during an evening date with Harry some months previously, in the heat of summer. Leaning off the bed to take a sip from his glass of ice water, Harry had come back up with an ice cube which he had introduced to her nipples. The effect of the sudden cold on her overheated skin, combined with the delicious flood of cool water that followed, had been so powerful Harry had spent a full half-hour lying flat on his back, wide-eyed and with trembling knees. After that, they had developed a routine somewhere between a massage and a drawn-out tease, which Harry liked to seductively refer to as 'the ice thing' and which Sasha had been gratifyingly eager to learn.

The actual moves varied from session to session, which was fortunate, as Sasha was a little too drunk and Ash a little too impatient to deal with complicated manoeuvres. The description Sasha was giving was suitably vague to allow for improvisation, while specific enough to give details which made Astra's eyes roll back into her head at the thought. By the time they reached Omega Zeta she was in a breathless state of anticipation, something which had apparently not gone unnoticed by Ash.

"You stop in there and get ice, Seychelle. I'll get her up to bed. Don't wait about, OK?"

Astra clung on to his shoulders, jolting uncontrollably as Ash took the stairs two at a time and barrelled through the central bathroom at full speed, pausing only to let her get her key out of her purse and unlock the bedroom door, which he kicked shut with such force that her bookshelves shuddered.

Astra found herself dumped unceremoniously on the bed, the mattress dipping slightly as she felt Ash climb up behind her. His belt buckle dug into her back as he pulled her flush against him and, with trembling hands, began to massage her shoulders.

"I can do this. I told you I could do this."

His hot breath teased the skin on her neck, causing the downy hair to stand on end.

"Oh God, Astra, I can make you feel so good—I can do anything you want…"

Melting under the soothing pressure of his hands, Astra rested her head on his chest, becoming dreamily aware of his erection pressed heavily into her spine. Ash's voice was starting to break as his breath stuttered.

"Fuck, I want you…I want you so *much*…oh God, I'm so…oh fuck…"

The door flew open and Sasha fell in, holding up a bowl of ice cubes in her right hand as she threw the door shut and locked it with her left.

"Got it. Ash, help me get her clothes off."

Ash stilled as he looked up at Sasha, breathing hard. Astra's eyelashes fluttered dizzily as the conversation continued over her head.

"Chelle, I can't—I need a minute to calm down—"

"For God's sake, Ash, you can do this."

"I'm not going to make it if I don't stop—"

"Ash, this is for her, not you. Bite your lip and take her fucking top off." Sasha crawled up onto the bed, kicking off her shoes, and reached for Astra's high-heeled boot as Ash, sucking in a deep breath, took hold of the hem of her silk vest top and slid it upwards.

It was uncoordinated, it was clumsy, but within five minutes Astra found herself naked, being supported against Ash's equally naked chest and having her shoulders massaged as Sasha gently began to rub one of her feet.

"Ooh..."

"That good?" Sasha whispered, pressing her thumbs along the sole of Astra's foot.

"Oh yeah." Astra threw her head back against Ash's shoulder, arching under the dual touch with a breathy moan. Moisture tickled the shell of her ear as Ash leaned in to softly bite the lobe, darting his tongue against her skin.

Sasha's fingers continued to knead the flesh of Astra's foot for a few minutes longer, trailing along the instep teasingly, before setting it gently aside.

"Ash, pass me the bowl."

Astra felt one hand leave her shoulder as Ash picked up the bowl of ice from the bedside table. Sasha's face loomed as she crawled forward, slipping an ice cube between her moist lips before lowering them to Astra's mouth for a cool, glistening kiss.

As their lips parted, Sasha slid downwards, trailing the melting ice over Astra's breasts, following the streams of water as they glided down over her stomach.

Oh!

Astra gasped, arching against the teasing cold. It trickled and sparkled and shimmered over her skin, leaving her shuddering against the scorching heat of Ash's chest.

"God—*yeah*..."

"You like that, I know you do..." Ash whispered.

"Fuck..."

"In a minute—my turn now—lift up, on your knees, yeah—"

Astra felt herself being manoeuvred upwards. Tucking her knees underneath her, she dimly became aware of Ash reaching for an ice cube as Sasha tormented her inner thighs with her mouth, now almost entirely empty of ice and dripping cool water.

A haze of pleasure settled over her senses, leaving her only vaguely aware of the trembling in her body, the aching need building in her gut as she arched in Ash's arms, crying out in wordless pleasure.

A second, burning point of cold sparked at the top of her spine, the breathy murmurs continuing unbroken, making it clear the ice had *not* gone in Ash's mouth.

"Yeah, that's it, do you like that? Oh, it's melting already, you're so *hot*—yeah, going down, down your back, like that—lift up, let me get to your ass—oh God, I love your ass..."

Astra rose up unsteadily on her knees, feeling Ash's hand catch her shoulder to support her as the cool fire blazed down, down, down, dripping over the soft rounded flesh of her cheeks. Ash's mouth pressed against the back of her neck as he let out his breath in a slow, shuddering sigh.

"Can't wait any more—I have to..."

"Do it," Astra gasped hoarsely, already twitching unconsciously as she felt him pressing against the back of her thigh. Instinctively she shifted to line him up with her entrance, pushing back against him. Ash moaned loudly as her movement caused him to slip in just past the head.

"OhmyfuckingGod!"

More ice. Sasha was trailing a fresh cube over her breasts, sucking softly on her nipples. Ash gripped her hips and thrust, thrust in to the hilt, biting down on her neck as he moaned, the vibrations pulsing through her skin. His right hand disappeared for a moment, then returned with a chilly wetness on his fingers as his mouth, filled with melting ice, pressed against her neck.

"Oh God—yes—" Astra threw her head back against his shoulder, groaning. "Please..."

And his left hand was still on her hip, steadying her as he thrust, while he moved his right hand, moved it downwards, and the cool moisture on his fingers met her own heat and wetness, dipping, swirling, caressing, *teasing*...

"God yeah—oh yeah—oh—*oh*..."

"Yeah, that's it," she heard Sasha whisper, her warm breath skating across the cold rivulets of water. "Come for us..."

"You...you're not..." Astra caught Sasha's waist and slid her hand downwards, meeting another, rhythmically moving hand, which batted hers away.

"I'm dealing with it. This is for you." Sasha caught Ash's eye over Astra's shoulder. "Doin' all right there, Ash?"

"Fuckin' fantastic," Ash groaned, sounding as though he was barely in control of his mouth. The ice cube had apparently either melted or fallen out.

"Oh God," Astra moaned, grinding back against him. It was too good—she was being hit by sensations from all sides, the cool tingle of the ice and the heat of their mouths and the pressure of Ash's fingers and the throbbing fullness making her clench and pulse and—

"*Oh!*"

She threw her head back, feeling Ash catch her around the waist and crush her against him, heard him cry out as her body tensed around him and squeezed, over and over.

Then Ash's hips jerked and he moaned as Sasha let out a shriek and slumped against Astra's shoulder, all three of them supporting each other as they shuddered in the throes of their orgasm.

Detaching from each other slumberously, they slid down into Astra's bed and allowed the darkness to overcome them.

* * * *

Astra lazily opened one eye as the bed dipped and rolled beneath her.

To her right, Sasha, wearing one of Astra's long T-shirts, lay sprawled with one leg half off the bed, her breath hissing rhythmically in her sleep. To her left, an empty space. Through the darkness she was able to make out the tall, lithe figure of Ash padding across the floor, presumably on his way back from the bathroom.

She glanced at the neon display on the alarm clock. 2:35 A.M. The bed dipped as Ash slid back into bed beside her, and Astra closed her eyes again.

Tired, tired, tired. Too much going on lately.

Thud.

Astra didn't bother to move. It was a sorority house — bumps and bangs in the walls were hardly an unusual occurrence.

Thud thud thud.

Astra felt Sasha stiffen beside her. The bed shifted slightly as Sasha rolled over, her mouth against Astra's ear.

"*What's that?*"

"I think—"

The sentence remained unfinished as, after a painfully silent pause, another series of knocks cut the air, followed by a raised voice.

"All right, you two, open up!"

Astra froze.

It was the House Mother.

The House Mother was *right next door*.

Sasha was still half in a doze, obviously no stranger to having her boyfriend thrown out of her bedroom. Neither was Astra, although Harry's winning smile had spared him a scolding on more than one occasion.

But this was Ash.

She was in bed with Sasha and Ash.

An image of Brad at the desk in his office, checking his croupiers' Facebook feeds, forced itself into her mind, and a cold hand gripped her heart.

If they were caught it would be around the house like wildfire.

And it would only be a matter of time before —

"*Fuck!* Ash, get out! Get out of here *now!*"

Astra heard the sound of a door opening, followed by raised voices and heavy footsteps — someone was being thrown out.

And then, before they could move, the knocking had moved to Astra's door.

Chapter Twelve

"Miss Scott." The voice was inexorable. "Open the door."

Oh shit. Oh shit. Oh shit.

"Wait a second," Astra called back, fighting to keep her voice steady. "I'm naked." Well, she was, after all.

Ash, with a swiftness that suggested familiarity with this particular danger, had already rolled off the bed and picked up Astra's robe, which had been lying on the floor. Shrugging his way into it, he paused to snatch a long T-shirt from the back of a chair and threw it to Astra, who caught it.

"I'm giving you ten seconds," came the voice, a distinctly sardonic tone now tingeing the words. "Get dressed and open the door."

Quickly pulling the shirt over her head, Astra darted a glance at Ash, who was now by the window, attempting to lift the sash with as little noise as possible.

"OK, I'm coming—"

Ash caught her eye, held one finger to his smiling lips, and winked.

Then, in a split second, he had thrown one leg over the sill and ducked under the sash, disappearing from view.

Sasha was still on the bed. Astra's mind span as she crossed to open the door, struggling for an explanation, but somehow it seemed less important now Ash had gone.

The House Mother stood in the corridor, arms folded, wearing a floor-length robe in a ghastly shade of green and with her hair pinned to the top of her head. Astra offered her most winning smile.

"Hi. Sorry about that."

A scuffle behind her, and then Sasha's head appeared over her shoulder. Maternal eyebrows were elegantly raised.

"Hi. Sorry." There was a definite slur to Sasha's speech. "We went to a bar. Was a little drunk. Lost my key."

"I said she could crash here," Astra added, dragging her own speech a little.

The House Mother eyed them both narrowly, and Astra found herself overcome with the urge to giggle. Beside her, Sasha snorted, and it was too much — Astra clamped her hand over her mouth to stifle a hysterical squeal.

"I see."

The disapproving glare did nothing to quell Astra's helpless laughter.

"*Well.* As you're obviously still drunk, I'll leave you to sleep it off." With a sharp look over Astra's shoulder into the empty room, the House Mother turned abruptly and swept away, robe swishing in her wake.

It was only when Astra found herself back in bed, door locked and herself flanked on both sides by smug best friend and shivering best-friend's-boyfriend, that she was able to relax without reflecting on just how close that call had been.

No-one could know. And so far, no-one knew.

So far.

* * * *

From the moment Astra reached the foot of the stairs, it was obvious the previous night's events had not gone unnoticed.

The sign on the noticeboard was brutally clear.

Chapter Meeting 7pm Tonight

Topic: Boys

"Subtle," Sasha murmured from behind her. "Like she's never thrown a guy out before."

"I definitely got the feeling she'd thrown Ash out before."

"Oh hell yes," Ash said with feeling, leaning his head between them. "Which is why I kept telling Sash to come crash at mine. They don't give a fuck at Alpha as long as we don't wake everyone up."

"Maybe we should just do that in future." Sasha put her hand on Astra's shoulder. "What do you think, Astra?"

"What do I—?" Astra's head had just gone into a tailspin.

"What do you think about crashing at Ash's in future?"

What do I think?

The thought was somehow scary.

Sleeping in her own room, or in Sasha's room, was one thing. Sleeping in Ash's room was quite another. It had an intimacy about it that made her stomach tighten even as it made her mind panic. It was one more step down a slippery slope.

No, a step *onto* a slippery slope, her mind immediately corrected.

And yet the thought of being caught, of the furore that would follow, of the inevitable Facebook flurry and career suicide, made the idea irresistible.

"I think it's a good idea," she heard herself say, and wondered at the steadiness of her voice as the image of Ash sprawled on his bed, guitar in hand, flickered briefly.

"Hey, Astra—you ready?" came Nicole's voice from the open front door.

"I'm ready."

"Good. I think I'm scaring people out here."

Stepping out onto the front step, Astra looked Nicole up and down with a wry smile. Kohl-rimmed eyes glowed with ice-blue intensity from under a heavy black fringe, complemented by the black cashmere sweater and dark blue jeans which were worn so long the black leather boots were barely visible under the hem.

Apparently Nicole was playing 'emo kid' today.

"No more than normal."

Nicole laughed and turned to leave. As Astra followed, a hand caught hold of her shoulder and twisted her round to face him.

"Astra?"

"Yeah?"

Oh God. It was Harry. He was desperately scanning her face, his hair mussed as though he had been running his hands through it repeatedly.

"Could we meet up after your last class? I just, you know…"

Astra's stomach dropped painfully. She really wasn't in the mood for a painful conversation, but apparently one was coming due.

"Yeah. Sure. I finish at two in Calliope."

"I'll meet you outside then."

"Okay."

"Okay."

For a moment they stared at each other, Astra tugging her hands inside her jeans pockets, Harry awkwardly shifting his weight from foot to foot.

"Hello?" said an irritated Chicago drawl beside them. "Class to get to?"

Jolting back into awareness, Astra dropped her eyes and made a show of looking at her watch. Harry laughed uncomfortably and gave Nicole a rather pitiful smile, which flickered and died at the steely look in her eyes.

"Right. Yeah. See you at two."

"See you at two," Astra echoed as Harry slid his eyes away from hers and made an unnaturally swift exit across the lawn.

"You two are useless," said Nicole definitively, taking Astra's elbow and guiding her away from the door and down into the street. "Now entertain me by explaining exactly why your limp-wristed boyfriend looks like he should be on lithium."

Astra sighed and wondered how she was going to fully explain toppy bisexual boyfriends in the five minutes before class was due to start.

* * * *

Astra and Nicole were forced to run to reach Calliope Hall in time for their reward management class, the disapproving eye of Professor Lindeman on them as they slid hurriedly into the back row. The explanation, therefore, was on hiatus until lunch. Astra saw this as something of a reprieve.

I just, you know… Want to talk, no doubt.

Why did Harry *always* want to talk about it?

Or rather, why did he always want to talk about it *after* the fact?

He had neglected to mention his curiosity until she had caught him coming out of Pink, by which point Ash had obviously been aware, so heaven knew who else had found out. He had insisted he was doing nothing wrong until she had confronted him about the incident in the alleyway, at which point he had been full of reassurances—until his guilt after her hospital visit had made him desperate to confess again. And now, for some reason, he was desperate to confess again, whether she wanted to hear it or not.

And she didn't.

In fact, she was getting fucking sick of it.

She couldn't rely on Harry for a damn thing. Hell, at this stage, he was her boyfriend more in name than anything else. His experimentation had taken over everything. And while he was out cavorting with whomever the hell he liked, slipping it into everything that moved under the impression it didn't count, she was being accosted in the street, run over by bikes, and left alone in hospital for hours at a time. If Ash hadn't answered his phone…

Oh, Ash.

Ash, Ash, Ash.

Ash was strong. Protective. He had carried her, taken care of her, made her feel safe.

Made her feel secure.

Once, Harry had made her feel secure, but she could no longer be sure of his presence. No longer sure of his honesty. No longer sure of his feelings.

Ash's honesty was now somehow reinforced in her head. Astra no longer believed he intended to blackmail her. He seemed to have too much invested in it to want to risk it.

He had been a constant presence for months, and now always there when she needed him.

And his feelings...

Oh.

There Astra came to a halt.

Ash was dating Sasha.

Yes, he obviously had feelings for Astra, and yes, she was fairly sure he had only started dating Sasha to piss her off after she had rejected him at that party. But that had been months ago. He had had plenty of time to develop deeper feelings for Sasha, assuming he was the type to fall in love.

He had *not* had the chance to develop proper feelings for Astra, other than those his possessive nature allowed. So it was unlikely he felt anything real for her.

You deserve better than that. Even if you don't want that from me...

Astra mentally shook her head and chastised herself. It was all very well for Ash to act as though he was offering more than he could give. He wasn't free to give it, and it was easy to offer it when he knew she would never accept it. Had she been in a position to accept it, he would probably have panicked and run a mile. He had, after all, been discussing a threesome at the time.

And what red-blooded male didn't fantasise about a threesome?

It didn't mean he felt anything else for her. He could, very easily, have been taking advantage of his girlfriend's intimacy with her hot best friend. It didn't involve much of an intellectual leap. Sasha, his girlfriend of four months had been...

Sasha.

Whatever Ash's feelings were, Sasha's were almost certainly deeper. Even if Ash wasn't capable of love, Sasha certainly was.

Ash was Sasha's boyfriend.

And, as long as he remained that way, Astra would hold on to Harry. Because, in the end, the security Ash provided was no more long-term than any other.

Harry was no longer hers.

But Ash wasn't hers either, and never would be, not without devastating her best friend.

And she would do anything rather than break Sasha's heart.

* * * *

Lunch was taken in the refectory and passed in a blur of motion. Surrounded by students chatting and carrying a tray, Astra considered herself safe to relax. Nicole was an enthusiastic vegan, so lunchtimes were usually spent in back-and-forth baiting between her and Jayla, who took great pleasure in eating grease-filled hamburgers in front of her.

However, today Jayla was conspicuous by her absence.

"She's throwing up," Nicole explained through a mouthful of tofu salad. "I told her to throw out that bolognese sauce, but would she listen?"

Astra had a suspicion Nicole would have blamed even the most obvious of hangovers on food poisoning when there was meat involved, but chose to ignore it in favour of concentrating on her stir-fried chicken.

Nicole was still extolling the virtues of veganism as they crossed the campus back to Calliope, only falling silent when they reached their Employment Law classroom. Professor Brandt's lectures, being delivered at high speed and without the aid of handouts, required full concentration at all times, which gave Astra an hour's welcome freedom from her wandering mind. Nicole spent the lecture apparently preoccupied, gazing off into space with her brow knitted in thought, which didn't bode well for either her grade or Astra's nerves.

On their way out of the classroom, walking shoulder to shoulder, Astra glanced across at Nicole to see she was still lost in her own thoughts. Astra shrugged and gathered her file to her chest and moved forward through the crowd. Harry was probably waiting outside, and the desire to simply have the conversation he wanted and leave was overwhelming.

As she neared the doors, Nicole caught her shoulder, pulling her against her side as she murmured close to Astra's ear, "Good luck with Harry, catch you later..." More jostling, and Nicole was swallowed up by the crowd, leaving Astra to be carried through the main doors into the sunlight.

Harry was waiting across the road, leaning against a lamp post. As Astra dragged herself out of the herd, she saw him catch sight of her and straighten up. There was a nervously hopeful look on his face.

Oh, God.

Harry was still cute. There was no doubt about that. His messy dark hair still fell attractively over his forehead, his blue eyes were still intense, his smile still adorable. He still wore his T-shirt and jeans with the grace of a gazelle, and there was still something about him that caused winged things to flutter around her stomach.

But it was supposed to be with excitement, not nerves. And it was impossible to see him, standing there on the sidewalk, and not imagine him wide-eyed and gasping, clutching muscular and unfeminine hips as he thrust, panting out the name of that night's random man...

Astra took a deep breath and crossed the street to where Harry was waiting, awkwardly shifting from foot to foot. She had intended to greet him with a hand to the shoulder, but Harry slid an arm around her back and kissed her warmly.

Wrong. *Wrong.*

It was clearly Harry's attempt to make everything alright. It lingered a little too long, and involved some uncertain darting movements with his tongue. Astra bore it as best she could, pulling back as soon and as gently as was polite.

"Hi," she said, smiling in what she hoped was a reassuring way.

"Hi," Harry echoed, a flicker of disappointment crossing his face. Astra inwardly groaned.

"Let's walk?"

"Okay."

Walking side by side and *not* holding hands, they set out across the quadrangle in the general direction of Omega Zeta.

"I wanted to talk to you," Harry began, and Astra suppressed a wince.

"About?"

Harry's answer was drowned out by a jeering yell from behind.

"Hey, Delfiiiii-no!"

Astra turned. Standing in a cluster, blocking the footpath, was a group of boys she recognised from the football team. Though she noted Ash at the back, studiously looking the other way, the speaker had been a swarthy, muscular student who was now moving forward, sneering under the black stripes that streaked his cheeks.

"You with a girl? That makes a change."

Harry was standing his ground, but Astra could hear his breath quickening. She cast a pleading glance at Ash.

"Bet you weren't with her last night, were you, Delfino?" The jock took another step forward, threateningly, and out of the corner of her eye Astra noticed Ash echo his movement.

"Leave it, Mancini."

Mancini paused, turned to stare at Ash in disbelief. "What?"

"Leave it." Ash had pushed through the crowd and was looking down at him from his superior height. "It's not worth it."

A pause, as the two eyed each other, before Mancini shrugged and turned away to smirk at Harry.

"*Well.* Looks like you've got a bodyguard, Delfino."

Astra let her breath hiss out in relief as the group began to move. *Thank God.*

In fact, thank Ash.

She was still limp with relief when Harry's voice rang out beside her.

"And what do I owe *you*, Ash?"

Oh God. Shut up, Harry…

Ash stopped and looked back coldly over his shoulder.

"It's not like you give a shit about me," Harry went on as Astra cringed. "And it can't be Astra. The last time I saw you speak to her, you called her a 'fucking tease'."

An unkind smile crossed Ash's face.

"Yeah, I'm sure you'd fucking love to believe I hate her guts, but I don't. I'm not the one who was pressed up against a wall while she was in hospital."

A deathly silence fell. Harry's stricken face proved he, at least, had laboured under the delusion Ash was unaware of his secret.

"Astra…?"

Oh God. Astra's stomach froze as Harry turned to look at her, his face distraught with imagined betrayal.

"Did… Did you…?"

"Oh, for fuck's sake, Delfino."

Ash's scornful voice cut through the air. Harry jerked around to face him, ready to snap out an immediate dismissal.

"No, she did not fucking tell me. Everyone on campus knows you're a fruit. You go out with guys from my house. I've heard guys from *your* house say you're a cockslut. *We all fucking know.*"

Harry's face was frozen, wide-eyed, biting down on his lip as Ash stared down at him with utter contempt.

"So don't give me shit about hating Astra. You're the one fucking around on her and acting like it doesn't matter. I'm the one who picked her up from the hospital when she was concussed while you were off with your latest fucktoy. I think I'm a *lot* better qualified to look after her than you are."

He abruptly held up a hand in Harry's face to cut off his stammering interruption.

"I'm not interested, Delfino. Go to hell."

Harry fell silent as Ash stalked away. He stared after Ash's retreating back for so long Astra felt obliged to say something.

"Look, I'm s—"

"No, don't apologise." Harry shook his head. "I deserved that."

Astra sighed. Here came the rest of Harry's guilt.

"I'm so sorry, Astra."

Ah, yes.

"I honestly didn't know anyone else knew."

Something snarled inside Astra's head.

"How could no-one else know? You go clubbing with guys from Ash's house! You take people back to Beta Phi! I was out last night and *heard* them talking about what a slut you were and what they'd heard you doing every fucking night. How could you possibly think *no-one knew?*"

Harry's mouth hung open.

"They heard me?"

"Well, you can be pretty loud, and if you will bring home screamers…"

"I didn't think—"

"No, you didn't fucking think, did you? So I have to listen to your frat brothers talking about how you've been sucking dick and eating ass for weeks, and get a soundtrack from your first experience topping in the process."

Astra rolled her eyes, the bitterness lacing her tongue.

"Assuming it *was* your first experience topping, because the last I heard, you weren't actually having sex with them, were you? I never actually hear about this until you've already done it."

"It *was* my first—"

Astra cut him off again, feeling her anger evaporating to be replaced with sinking despair. "Please, Harry, tell me how I can believe a word that comes out of your mouth."

White-faced, Harry stared dumbly at her, eyes glistening.

Fuck.

She hadn't meant to go so far. Apparently it had all been waiting for a suitable opportunity to come out in one blinding rush.

What was Harry going to say now?

"Shit."

Astra held herself steady as Harry's face threatened to crumple.

"I've really fucked everything up, haven't I?"

Lowering her head, Astra let out a trembling breath. This sounded like it was leading towards a painful break-up.

She didn't think she was ready. As Harry hid his face behind one hand, biting down on his lip as it quivered with emotion, she dropped her head and started to turn away. Looking at him was excruciating.

"Astra—no. Wait."

She paused, but kept her head lowered.

"Astra, please!" Harry sounded desperate. "Look at me."

Do I have to?

With an inward wince, Astra turned back to face him. Harry had managed to regain his composure, although he was still pale and red-eyed.

"Look. You're right. I've been an arse, and I really don't blame you for not trusting me, and I wouldn't be surprised if you never wanted to see me again."

Here it comes, Astra thought, feeling her stomach twist painfully.

"But if you'll give me another chance, I can make it right."

What?!

The shock of this statement caused her mouth to fall open, which Harry apparently took as a sign of encouragement. Astra found herself being pulled forward into a half-embrace, Harry clinging to her shoulders as words spilled enthusiastically forth.

"I'll stop going to the clubs."

"You don't have to do that."

"Please." Harry slid his hands up to rest loosely around her neck, fixing her with a pleading gaze. "I can—"

"Look, let's just stick to what we were doing. Dating other people."

Harry froze, his eyes moving over her face.

"Are—are you seeing someone else?"

Oh God. She had always found it difficult to resist those blue eyes.

"Yes." She took a deep breath. "I am."

"Who is it?"

Oh, hell no.

The thought of telling Harry what was happening made Astra's mind recoil. Harry hated Ash. The knowledge that *he*, of all the men it could have been, was seeing his girlfriend, even to the casual degree they had been...

"It doesn't matter. It's just dating."

Harry held her gaze for a moment, then looked down.

"All right." He paused to catch his breath. "You know I love you, don't you?"

The words hung in the air as Astra struggled for speech.

"I…"

Beep-beep!

"Oh!"

They jerked apart abruptly as Astra's cell phone beeped in her pocket.

"Sorry. My cell."

"Course. Yeah."

She flipped the phone open and pressed a button to bring up the text message, which she could now see was from Sasha.

Ash's room tonite?

"Who's that?" Harry asked, moving round to see the message just as the screen fortuitously darkened.

"Sasha," said Astra in relief. "Just wondering where I am."

"Oh, right. I'll walk you back there."

"Yeah."

Harry caught her hand as they began the walk across the quadrangle towards Omega Zeta. Smiling, Astra slid the cell phone back into her pocket.

Her stomach did an inelegant backflip at the thought of sleeping in Ash's room.

"You okay?"

Astra smiled dreamily at Harry. "I'm okay."

Oh, yes. I'll be okay. Her eyes drifted towards the other side of the field, settling on the solid stone building that housed Alpha Nu Mu. Some lights were on in the upstairs rooms.

Oh, Harry, I'm more than okay.

Chapter Thirteen

Sitting on Ash's bed, her back resting against the headboard, Astra casually watched Ash dig through his bedside cabinet for a pizza menu as her hands absently wrestled a pillow on her lap. By her feet, Sasha lay on her stomach across the end of the bed, reaching down to unpack a plastic bag full of bottled beer and wine.

Nearly two weeks.

Two weeks of switching between Harry's and Ash's rooms, a practice which had only served to point up the problems between them.

Nights with Ash and Sasha had been relaxed and warm, spent drinking beer and eating take-out, laughing and joking as the room began to spin and the light spilled from the window, holding them in a glowing cocoon that protected them from the dark outside.

Ash was remarkably relaxed when on his own turf. He had taken great pleasure in initiating Astra into the intricate male bonding rituals shared by the jocks of Alpha

Nu Mu, including such steps as punching each other in the corridor, shouting obscene comments through the walls and doors when someone had a female visitor, and the ancient art of nicknaming, which served to emphasise many complex in-jokes while reinforcing the fraternity hierarchy. Ash had been the recipient of many ribald remarks the first night he had arrived back with two women on his arm, but had also been threatened with a painful death if anyone suspected him of enjoying anything other than Astra's conversation. Sex, therefore, took place either in Sasha's room or in breathless silence.

And sex, now Astra was in such close proximity to him, was clearly the root of one of Ash's major issues.

Up until that point, Astra had only ever viewed the premature ejaculation rumours as a source of humour. Her mind had been abruptly changed after an evening when Ash, over a slice of Meat Feast pizza and vast amounts of alcohol, had been holding forth on the back stories to some of his fraternity brothers' nicknames.

"...and Hinson down the corridor, we call him Shamu, because his pants come off every time he drinks. So every time he gets drunk, he frees willy."

Astra had collapsed on the floor in giggles.

"Oh God, that's too funny. Do you have a nickname?"

The flash of Ash's cold mask had penetrated even Astra's glittering Goldschlager haze.

"No. I don't."

"No? So what do they call you?"

"They call me Ash. Or Drake." Ash had picked up the pizza box. "Want more?"

Astra had left it at that, but had been sharply reminded of the conversation by a loud bang on the door half an hour later.

"Hey!" a leering male voice had shouted. "You getting any, Quick-Draw?"

"More than you, Malone!" Ash had shouted back, fixing Astra and Sasha with a look that dared them to open their mouths. An uneasy silence had prevailed for a few seconds, but their alcoholic glow had taken precedence and Sasha had kissed Astra, leaving the awkward moment to be mulled over later.

Ash had never mentioned the incident again, but it had hung silently in the air until the next time the three of them had had sex, when amidst the burgeoning excitement and the slide of slick flesh Astra had watched him, noticing for the first time how as soon as his control began to slip Ash's cries would become strained and his muscles tense. Gripping the sheet, he would fight to hold back with increasing desperation until finally his body shuddered in his moment of surrender.

Even then, Astra thought, he could never fully let go.

In one sense, it was a good thing Ash wanted to last until both she and Sasha were satisfied. But even when they were both focussed on pleasuring him, it was clear to Astra the spectre of that one humiliation haunted Ash, hounding him into restraining himself past any reasonable point of endurance.

It was a spectre Astra would have dearly loved to exorcise, had she not been uncomfortably aware it was Sasha who deserved that dubious honour.

With Harry, in contrast, evenings were spent ignoring elephants in the room—Harry struggling to pretend he wasn't still yearning to go out to Pink, Astra struggling to pretend she cared about him enough to give a damn about what he did with his spare time.

The nights she had spent in Harry's room had felt like eternal purgatory.

Astra Scott, you have sinned, and are condemned to spend all eternity pretending to enjoy passionless sex with this man, wondering if he knows you are superimposing another man's face over his, while being secure in the knowledge he is superimposing another man's face over yours.

Ugh.

The knowledge that all of Harry's fraternity brothers knew what he was doing was bitterly humiliating, as were the sidelong looks she had initially received as she passed them on the way up the stairs, Harry ahead of her, flushed, sweating and clearing a path with his defensive glare. Those had stopped a few days later, when she had attended a party at Omega Zeta and run into a group of Beta Phi guys doing shots of Sambuca.

"Got a shot for me?" Astra had seductively asked, leaning over the table and feeling gratified at the wide-eyed looks caused by the flash of her cleavage.

"Um — sure…" one of them had stuttered, offering a shot glass and his lighter at the same time. "Do you want me to…?"

"Oh yes," Astra had purred, one eyebrow raised. "I like them *flaming*."

Since then, even though comprehension was beyond them, the brothers of Beta Phi had apparently decided Astra must be getting *something* out of the relationship. Interaction between them was now reduced to nods and the occasional 'hi' in passing.

Fortunately for Astra, contact was increasingly limited.

Harry had initially set forth to become the perfect devoted boyfriend, keen to involve Astra in as many aspects of his life as possible. Keen to introduce sexual techniques using fingers and mouth that he would presumably be missing. Astra had briefly considered mentioning the strap-on dildo, but somehow felt no inclination to do so. It seemed to belong to another existence, another world.

The situation had lasted for all of one week before, with much twitching and lowered eyes, Harry had casually asked her if she was planning to go out with Sasha that night.

"Oh? Do you have plans?"

"Well, yeah. Some of the guys are going out tonight and…"

"Are they?"

Harry looked up at Astra with an uncomfortable, slightly desperate expression. Something seemed to uncoil in her stomach.

"Yeah, I'm out with Sasha tonight."

In fact, she suspected Harry knew she wasn't fooled, and had never expected her to be. When she had agreed, the relief on his face had been plain, although Astra had briefly wondered if she had also seen in his eyes a trace of resignation. Had he realised she no longer wanted to spend the night with him?

Was he trying to make *her* the reason he was being driven back to Pink?

Regardless, Astra had spent that night with Ash and Sasha, and had done so without murmur every night afterwards. If Harry had expected any other response, he had made no comment. Confessing about Ash would have had Harry in a jealous fit, Astra knew, but the prospect of an emotional outburst held no pleasure for her. Instead, she had kept their few meetings that week — two lunches in the refectory — entirely superficial, steering the conversation away from personal topics, staving off any attempts at intimacy.

She was going to have to end it with Harry, it was as simple as that.

"Astra? Do you want the same again?"

Astra glanced up at Ash, who had found the pizza menu and was waiting, cell phone in hand, for her response.

"Yes please."

Ash gave a decisive nod and stepped away to dial as Sasha shuffled back into a kneeling position on the bed, a bottle of wine in each hand. Gesturing first with the bottle of red in her left and then the bottle of white in her right, she looked at Astra in wide-eyed query. Astra eyed them both—a Cabernet Sauvignon and a Pinot Grigio—and pointed at Sasha's right hand.

"That one."

Glass clinked on glass as Sasha replaced the red and dug out two tumblers. Stretching out on the bed, Astra let her gaze rest on Ash, hoping her feelings wouldn't show in her eyes.

Breaking up with Harry would leave her on her own.

If asked, Sasha would almost certainly have insisted she wasn't alone as long as she had them. But the pronoun *them* only served to prove Ash and Sasha were a unit, while Astra was merely an optional extra.

Changing the situation with Harry might rock the boat and destroy what little she had. If Ash *did* want her—but then Sasha clearly wanted him—it could damage their relationships irreparably. But she was damned if she was going to stay in that corpse of a relationship any longer.

Of course, Sasha had wanted to bring Ash in with them. Oh, sure, Ash had made the original discovery and asked to join in, but Sasha had been keen enough. Astra had been talked into it. That was it.

"Astra?"

Astra looked up at Sasha's question, feeling unreasonably ill-used, and glowered at the proffered glass of white wine as she attempted to tuck her strangely pouty lower lip back in.

"Drink?"

Astra reached out and took the glass.

"Oh, God, yes."

* * * *

Holding the door open with his back, Ash shuffled into the room with an armful of pizza boxes and polystyrene containers to find Astra pressing Sasha up against the side of the bed.

"Starting without me?"

"Be with you in a minute—" Sasha ground out, before breaking off in a breathless moan as Astra's mouth latched on to her neck.

"For fuck's sake."

Arching her body forward against Sasha, Astra became dimly aware of the thud of cardboard against carpet as a warm body pressed against her back. There was a brief moment of fumbling before Sasha slid her hand along her inner thigh, brushing aside her skirt and hooking her panties to one side. Astra buried her head in Sasha's neck and squealed as she was suddenly entered in one thrust.

"Oh God," Sasha groaned, moving restlessly underneath her. "Please…"

Astra stretched out her left hand towards the plastic bag beside them and encountered Sasha's hand, which was nearer. She drummed her fingers on Sasha's knuckles.

"Pass me the—"

"Yes—"

As Astra's mouth met Sasha's again, her hips rocking with Ash's movements, Sasha pressed a pocket vibrator into her hand. She passed it from left to right, wrapping her left arm around Sasha to crush them together as she slid her hand between them to press the buzzing toy against Sasha's centre.

"Oh, *fuck!*"

"Yeah—"

"God, *yeah*—"

Panting, moaning, gasping, they ground their bodies together until Sasha bucked and cried out, arching up to trap the vibrator between them so Astra fell over the edge a few moments later, muffling her shriek in Sasha's shoulder. Ash was still thrusting, biting his lip to stifle his moans.

Through the haze of her climax, the buzzing in her fingers gave Astra an idea. She slid the vibrator out from between her and Sasha's bodies and held it up over her shoulder.

"Ash, do you want—with this?"

The rhythmic thrusting stuttered for a second.

"Oh, God, yeah—"

Astra slithered out from under him, feeling the slide as Ash detached from her body and slumped forward onto Sasha, flushed and gasping as he lifted his hips, the soft curves of his cheeks bared as the waistband of his jeans slipped lower. She roughly pushed them further down, parting his smooth buttocks with both hands as she tucked the vibrator between her thumb and forefinger and lined it up against the newly revealed pucker.

Ash groaned, arching his back to lift his bottom further. "*Fuck!* Do it!"

The only time he lets himself go is when he's submissive.

Astra's lips twisted as she slid the tip of the bullet inside, dipping it in and out as Ash let out a tortured moan, burying his head in Sasha's shoulder in a desperate attempt to avoid being overheard.

"Oh, you *bitch*, please — God, I can't, I *can't* — Don't make me wait — Oh, you fucking tease..."

You're a pricktease.

Oh, you tease...

With a snarl, Astra shoved the vibrator inside up to the hilt, a predatory smile on her face as Ash jammed his fist in his mouth and immediately convulsed, stifling his cries as he spurted his juices hotly all over Sasha's stomach.

"You don't think we were a little, uh — loud?"

Ash eyed Sasha and shook his head as he slowly stirred, raising himself on one hand while hoisting his jeans with the other. Fastening himself up, he stretched out and caught the pile of delivery boxes with one hand, dragging them into the centre of the room as Sasha and Astra moved to sit around them, Sasha wiping her stomach with a nearby discarded T-shirt.

"If no-one's banged on the wall or yelled at us yet, then no. Give me a hand with these."

Astra leaned in to help, revealing two large and heavily-loaded pizzas, a garlic bread, and two portions of fries as Sasha moved to refill their glasses and open Ash a beer.

For the next ten minutes, the conversation revolved solely around food and beer. Astra thought she had eaten more pizza and drunk more wine in the past two weeks than she had done in an entire year's worth of sorority and fraternity parties. Despite this, she was feeling rather dreamy and giggly by the time most of the pizza was gone, and was just reaching for another slice of the Supreme when Sasha lost her balance and fell against the guitar stand. Ash, sitting opposite, was too far away to grab it. Automatically, Astra's hand shot out and caught the Gibson Standard by the neck.

"Hey, watch out! Those things are expensive."

"More expensive than Astra's?" Sasha asked, slurring her words slightly.

"No," said Astra, replacing the guitar with an abrupt jerk of her wrist. "About the same."

"Oh?" Ash raised his eyebrows. "What kind have you got?"

Astra was a little surprised Ash hadn't noticed the guitar in her room, despite the events that had been taking place at the time. The guitar had been lying on the floor next to him while he had been wrapping her in her duvet.

"I *had* a Stratocaster."

"Had?"

"It got knocked over. The neck's broken."

There was a brief, awkward silence while Astra wrestled with her quivering lip. She was a little too drunk for this. The Stratocaster had been one of her most prized possessions. When she had found it on the floor the previous week while picking up more clothes, she had returned to Alpha reasonably calm, having spent a full hour cursing and throwing toys at the wall.

How it had been knocked over remained a mystery. As far as she knew, no-one could have been in her room.

"Can you get it fixed?" Sasha asked finally.

"Yeah, I can get a new neck for it, but it costs money."

"You can use mine if you like."

Astra raised her head to give Ash an incredulous look, remembering the last time she had dared to pick up his guitar.

"Seriously! Just don't play any fucking Michelle Branch on it."

Figures. Astra's eyes glinted mischievously. "Can I play with your whammy bar?"

Ash's expression didn't waver. "If I can play with your flange pedal."

Astra arched an eyebrow, which was met with one of Ash's own.

"Oh, you're honoured," said Sasha, reaching for the garlic bread. "I've gone along to his band rehearsals for months and never been allowed to touch the thing. Ash thinks it's the Holy Grail."

"That's because the first time you picked it up, you fucked around with the keys and I had to spend ages retuning it." Ash fixed Sasha with a frosty look which was completely ineffectual against Sasha's sweet, slightly drunken smile. "Anyway, you've never been to see us play, have you?"

"Nor has Astra. We should go next time. She likes rock."

"Do you have one coming up?" Astra asked.

Ash nodded. "Next week. We're playing a place in town not far from the casino. Come if you want—we're pretty good."

"I might just take you up on that."

"You do that." Ash raised an eyebrow at her, his voice rich with meaning. "They tell me I do a good Axl Rose."

Ooh.

Astra held his gaze as the previous incident flashed through her mind. Ash sprawled on his bed, legs spread wide, jeans barely buttoned, a burgundy shirt falling off his bare shoulders, and that voice — that voice —

Oh God.

Sasha was offering the garlic bread, blissfully unaware of what was going through Astra's head. Astra took a piece, hoping it would help soak up the alcohol. She had a feeling if things went on as they were, she was going to betray herself completely.

And that would *not* happen if she had any say in the matter.

"What time is it?"

Ash put down his beer and looked at his watch. "Ten to twelve."

"Oh good. We haven't missed it then." Sasha was lying on her back on Ash's bed, her head hanging over the side so her blonde hair brushed the floor. "There's supposed to be a lunar eclipse tonight. We should go out on the fire escape and watch it."

"When is it?" Astra asked from her position slumped against the wall.

"About half past midnight."

"Thank fuck for that," said Ash, picking up his beer again. "I can still remember when you kept me up until three AM to watch that stupid meteor shower."

"Hey, it was pretty!"

"I had practice at eight! I nearly passed out."

"Well, you don't have a morning practice tomorrow, so shut up. I know how interested you are in all things astral."

Astra raised her head from her wineglass in time to see Ash dart a fierce look at Sasha, who smirked in response. Having surprised several similar bits of byplay over the course of the past two weeks, she had given up trying to understand them.

She was, however, curious about one point of the conversation.

"How come you didn't enter the draft, Ash?"

Ash turned to her with an expression that clearly showed he didn't think she knew a football from her rear.

"How do you know I didn't? I could have done."

"Because my brother had to go off to camp when he entered. You haven't."

Ash's look of patient acceptance of her idiocy now changed to one of incredulity.

"What's your brother's name?"

"Dash. Plays for Northwestern."

"*Dashiell Scott?!* He's your brother?"

Astra fought it, but couldn't keep the smug smile from crossing her face. If Ash knew who Dash was, he would also know he was a particularly successful linebacker whose entry into the draft this year was a full year before the end of his college career. Not only could her brother probably kick Ash's ass, he was clearly a more respected college football player.

"Who's Dashiell Scott when he's not at home?" Sasha asked from her upside-down pose.

"He's a Northwestern linebacker," said Ash with a dismissive wave of his hand, still looking at Astra. "So you *do* know —"

"Are you a linebacker?"

"You know I'm not a fucking linebacker. Do I look like a linebacker? Dashiell Scott is built like a fucking wall."

Astra chose this moment to step in, as Ash was eyeing Sasha as if he wanted to clear her intoxicated head by submerging it in the sink.

"What position do you play?"

"I'm a running back. Occasionally a wide receiver."

"Nice," said Astra appreciatively. "So why didn't you declare for the draft?"

Ash studied her for a moment, obviously weighing the benefits of explaining this to a woman who actually knew what he was talking about.

"I wouldn't have been picked. I'd been suspended from too many games. So I figured I'd finish out the year and then declare for it next year. Besides, I had..." He mumbled the last few words, which Astra made out to be "disciplinary issues".

Well, of course he'd had disciplinary issues. Ash was renowned for nasty tackles and stamping on other players. If anything, Astra was more surprised he hadn't mentioned academic issues. She had a fair idea players who didn't keep up their GPA weren't eligible.

And Sasha *had* told her he was barely maintaining his grades. Maybe he'd employed a ringer.

Or maybe he's not as dumb as I thought he was.

"I thought you had a sister," came Sasha's dreamy voice, breaking through Astra's thoughts.

"Yeah. Emmy." Astra caught herself before rolling her eyes. Sasha had seen her family photos and talked about them many times, but went into 'rambling' mode after several drinks. "But I also have Dash."

"Oh, yeah."

Ash threw a scathing glance at his girlfriend before turning back to Astra.

"So if you're into football too, did you play with him?" He paused, then covered his face with a groan. "Hold on. That didn't come out right."

Astra giggled.

"No, I was a cheerleader. Why? Do you have brothers you like to play with?"

Ash parted two fingers and peeked at her between them.

"I have brothers, yes. Brett is a guitar god and a hockey player, so I've only *played* with him on the Gibson. Jay doesn't do sports, 'cause he's a fucking wiener. And no, I haven't played with his wiener." Raising one eyebrow, Ash slid his hand down from his face to reveal an evil smile. "But I did play with his girlfriend."

"Which is why he hates you," Sasha put in.

"Which is why he hates me," Ash agreed.

Astra raised an eyebrow and made a sweeping 'you have the floor' gesture with an open palm, leading Ash to elaborate further. The Drake house in Florida had been three stories tall, with bedrooms on the second storey for the two younger brothers and Ash's parents, while the oldest, Jay, had reigned supreme in the attic. His habit of partying all night in bars meant Jay had a steady stream of drunken bed partners whom he would bring home at 2A.M and entertain with much noise and creaking of bedsprings, while the seventeen-year-old Ash lay wide-eyed and envious in the room below.

"I mean, God, I was a virgin, I had no idea what he was doing to them but they were screaming louder than him, so he must have been good. Anyway, one night he brought this blonde chick home, Dana—plastic tits and red lipstick—"

Astra rolled her eyes. "Sounds *lovely*."

"Ah, fuck off. Well, they went upstairs and nothing happened. I was lying there bored and half asleep when my bedroom door opened and Dana came in, gave me this *look* and said Jay was too fucked to get hard and had passed out, and did I want to...you know. And next thing

I knew, she'd pulled the covers off me, got my boxers off and was putting a condom on me *with her mouth*.

"Well, fuck, I was seventeen! I still don't know how I lasted as long as I did. She must have been halfway there already. But the next morning she told him his brother was a better fuck than he was, and Jay came storming down to kick my ass."

"And did he?"

Ash snorted. "Yeah, right. He's three inches shorter than me and weighs about fifty pounds wet through. I gave him a black eye and told him to go fuck himself, and he's hardly spoken to me since."

Laughing, Astra shook her head in resigned disbelief. It seemed strangely appropriate that Ash, who was so firmly convinced of his own irresistibility to women, would have lost his virginity by nailing his older brother's girlfriend. Not to mention that, even as a seventeen-year-old virgin, he had apparently been better in bed than a more experienced ladies' man.

Her own virginity had been taken at the age of eighteen, by a former steady boyfriend who had taken her out driving after their senior prom. Comparing notes with her friends afterwards, she had concluded either high school boys were uniformly terrible at sex, or the moment had been ruined by it taking place in the back seat of a car. He had gone away to college in Georgia and had broken contact until the following summer, by which point Astra had had a number of boyfriends and had no intention of meeting up for an inept knee-trembler.

At the reminder of former boyfriends, a brief image of Harry flashed across her mind.

Harry breathing hard, that catch in his throat... Harry's eyes drifting closed in pleasure... The down on his neck... The taste of his skin...

Nothing.

There was nothing but a cold, hard throb where before there had been softness and light.

Damn it. Astra's eyes hardened as she gripped her wine glass, letting out her breath in one long, sharp gust. Glancing upwards, she found herself under Sasha's unsettlingly knowing gaze.

"That was a heavy sigh."

"Was it," said Astra flatly.

"I think we need some air." Sasha pushed herself up on her hands and knees and made to slide off the bed. "Let's go out onto the fire escape. It's nearly time."

Astra put down her glass and rested her hands on the floor as she made to stand up. Belatedly, she realised her balance was still off as she lurched violently forward, almost falling flat on her face before two warm arms caught her round the waist.

"Whoa! I got you."

The world span crazily as Astra was pulled upright, affording her a lopsided view of Sasha's leg hanging over the sill as she climbed out of the window. Ash's arm tightened around her stomach, pulling her back against his firm chest.

Oh God.

"Thanks," Astra gasped, forcing herself to ignore the heat of Ash's skin through his shirt as it pressed against her back.

"Here, I'll help you with the window."

"Oh, good."

As they awkwardly approached the window, moving like contestants in a three-legged bar crawl, an uncomfortable silence hung between them.

Astra bit her lip. Ash's muscles were tense—he was building up to something. The need to deflect wrestled with the need to wait.

"You were—"

Ash broke off, apparently to rearrange his thoughts.

"You were thinking about him, weren't you? That's why you sighed."

"Just thinking about—" Astra paused, wondering whether to be honest with him.

"About what?"

"How I'm going to have to dump him."

Ash's grip tightened further.

"You're going to dump him?"

"Yes."

By now they had reached the window. Astra hooked her hands over the sill as Ash's arms shifted position, ready to lift her.

"I thought you were still in love with him."

Astra stiffened.

"I don't know what I feel any more. Lift me."

As her feet touched the concrete floor of the fire escape, a gust of cold air swept over her, causing her to shiver as gooseflesh rose on her arms. Ash leaned away from her for a moment and returned with a leather jacket draped over one arm. Vaulting over the sill in an effortless show of strength, he raised one eyebrow and settled the coat around her shoulders, holding it in place as Astra slid her arms down the sleeves.

"Move it, you two!" Sasha called, her voice floating back to them from around the corner of the building. "You can see better from here."

The moon came into view as Astra joined her, Ash coming up on her other side and leaning on the railing. Feather-light wisps of cloud were drifting softly across the lunar surface, a slice of creamy white in the cool darkness, already beginning to take on an amber glow.

"Look," Sasha breathed. "It's starting."

A soft breeze stirred the trees below them, caught in the cool wash of light from the streetlights. Astra let the wind blow her hair out of her face as she tilted her head back to gaze up at the sky, an endless arch of velvet black studded with stars and hung with one great lamp, slowly, softly reddening as the eclipse took hold.

"Astra?"

Ash's whisper at her ear stirred her from her thoughts, but her eyes remained locked dreamily on the blushing moon.

"You don't think it's weird, do you?"

"What?" Astra breathed back.

"Me." A beat, stiff, uncomfortable. "In the ass."

"Oh. No."

"Does *he* like it? When you... I mean..." Ash paused for a moment, apparently collecting himself. "Does he like you to—"

Astra decided to take pity on him. "I've done it. He likes it."

"Do you think it's—*gay*?"

It was almost comical. Ash sounded as though his entire existence rested on her answer.

"*He* might be. But if you like women doing it, not men..."

"No. *God*, no. Not men." Ash straightened up beside her with a shudder at the thought. Astra hid a smirk.

"You're alright, then."

A pause, and then Ash's mouth brushed her ear for a second time.

"You won't tell anyone, will you?"

His voice trembled slightly, and Astra forced herself to stay still rather than shake her head in disbelief. He was *scared*, actually scared she might tell his fraternity brothers and jock teammates. And here she had been worried he would blackmail her.

It seemed so long ago now.

"Course I won't."

Ash straightened again, letting out a suspiciously quavery breath.

"Yeah. Course."

Idiot. Who could I tell?

The moon was now a deep, deep red, at the darkest point of the eclipse. It filled Astra's gaze, passionate, hypnotic.

"It's beautiful," Sasha breathed in admiration. "Don't you think?"

Astra tore her eyes from the sight, drawn out of her thoughts.

"Yeah," she said. "It's beautiful."

* * * *

The piercing tones of *Milkshake* emanated from Astra's bag as the three of them clambered back through the window. Astra crossed the room swiftly and pulled out her cell phone, thanking her stars it had been at the top.

"Who's that?" Sasha asked as Astra scanned the screen before hitting 'accept' and holding the phone to her ear.

"My voicemail."

The slightly too-loud voice of Brad rang in her ear.

"Astra, hi. Listen, we need you to work tomorrow night. Jackie's called off with a broken leg. If you could come in at seven, that'd be great. Thanks." *Click.*

Sasha and Ash were both watching her curiously. Astra briefly recounted the message and saw an expression of interest cross Sasha's face.

"I've never been to a casino before. We should go, Ash."

The look on Ash's face was considerably lacking in enthusiasm.

"Does that mean I have to wear a suit?"

Astra raised an eyebrow. "Do you *have* a suit?"

"Yeah, but it's too tight."

"Oh, quit your bitching," Sasha said airily, cuffing Ash on the shoulder. "I want to go."

Astra looked from one to the other and sighed inwardly. They had such *ease* with each other, such…connection.

So much she didn't have.

Oh well. At least I have the job.

And willingness to come in at the last minute would always look good on her record. Maybe tomorrow night would be the night the decision was made.

She ignored the little voice that muttered secret wishes Sasha and Ash would make other plans. It was a large casino. She might never see them.

But the thought of working while they were there, teasing each other at the craps table, stealing a kiss behind the fruit machines, was enough to make her heart drop.

Please, you two. Do something else. I can't watch that. I can't.

Chapter Fourteen

At ten to seven the following evening, Astra slipped through the side entrance of the Fountain Casino.

The employees' corridor was crowded and bustling. Members of the previous shift passed Astra on their way out, as around her croupiers and bar staff adjusted their uniforms, pinned up their hair and clipped bottle-openers and radios to their belts. Confident in her own appearance, Astra made straight for the break room and joined the rest of her shift members, who were waiting to be assigned positions.

"Hey," she muttered as she stood in between Ally and a barman named Ken. A chorus of equally automatic 'hey's rippled around the room in response as Brad entered the room, moving through the group to stand in front of them.

"Good evening, everyone."

"Evenin'," came the mumbled response from the group.

Astra maintained her practiced expression of polite enthusiasm as, hoping she was being inconspicuous, she scanned the faces of those in the room.

I wonder if any of them are up for promotion?

Brad picked up his clipboard and began counting down the page with his biro, glancing upwards occasionally to compare faces to the names on the schedule. With a satisfied nod, he cleared his throat and fixed the group with a cool stare.

"Places, everyone. Blackjack tables, one to five: Jason, Tanya, Jodie, Astra, Becky. Poker tables, one to three: Ally, Ryder, Simon. Craps tables: Lucy, one; Zack, two. Roulette: Darren, one; Kelly, two. The rest of you are on the floor tonight. Bar staff, two to a till..." He pointed with his two index fingers at two barmen on his left, then began to move along the line. "*You*, till one; two; three; four; five. Okay, let's do it. Astra, might I have a word, please?"

Astra dutifully remained in place as the other croupiers and bar staff filed past her.

The memory of Ash and Sasha disappearing together through the front entrance nagged at her brain. Maybe Ash would be blinded by the flashing lights and glue himself to the first slot machine he reached.

Or try something clever and get thrown out.

Brad had put down his clipboard on the table and was now unfolding a piece of paper which he had drawn from his inside pocket. Astra caught a glimpse of the official casino letterhead.

"Now."

He turned a professional eye on Astra, who straightened and tried to look as competent as possible.

"You may recall we discussed your undergoing management training with us?"

"Yes."

"Yes. You were on the list along with several other people who I've been watching. The senior management team have been studying the reports and were particularly impressed with your dedication to the casino after your accident."

Astra adopted a polite smile, wishing Brad would get to the point.

"Anyway. We have three places available for management trainees, starting in October, and we would like to offer you one of those places."

Astra bowed her head slightly, giving herself time to control her expression.

"Thank you."

"Now you don't have to accept straight away —"

Is he kidding?!

" — you'll be sent out an official offer letter, and if you could let us know within a week, that would be good." Brad folded the paper back up and tucked it back into his jacket. "Okay, out onto the floor with you, Miss Scott."

And, before Astra could regain her scattered wits, she was being ushered out of the break room and into the corridor, where she had just enough time to gain the impression of black eyeliner and dirty-blonde hair before she collided violently with a warm body.

"Ally," Brad said with an air of resignation. "Would you mind moving out, please? Vonda's shift finished five minutes ago."

"I just wanted to ask —" Ally argued.

"*Now*, Miss Brass. Relieve Vonda on table one and I will talk to you later."

The door slammed shut, abruptly ending the discussion.

Astra's mind whirled, fighting to process this new development before taking her table, but Ally seemed determined to talk as they walked down the corridor towards the door that led into the casino area.

"So you've been offered a place? You're going to be management?"

"If I complete the training."

"Did Brad say who else—?"

Astra cut off the query with a sharp push to the door, its hinges squealing in protest. Immediately ahead of her was the first poker table, where a round-faced girl with a mane of black hair was winding up a game. As the door shut with a bang, she looked up at Ally and made an impatient gesture.

"Best get out there." Astra nudged Ally supportively with her shoulder, hiding her relief. "She looks mad."

Ally rolled her eyes expressively and set out towards the table as Astra turned left, passing two other tables on her way to blackjack table four, where a dark-haired, skinny young man was just dismissing two intoxicated-looking patrons.

"Thank you sirs, please enjoy the rest of your evening. Astra, hi."

"Hi, Barry." Astra smiled up into his pointy face. "Busy so far?"

"It's picking up," Barry responded, stepping aside as Astra took her place at the dealer's spot. "Glad you're here. We'd have been swamped otherwise."

"Yeah, I heard Jackie called out."

"Fell down stairs when she was drunk, apparently. Brad wasn't happy."

Another case of Brad's disapproval of bad behaviour. Astra inwardly thanked every deity she could think of that her own life was, so far, private.

The sound of chairs ruffling the carpet brought her back to herself, and Barry turned away with a brief 'see ya!' as Astra switched automatically into croupier mode, smiling in greeting at the two men who had joined the table.

The game was on.

* * * *

Astra turned to reload the automatic shuffler and took advantage of her newly-empty table to check her watch for the fifth time.

Nine twenty-five.

She had been on the table for nearly two and a half hours. In that time, she had had two men thrown out for fighting, both convinced the other was cheating, three clients had bet and lost so heavily Astra suspected they were using the company expense account, and one rather trashily-dressed woman in her forties had played such a careful game she had managed to sit through ten hands without winning a single thing.

Astra had never understood this point of view. In gambling, the risk was *everything*. Where was the fun if one never took risks?

The glowing air around her echoed with voices, numbers being called, victorious laughter. High stakes and tension at the poker tables, the jangling music, glittering lights and rattle of coins at the slot machines. On the turn of a card, she could make a man's fortune or break it to dust.

This was her dream. Her life.

Out of the corner of her eye she noticed figures approaching and preparing to sit down. Astra turned to face them, suddenly extremely grateful repetition had made her opening greeting so smooth as her eyes briefly narrowed in recognition.

Ash had joined the table.

You bastard. You fucking bastard.

He was banking on the fact she wouldn't respond. He thought this was the one table where he could cheat all he liked and not get thrown out, because it was *her* table.

And if she was caught turning a blind eye, she would be risking her entire career.

That smug, selfish asshole.

Astra let her body take over the rehearsed movements of the exchange of cash for chips and the opening deal, steadfastly refusing to look at him.

He had taken the seat directly opposite her as if to flaunt his presence. She focussed on the slide of the cards and the expressions of the other two players, deliberately keeping her mind clear of emotion as her thoughts raced.

If he starts counting cards… No, he won't do that. He hasn't got the maths skills.

Oh God, please tell me he isn't going to do that.

Where's Sasha?

As her hands automatically made the flowing motions for the second deal, she scanned the room, including the men in front of her. A fleeting glimpse of glittering silver, possibly Sasha's sequinned mini-dress, caught her eye from one of the craps tables. Passing her gaze back along the table, she inwardly winced.

Oh yes, Ash was counting cards.

And he was really *bad* at it.

Astra gritted her teeth and continued to deal, hand after hand, chip after chip, each time darting glances at Ash while never meeting his eyes, until her jaw was clenched so tight it was beginning to hurt.

This was getting fucking ridiculous.

Ash was taking twice as long to decide what to do with every new card, too busy trying to recalculate his count every time. He was staring at each card as though trying to memorise its face. The other two men were beginning to eye him with suspicion, and from the coolly smug expression on Ash's face, he had no idea he was being so obvious.

If she didn't do something soon, someone would complain.

Feigning a turn towards the shuffler, she glanced up at the bar and made eye contact with one of the barmen, raising one eyebrow and gesturing slightly with her head.

Get over here!

The barman nodded once, briefly, and put down the glass he was polishing. Satisfied, Astra turned back to her three patrons, resisting the temptation to smirk in Ash's direction as she started the next hand.

It was almost pitiful to watch, she thought. The man on her left had drawn a ten and a five, and she could actually *see* out of the corner of her eye that Ash was staring at his cards, looking back at his own, then darting his gaze at the man on her right, struggling to calculate what was likely to come up next. The barman loomed behind him, and Astra kept her face turned towards the first man, sliding him a card as he signalled for a hit.

"Can I get you a drink, sir?"

Ash started guiltily, then a dark flush crept over his skin as he attempted to respond nonchalantly.

"No, thank you."

Deliberately keeping her expression neutral, Astra turned towards him, watching him steadily as the barman moved on to the next man. Ash had paused, still slightly facing away from the table, two fingers tapping in agitation on the baize. After a moment, slowly, stiffly, he turned back to face her, eyeing her under darkly lowered eyebrows.

Astra briefly allowed her glee to show in her face. Ash's expression darkened even further.

Aw. Did we lose our count?

With a studied air of casualness, Ash chose to stick on his hand of eighteen, but showed no surprise or disdain when he lost. Instead, he stood, locked eyes with Astra for a moment, then gave a curt nod before striding away towards the slot machines.

Astra wasn't sure if she was disappointed or relieved.

* * * *

"Astra."

A hand descended on her shoulder. Astra turned and found herself face to face with Dinah, one of the croupiers Brad had assigned to floor duty.

"Brad wants you to swap with me for an hour."

"Oh, okay."

It wasn't uncommon for croupiers to be switched mid-shift but, with their earlier conversation in mind, Astra wondered if Brad was testing her versatility. As she stepped to the side, allowing Dinah to take her place, she caught herself looking her coworker up and down.

I wonder if she's also been offered a place.

The question struck her as having a simple answer —
"Unlikely." Dinah, a short and pretty woman of Chinese
ancestry, rarely worked the evening shift and had only
been trained on the blackjack tables, having shown an
inability to retain the rules of craps or handle a roulette
ball with any accuracy. She was generally assigned to floor
work, occasionally being used to cover breaks or, as in this
case, to switch off with the blackjack croupiers.

Leaving Dinah to handle the table, which was again full,
Astra made her way out onto the floor, dodging around
the patrons gathered at the nearby craps table. She briefly
wondered where Ash and Sasha were before forcing her
mind back onto her work.

She couldn't risk being seen talking to them while on
duty.

She could, however, risk talking to a member of staff.
May as well get the practice in for when she was
management.

Standing against the wall by the first bank of slot
machines were a lanky, freckled redhead with prominent
front teeth and a slim, blond man with a pointed nose,
wide, blue eyes and one hand resting on his cocked hip.
The redhead was gesticulating wildly as she talked, clearly
complaining about something, while the young man was
leaning back, head tilted sideways and eyes cast to the
ceiling in an affected attitude of boredom.

Astra crossed behind the fruit machines and greeted
them.

"Hey, Carmel. Tony."

The redhead paused mid-whine. "Hi, Astra."

"Hi, Astra," Tony added, an expression of relief crossing
his face.

Astra bit her lip to hide a smile as Carmel opened her mouth again. It generally wasn't necessary to say anything beyond 'mmm' when talking to Carmel. She was more than capable of carrying on a conversation all by herself.

"I didn't think you were on floor work tonight. Oh, have you been switched off? It's been really slow tonight. Hardly worth it really."

"Have you been down here all night?"

"Oh God, yeah," Tony answered, rolling his eyes dramatically as Carmel tucked the tissue back into her pocket.

"We've been walking up and down here for *hours.*"

I'll have to work on that. They could have been switched off more often.

"And there was this guy who was such a fucking *asshole.*"

"Wasn't he, Tony? Ugh." Carmel pulled a disgusted face. "Tony tried to stop him punching a machine, and he called him a fag! Can you believe that?"

Astra broke away from her thoughts, struck with genuine outrage.

"No! Really? What an ass."

"I know." Carmel nodded indignantly, gesturing towards the front entrance. "We called security on him."

"They throw him out?"

Carmel smirked, obviously relishing the memory. "Right on his face."

Oh, that must have been sweet to see.

Astra's satisfaction at the thought abruptly dissipated as another image materialised in her mind—one of blond hair, a lean body and a too-tight suit, wrestling with two burly security guards, shouting and cursing in the deep, rough voice of a testosterone-enhanced jock.

Shit. What if Ash had got himself thrown out?

He was certainly violent enough to punch a slot machine, and she knew plenty of jocks who were capable of throwing around homophobic slurs, even if she had never heard Ash use them—even about Harry…

No, surely it couldn't have been him.

Carmel had paused in her speech to lean around the bank of machines, scanning the row for any punters in need of help. To Astra's surprise and amusement, her eyes suddenly widened in excitement and she leant back towards them, one hand cupped slightly round her mouth as her voice dropped.

"Oh my God, it's that guy. He goes to your college, Astra. Down there—blond guy, footballer type—"

Astra twisted around, squinting over her shoulder, and to her great relief spotted Ash at the far end of the row, casually leaning on a machine with one hand as he entered quarters with the other. His face bore an expression of firm determination that briefly made her stomach flop.

"Ash? I didn't know you knew him."

"Oh yeah," Carmel glinted, her voice taking on a distinctly salacious quality. "I met him at a party back in May last year. We got on *very* well."

Astra had a momentary fantasy of Carmel's face being slammed in a door. Covering her irritation, she adopted an expression of prurient interest.

"*Reeall*-ly? So how was he? I heard—" she glanced casually over her shoulder as if checking for eavesdroppers "—that he can't last five minutes."

"Oh no, not at all." Carmel smiled, the face of a ragged and bucktoothed cat who had somehow managed to steal the cream. "He lasted *ages*. And he was *good*. He had this thing he did with his tongue..."

Astra smiled knowingly back at her, wondering if she could find some excuse to get the red-headed bint fired as soon as she became a manager. Maybe she could just poison her lip gloss.

She was considering asking another question when Tony suddenly straightened up and looked over Astra's shoulder. Automatically, Astra and Carmel both snapped to attention, Carmel moving towards the second bank of machines as Astra started down the row behind her, glancing briefly to her left to glimpse Brad making his way through the bejewelled and suited masses at the craps tables.

Spotting Ash still standing at the far end of the row, she approached him, walking past him and around to lean her back on the side of the slot machine, thereby ensuring anyone who glanced down the row would not see the two of them together. Ash, concentrating on his game, didn't notice her presence until his cell phone signalled with a jarring blast the arrival of a new text.

Will the man with the ten-inch penis please report to reception?

Straightening up to pull the phone from his trouser pocket, Ash caught Astra's sardonically slitted eye and responded with a playfully raised eyebrow. Astra suppressed the urge to shake her head in confusion. Ash being playful was something she still couldn't quite grasp.

"Who's that?"

"Seychelle. Just checking in. She says—" Ash scrolled down to the bottom of the message, "—that she's won fifty bucks on the craps table."

"What about you? Won anything?"

"Well, not at blackjack, you bitch." Ash returned the phone to his pocket before reaching into his jacket. "Oh yeah, that reminds me." He pulled out a balled-up pair of green boxer shorts, which he jammed into Astra's hand.

"These? Are not mine."

Astra held the boxers up and looked at them.

"Oh yeah. These are Harry's. He must have left them in my room and you picked them up. Sorry."

"They're Delfino's? That would explain why they spent most of the night up my crack."

Astra gave him a patented Look. The comment reminded her of what Carmel had said, and she took a moment to compose her face before leaning in closer to Ash's ear.

"There's a staffer over there who you've slept with, apparently."

"Which one?" Ash turned his head to see where she was looking. Carmel had rejoined Tony against the far wall. "God, no, he's not my type."

Astra lightly slapped his arm. With a grin Ash responded, bumping her with his shoulder.

"Not Tony, you dick. Carmel."

"Oh, the firecrotch." Ash cast another glance along the row, running an appraising eye over Carmel's elongated figure. After a moment his eyes widened in recognition, his mouth suddenly twisted and he jerked his head away as if tricked into viewing the results of a ritual disembowelling. "Yeah. I did. But I was drunk. Very, very drunk."

Astra bit her lip to stop herself smiling too brightly.

"She was very complimentary about you. She said you lasted ages."

Ash rolled his eyes and adopted an expression of patient resignation.

"Well, yeah. I did. I guess she never figured out why. Like how she didn't stop *talking* from start to finish. And she just lay there like a sack of potatoes, digging those pointy nails into my back and squealing like a fucking banshee. I had to think of Angelina Jolie before I could come at *all*."

Maybe those fantasies about slamming Carmel's face in a door had been premature. Astra eyed her co-worker, imagining the scene, and decided this would make working with Carmel much more palatable from now on. Certainly she would have no difficulty mustering up a smile when dealing with her.

He had this thing he did with his tongue...

She deliberately ignored the fluttering in her stomach, which was most definitely not caused by the painful image of Carmel in Ash's bed, and certainly had nothing to do with the sudden sharp image of white-blond hair trailing along the insides of her thighs—

Inwardly cursing, she leaned again on the side of the machine, a position which outwardly blocked her from view while also allowing her to conceal her flushed face behind a veil of hair. The clatter of coins and trilling music to her left told her Ash had turned back to his game.

I need to get away from him. I have to—

The machine behind her jolted violently under a sharp blow to the 'hold' button.

"Fucking thing."

Astra glared at him. "Don't smack it around."

Without looking at her, Ash muttered something under his breath.

"What?"

"I *said*, I don't like you working here." Ash slapped at the machine again, his eyes fiercely fixed on the flashing lights. "I don't like you walking home in the dark."

Slam.

"Ash." Astra fought to interrupt him between thuds. "It's not a problem—"

"Yes it is. You'll still be here when this place closes."

Slam.

"I'll have to leave, and you'll still be here. And anything could happen."

"Look—"

Astra's hand shot out to catch Ash's wrist as he made to pound the buttons again. Caught off-guard, Ash tried to stop, but had put too much force behind the blow. Both winced sharply as Astra's wrist collided with the corner of the machine with a sickening thud, jolting from her a pained cry.

"Fuck! Sorry."

She tried to cradle the injured wrist against her chest, but Ash kept hold of it, turning it this way and that, running his fingers over the bones, caressing the sensitive skin until her fingers began to stir distractedly, the downy hair on her arm standing on end as her flesh tingled.

"Ash—"

"Keep still, you," Ash muttered, his voice rough. "You might have broken it."

"It's fine."

"It's not *fine*," Ash snapped. "I might have hurt you."

"Ash." Astra took a risk, sidling between him and the machine and resting her other hand on his forearm, feeling the firm muscles beneath the smooth material of his jacket. "It's fine."

Ash stilled, his skin flushed pink, then drew her hand up and kissed the inside of her wrist. Astra's hand tightened reflexively on his arm.

Oh, God...

"I'm scared for you."

She stared up at him, helpless to break his gaze.

"They — they book us taxis now. It's fine."

"I don't *care*," Ash said fiercely, "because I'm not leaving. I'll wait for you at the side entrance until you're finished. You're not coming out alone."

Astra opened her mouth but found herself speechless, Ash's heated eyes boring into her, daring her to protest. Her stomach clenched with such force it was almost painful as desire struck her in a sharp rush, the hand Ash still held beginning to tremble.

Ash leaned in closer, releasing her left hand to fall onto his shoulder. "I'm *not* leaving you alone," he repeated, his voice low and rough, and Astra's control broke, clutching at him as her body arched desperately towards him.

Ash...

Arms encircled her, pressing her against his hard body as she felt herself tugged forward and twisted sideways, her face buried in the soft skin of his neck. Raising her eyes, she realised they were now at the side of the row of machines, slightly shielded from view. Ash's grip loosened briefly, allowing Astra to fall back, then he jerked his hands to her face as their eyes locked together, both breathing hard, her fingers unconsciously kneading at his forearms.

For a moment she thought he was about to say something, but then Ash pulled her forward and kissed her, and all thought left her mind as she slid her hands around him, clinging to his shoulders as their bodies crushed together.

She threaded her fingers through Ash's hair, caressing the nape of his neck. Ash moaned and slid his hands lower, resting on her waist, fingers twitching as if with self-restraint. His body surged forward, pressing her uncomfortably against the side of the machine, and Astra's protest was swallowed in a gasp as she felt his tongue slide past her lips, locking their mouths together.

It was Ash who finally broke the kiss, guiding Astra's head to his shoulder as his arms wrapped around her and held her tightly to him. Still trembling, Astra turned her face into his neck and nuzzled against the soft skin, feeling the muscles vibrate softly as Ash groaned.

"Don't, I won't be able to stop. Just hold still a moment, okay?"

Astra stilled as Ash's hands softly caressed her back, feeling her breath slowing as the tension between them eased. His voice continued in her ear.

"Go back to what you were doing. If I don't see you before, I'll be outside when you finish." Ash's voice paused, then darkened as he went on. "I have to sort something out."

Shit. Sasha. Astra stiffened automatically, pulling back, but Ash's grip tightened, holding her flush against him.

"Don't do that. It's fine. Really. Let me handle it."

Astra automatically opened her mouth to object. How could Ash possibly claim it was *fine?* Sasha was her best friend, for God's sake. It was patently ridiculous—

"It's fine," Ash said again, more firmly, and Astra broke off her protest to lean back and look him straight in the eye.

Ash's gaze was clear and steady. His features were set in determination, but with a tension in his jaw and brow that suggested a struggle for control. There was no trace of the arrogance Astra had expected, no twist to his mouth or knowing glint in his eyes. Whether he was right or not, Astra felt he believed it.

And also that he knew something she didn't.

"All right," she said finally.

"Good." Ash scanned her face for her moment, then pulled back with a final squeeze to her shoulders. "Okay. Get back out there before they miss you."

Astra darted a glance down the row of machines and, seeing no other staffers in evidence, slid out from her hiding place, automatically straightening up and adopting a neutral expression as she began her walk back across the casino floor. Beneath the mask, her heart was bouncing.

Ash...

A swift check of her watch told her she had ten minutes before she was due to retake her table. Uncomfortably conscious of possibly swollen lips, flushed skin and Harry's boxer shorts balled up in one hand, Astra made a beeline for the employees' corridor, where there was a private bathroom.

As she passed poker table one she noticed Carmel had taken over. Presumably she had been switched with Ally. Good. Astra made a mental note to get straight back onto her table as soon as she had made herself presentable, rather than risk running into any over-curious individuals on the floor.

Five minutes later, her hair and make-up retouched and Harry's underwear disposed of, she opened the bathroom door and immediately cringed. Echoing from around the corner at the far end of the corridor were the unmistakeable Valley Girl tones of Ally Brass. She sounded like she was talking on a cell phone.

"… finishing at midnight. Yeah, I'm getting a cab."

Astra slowly began to tiptoe out into the corridor, holding her breath. If she could just get back out onto the —

Shit. Ally's voice was getting louder, accompanied by footsteps.

"…Okay. Bye then."

Recognising the inevitability of the situation, Astra let the door shut behind her just as Ally rounded the corner, snapping her phone closed.

"Oh. It's you."

"Ally." Astra gave her a nod, professional yet curt, and turned to walk away, but the hurried clip-clopping behind her told her Ally was determined to catch up.

"Did you know Becky's been accepted for management training, too?"

"No." *Go away.*

"Do you think they'll offer permanent jobs to everyone who trains?"

Astra kept her face forward as she walked, but Ally's eyes were boring into her cheek, bright and expectant.

"I don't see why not."

"Do you think," Ally continued, quickening her pace a little to put herself ahead of Astra, "that they'll offer *you* one?"

Astra stopped and looked her straight in the eye.

To hell with this.

"Yes, I do." She deliberately made her voice casual, yet with a hint of challenge. "Why?"

Ally eyed her for a moment, then folded her arms and fixed her with a smirk.

"Well, the thing is, Astra, I just can't see myself respecting you as a manager." The smirk widened. "Sorry about that."

For a moment, the anger threatened to overwhelm her.

Then, as Astra held Ally's gaze, an image popped into her mind of a strong, masculine figure, radiating confidence and arrogance in the tilt of the hips and the jutting peak between, of Sasha sprawled beneath her, knees raised, welcoming every thrust...

And the weakness vanished, replaced by control.

"Well, I'm sorry to hear that, Ally." Her voice came out deeper, unwavering. "But the fact remains that I will *be* a manager, and if you feel that will be a problem, maybe this isn't the best job for you."

Wow, said a voice in the back of her mind. *Was that even me?*

I guess it was.

Walking back out onto the floor, a quick glance at her watch showed she was just in time to take over from Dinah, and Astra found herself moving back into her croupier role with the ease that came from complete confidence in her ability.

One more hour until the end of her shift. She could tell already it would pass quickly—the bustle, the ebb and flow of dealing and collecting, would make the time move with barely a thought.

Which would allow her thoughts to wander.

And it was strange, gratifying, bordering-on-ecstatic, in fact, to realise that in between the heated mental glimpses of Ash's glowing eyes and flushed skin, the memory constantly resurfacing was of Ally's shocked, recoiling face.

Chapter Fifteen

Sasha had listened to the story of Astra's evening — the sanitised version, at least — with expressions of excitement at the offer of training, and glee at the description of the look on Ally's face.

Astra had left at midnight to find two lingering figures at the side entrance. Since they had waited deliberately to walk her home, it had seemed only fair to offer them a ride. Exhausted, Astra had fallen asleep in the back of the prepaid cab Brad had ordered, waking briefly to find herself being carried up the stairs of Omega Zeta by Ash, Sasha padding languidly alongside him, dreamy-eyed and wearing a strange smile Astra was too sleepy to attempt to interpret.

Now, in the late hours of Sunday morning, Astra stirred comfortably in Sasha's bed, feeling the morning light slowly steal its way into her consciousness. She rolled into a luxurious stretch, the slight tension in her shoulders and tingling in her feet a lingering reminder of the night she had spent standing.

"'S too early," Sasha mumbled from her right, face buried in the pillow and obscured by a mass of feathery blonde hair.

Astra held her pose for a moment longer, then relaxed, dropping lightly back onto the mattress. As she allowed her eyes to open gradually, growing accustomed to the light, she felt a slow, unrestrained smile begin to spread across her face.

It felt so *good* to wake up and remember the night before.

The image of Ally's outraged eyes and sagging jaw brought with it a wave of pleasure. Astra didn't expect this would be the end of her insubordination — Ally was too proud to allow that, too eager to save face. But having made the first smackdown, Astra knew she could do it again, and the more often it happened the easier it would be, and eventually Ally would either retreat or — more likely — quit.

Even though she knew things were far from over, Astra felt almost *limp* with relief.

Her eyes rested on the lower edges of Sasha's calendar, which hung on the wall behind the bed. Arching her back, she stretched up one arm and unhooked it, bringing it down onto her chest as she shuffled into a half-sitting position. In perky, rounded handwriting Sasha had noted down every one of the sorority's activities for the month.

Chapter meeting
Forget the Finals Costume Party
Bake sale and After Party
Around-the-World Themed BBQ

The bed shifted as Sasha rolled onto her side and propped herself up on one elbow, apparently unable to ignore the daylight any longer.

"Whatcha doing?"

"Reacquainting myself with my social calendar."

Sasha leaned her head on Astra's arm and looked at the page.

"You've hardly been a recluse. We've been to stuff."

"Yeah, but—" Astra drummed her fingers thoughtfully on the paper. "It's nice to be able to think about it. Instead of stressing about the job."

"It is nice, isn't it?" Sasha tapped the calendar just under the word *Costume*. "I've been looking forward to that one. Forget the Finals. God knows I need to." She rolled her eyes and twisted her mouth, blowing her bangs up into the air. "I've got *so* many exams."

There was a grunt from the other side of the bed as Ash stirred, followed by a formidably loud fart. To her surprise, Astra found herself collapsing helplessly into giggles, which continued unabated in the face of Sasha's elegantly raised eyebrow until Sasha shook her head, an indulgent smile spreading across her face.

"It's good to see you happy."

Slumping back against the headboard, Astra allowed her laughter to be swallowed in a blissful sigh.

"It's just good to have one less thing to think about."

Sasha nodded slowly, her smile still in place, but with her head tilted in thought as her eyes scanned Astra's face. Astra managed to restrain herself from squirming under the scrutiny.

"What else did you have to think about?" came Ash's sleep-roughened voice, followed by his face as he sat up. His white-blond hair floated around his head, forming a staticky fuzz Astra thought was unreasonably cute. "Delfino?"

"I don't think about him," Astra replied reluctantly. "Not if I can help it."

"Is it still open between you two?" Sasha asked.

"Yeah. We just don't talk about it."

"What *do* you talk about?" Ash's mouth twisted into a sneer. "I don't know why you don't just dump the guy."

Astra sighed deeply.

"I keep meaning to. He talks me out of it."

"Riiiight." Ash's eyes turned steely. "Course he does."

"Oh, stop fucking me up, Ash."

Astra folded her arms stubbornly across her chest, deliberately blocking Ash out with an imaginary set of blinkers. She allowed her gaze to fix on one of Sasha's shelves on the wall opposite, focussing on the collection of dance team photos, fluffy toys and cookbooks that lay haphazardly on top of each other. *Fuck off. I'm not looking at you.*

She was so *sick* of the Harry situation. It had been too long since she had been able to go out, go dancing, get drunk, just *relax*. Why couldn't Ash just leave things alone?

Unless he wants me to dump Harry so he can date me himself. But he doesn't. He's with Sasha.

Unless —

"Look, I'm —"

"Ash, " Sasha interrupted, holding up one palm. "Drop it."

Ash looked mutinous.

"Don't tell me to —"

Palm still upraised, Sasha gave him a look that would have stopped a tiger in its tracks before rolling over onto her back. She rested one hand on Ash's arm and the other on Astra's shoulder, silently commanding attention from both.

"What does it *matter* whether Astra's still dating Harry or not?"

Astra raised intrigued eyebrows, inviting her to continue.

"We don't have to stop hanging out together." Sasha slid her eyes towards Ash. "We don't have to stop sharing a bed."

Something flickered briefly in Ash's eyes. Sasha held his gaze for a moment before, slowly, he subsided, an expression of reluctant acceptance on his face. Astra resisted the urge to roll her eyes.

What a surprise. He's happy now he knows his sex life won't suffer.

Ash darted a knowing glance at her, flicking his eyebrows briefly, and Astra felt her stomach clench at the memory of the scent of his neck, moving his hands on her skin as he caressed the inside of her mouth with his tongue.

Has he told her? He can't have told her.

Sasha was still talking, oblivious to the heated looks passing over her head.

"You're not letting Ash get to you, are you?" Sasha jolted suddenly and let out a sharp breath as Ash's elbow connected with her ribs. Throwing a mock-glare at him, she rolled over onto her side again, deliberately presenting Ash with her back.

Smiling involuntarily, Astra fought to regain the feeling of euphoria that had filled her from the moment of her waking.

"It doesn't matter," Sasha said again. Fixing her eyes on Astra's, she reached out to rest one hand on her arm. "Dump him or don't. Whenever you're ready."

"Yeah. You're right."

"I know I'm right," agreed Sasha, ducking as Astra aimed a teasing cuff at her head. "You know what else?"

"What else?"

"You need a night out."

Astra automatically glanced down at the calendar, only to find Sasha's hand firmly placed in the middle of the page.

"Not with the girls. A proper night out." Sasha twisted over her shoulder as Astra shared a mystified glance with Ash. "Ash, when are you playing that gig?"

* * * *

Flip.

Harry stared disconsolately at the brightly-lit screen on his cell phone before snapping it closed again.

For God's sake. Just ask her to lunch.

Flip.

Snap.

He shifted restlessly on the bed, the fingers of his left hand drumming on the duvet.

Flip.

It's been three days. If you're not going to spend the night with her, you have to at least do lunch.

Harry grimaced involuntarily. He had met Astra for lunch twice that week in a valiant attempt to make up for his nocturnal activities. The experience had been disconcertingly easy. Astra was cheerful, she was breezy, she chatted about superficial topics such as coursework and parties, and never once did she mention anything of importance. The intimacy of a lingering glance was replaced by a darting green flash. Instead of a hand on his arm or her knees touching his, she retained a casual distance better suited to friends than lovers. She kissed him as though she was thinking about her shopping.

The thought of what it might mean, what it almost certainly meant, made a cold hand clutch at his heart.

Flip.

And yet the thought of doing what was necessary to halt the atrophy of their relationship —

Harry cursed, with all the forceful British vocabulary he could muster.

Snap.

A knock on the door interrupted his glare at the phone.

"Hey, Harry!"

Throwing the Nokia down onto the bed, Harry rolled until his feet hit the carpet and crossed to the door. He opened it to reveal a tall, skinny blond whose pointed face was dominated by a wide gash of a mouth and an overly-long nose.

"Hi, Jez."

Jez was a fellow Computer Science student who was also the treasurer of the campus LGBT Society. Harry had been clubbing with him enough times to know he was fairly indiscriminate about who he slept with, and had had enough drunken conversations with him to know he was, as he put it, 'neither pitcher nor catcher'.

"Hey, fuckface." The broad slash of Jez's mouth parted to reveal uneven teeth. "Coming out tonight?"

"Where? It's Sunday."

"Rich and Trey are going to that new place out by Taco Bell. Sunday is retro night. Up for it?"

Harry opened his mouth to answer, then paused. Just inside his field of vision, the cell phone glinted accusingly amid the rumpled edges of the quilt.

Jez snapped his fingers. "Oh yeah. One other thing."

"Mmm?"

"Tuesday night, are you free? We're going to see a band play out by the casino —"

Another glint, and Harry's fingers reflexively gripped the pocket of his jeans.

" — they're called Autarkis. Group of guys from Alpha Nu Mu. I hear they're good." Jez rolled his eyes expressively. "Plus some of the guys want to do the lead singer. I've not seen him, but I'm told he's a twink."

His flash of anger at the mention of Alpha Nu Mu dwindled at Jez's last words.

"Yeah?"

"Yeah. Real hot one." Jez's eyes sparkled at the poorly-concealed catch in Harry's voice. "Interested?"

The excitement was already spreading in Harry's stomach.

"I'll come."

"And tonight?"

Harry darted a glance towards the bed, where the cell phone lay, dull and lifeless, half hidden in the folds of duvet.

His gut clenched almost painfully.

"Yeah. I'll be there."

* * * *

"Put that down," said Ash firmly as he re-entered the bedroom, hair freshly gelled, to find Astra practicing a Michelle Branch track on his guitar.

"She's really good," Sasha protested.

"I don't care. I'll be playing some *real* rock songs on this tonight, not 'All You Fucking Wanted'."

Without bothering to look up from the Gibson, Astra rested her hand on the strings before breaking into the opening bars of *Smells Like Teen Spirit*.

"Oh, all right." Ash's voice was resigned. "Now give it back. The cab's waiting."

The ride to the venue was brief and uneventful, made slightly more entertaining by Sasha's insistence that Ash sit in the centre with both sets of female legs across his lap. Ash passed the time by giving terse directions to the taxi driver while cradling his canvas-sheathed guitar against his crotch, fidgeting with the neck in a way Astra found vaguely distracting.

"Left here," said Ash finally. "It's this one."

The cab pulled up outside a tall, slightly seedy-looking building, decorated lavishly with graffiti and posters advertising local bands. A green-haired youth poked his head out of the door, above which was a cineplex-style sign that read, The Tombstone.

"Ash, you fuck! We need to sound check!"

Ash hastily pushed a handful of notes into the driver's hand and climbed out of the cab, already shouting back at his bandmate as Astra and Sasha scrambled after him.

Three other young men were on the stage as they entered, two setting up their instruments while a third made gestures towards an invisible lighting technician. Ash hauled them across the as-yet sparsely-populated dancefloor, unzipping his guitar en route and throwing the cover behind an amplifier, his argument with his friend pausing only to introduce the green-haired boy as, "Jamie, our lead guitarist". The remaining band members were introduced in a blur of pointing, pointing, pointing, which led Astra to immediately forget all their names.

"Come on," said Sasha, bumping Astra's shoulder. "Let's get a drink."

The bar was on the far right of the venue, built from a mixture of black formica and metal and adorned with several of the plastic glasses Astra was used to seeing at concert venues. Seeing Sasha pick one up and eye it with her nose wrinkled, she ordered two bottles of beer.

"You're really not used to these places, are you?"

Sasha shook her blonde head. "Give me a cocktail bar any day."

They moved over to the centre of the dance floor as the room slowly began to fill, Astra manoeuvring them into a space with a reasonable sightline. The atmosphere in the room was building, the buzz of chatter and the breathless excitement flowing like electricity. Astra was a conduit, her eyes and skin sparkling, her gaze focussed on the stage where Jamie and Ash were finishing their sound check with a series of increasingly complex riffs, facing off against each other, each determined to triumph.

"Can you do that?" Sasha's voice asked in her ear, only just audible over the crowd.

"Oh yeah, totally."

She felt rather than saw Sasha shake her head dazedly before turning around to scan the room, which was rapidly becoming packed with people. Suddenly the figure beside her stiffened, and Sasha's hand gripped her shoulder.

"What is it?"

"Guess who's over in the corner."

"Axl Rose."

"No, although he's probably just as good a dancer. It's Harry. Don't turn round."

Astra's stomach twisted in a way that was both familiar and surprising, because it lacked passion. Where once there had been heat, jangling nerves, now there were only cold ashes and disinterest.

Indifference.

Revulsion.

"Fuck him."

"What?"

"Fuck him. He can do what he likes." *And so can I.*

The lights abruptly lowered, drawing Astra's attention back to the stage as the air filled with excited hooting. Over the roar of the crowd, the voice of an unseen emcee was shouting something about welcoming them onstage, incredible local talent, Autarkis —

— and Ash was stepping up to the mike, guitar in hand.

Harry stared at the stage in stunned disbelief, feeling an encroaching anger beginning to boil at the edges of his consciousness.

Of all the people it could have been, it had to be fucking Ash Drake.

For a moment the voices of his friends around him were still audible, discussing the relative merits of each band member's physique, before being drowned by the growl of electric guitars and the painful crashing of drums. A squeal rose up from the crowd, growing louder, layer upon layer, as the tall blond figure in slim jeans and a black T-shirt stepped up to the microphone, his muscles enhanced by his firm grip on the guitar.

Harry had never felt such loathing in his life.

Ash's voice was dark — rough, yet controlled, flowing through the notes of *Lithium* as though the song was part of him. He held himself with little movement, arrogance running through his toned body from his lowered eyes and sneering mouth to the cocky tilt of his hips. His voice swelled aggressively as the chorus neared, one arm jerking to swing the guitar around to his back, then both hands were on the mic as, with the first "*Yeah*", he exploded into life, becoming almost violent in his intensity, his blond hair lashing his face as he surged forward towards the baying crowd—

— and Harry winced as he realised he was actually shaking.

Ugh! No!

Behind him he could hear Jez and Trey engaged in a fierce discussion.

"He is so not a twink. I bet he's straight."

"Hey, I know he's got muscles, but that hair is to die for. Do you think he's a bottom?"

"Oh, no. Too aggressive. He's got to be a top."

"Mmm, I don't know… That ass is just begging for it."

Harry rolled his eyes, deliberately focussing on the other members of the band. There was no way in the world he was going to spend the evening discussing the sexual preferences of a man he knew to be not only straight, but unnaturally protective of *his* girlfriend. His fists clenched reflexively.

"So this is where you hide out," said a familiar voice, deep and gravelly, and a rush of heat flooded Harry's stomach.

Marcus.

"I didn't think," the voice continued, taunting, "that blonds were your type."

Harry's breath caught.

"They're—They're not."

"Sounds like Dumb and Dumber disagree." The voice laughed coolly. "You sure do pick 'em, Delfino."

Harry ran his hand through his hair, fighting to steady the trembling in his limbs.

"So what are you doing here then?"

"Looking for you." Goosebumps rose on Harry's skin as he felt the pressure of a warm body against his back, the voice lowering as it spoke closer to his ear, breath tickling his neck. "Needed a reminder of that hot little ass."

A furred, muscular arm pressed across his ribs, drawing him back against a broad chest. Harry gasped as two solid hips moulded to his, his groin immediately tightening in response to the hardness he could feel against his buttocks.

"You know," the voice continued persuasively, "there's a yard out back. Very quiet." Hips thrust forward sharply and Harry groaned, his head dropping back on Marcus's shoulder. "I'll make it worth your while."

Harry caught a glimpse of a smirking Jez as he was drawn back through the crowd, but found it no longer seemed important. His attention was stolen by the throb in his crotch, the weakness in his legs, the coiled excitement in his stomach.

A hand slid around to squeeze his erection as they reached the side door, and Harry was lost to his desire.

Sasha's breath tickled Astra's ear.

"He's good, isn't he?"

Mouth dry, barely able to breathe, Astra could only nod. Sasha leant back and let out a whoop as the eighth song, *Mr Brightside*, came to an end.

To watch Ash on stage was like watching a stranger. The intensity of his focus, the passion in his voice, was breathtaking in its unfamiliarity. His eyes swept the audience during the instrumental sections, resting on this girl, that girl, another girl, his arched eyebrow and the twist to his mouth implying every female in the room was his for the taking. As the song finished, he threw his head back, one arm raised, his body stretched taut as the cheers began, and Astra withdrew a little from Sasha, not wanting her to see she was physically shaking.

Her desire for him was so strong she could have *screamed*.

The emcee's voice shouted about a twenty-minute intermission, then Sasha's hand was in hers, dragging her towards the stage where the band was already preparing to leave under the glare of the newly-raised lights.

Ash glanced up as they approached, halfway through replacing his guitar in the stand. A lazy smile crossed his face.

"Hey, you two. Enjoying the show?"

"You were amazing," Astra said breathlessly before mentally kicking herself.

"That's what all the girls say."

"Hmm," Sasha drawled in a tone that suggested she knew better. "What's the name of your drummer again?"

Ash flashed her his middle finger before turning back to Astra.

"What do you make of Jamie's guitar then?"

Astra looked across to where a glittering blue Telecaster was propped up at the other end of the stage. Not sure if he was referring to the actual guitar or Jamie's musical skills, and having been almost completely unaware of anything besides Ash in his role as the frontman, she decided to be diplomatic. "He knows what he's doing."

Ash cocked his head in a gesture that demanded further comment.

"Like the blue. I've never played on a Telecaster before."

"Do you want to?"

"Excuse me?"

Ash casually flicked his thumb at the green-haired young man as he passed them in the direction of the bar.

"I told him you played guitar. He said, if you want, he'll step off for one song and let you get up there."

Astra turned her gaze back to the Telecaster to give herself a moment's thinking time.

It wasn't the first time she had been asked to play in public, but it would be the first time outside the familiar surroundings of a music school recital, away from the security of rehearsal time and the safety net of a family-filled audience.

And the thought of herself onstage with Ash—

Beside her, Sasha gave a breathy, excited gasp, and a brief image of Harry flashed through Astra's mind. Her insides curled up and died. Sasha had Ash, Sasha was loved, Sasha was happy.

Another flash, this time of Ash onstage, his back arched, microphone tilted towards his mouth as it opened in a dark, raw scream.

"Which song?"

Ash's eyes widened slightly as his smile brightened.

"*Teen Spirit* work for you? Jamie does that one on his own."

"Works for me. Unless you have a weird arrangement?"

"Nuh-uh. Go get a drink. Second song after the interval."

The bar was already crowded, but Astra and Sasha were pretty, and two more bottles of beer were easily had from the enthusiastic bartender. Astra drank hers in silence, eyes glazed as she allowed herself to slide into the trance she preferred when preparing for a performance.

Smells Like Teen Spirit. *Just lead guitar and bass.* Visualising her Stratocaster, she mentally ran her fingers across the strings, picking out the chords she would need, gliding one hand along the frets.

Here we are now.

Entertain us.

"That drummer's cute," Sasha said, the bottle of beer halfway to her mouth.

Drums come in after the guitar.

Out of her corner of her eye she noticed Sasha start to say something else, pause, and stop, an indulgent smile kinking her mouth.

Bass and guitar behind the vocal.

The crowd around them was starting to move. She felt Sasha's hand touch her arm, softly stirring her from her reverie.

"It's time."

Astra's insides flooded with cold, her breath rushing out of her.

I can do this. I can do this. I can do this.

Second song.

"*Hel*-lo," Jez drawled as Harry, flushed and with hair disarranged, stumbled back through the crowd, flinching a little from the glare of the stage lighting. "I see *someone's* been totally fucked."

"Piss off," Harry mumbled, bumping Jez with his shoulder. He squinted at the stage, where Ash, guitar back round his neck, had positioned himself behind the microphone stand and was tapping the mic with one finger, talking over his shoulder to the green-haired lead guitarist.

Dumb jock.

The drums crashed, briefly, then guitars snarled into the opening riff of a Thin Lizzy track.

Standing outside, the brick wall digging into his back, cool air playing on his crotch, Harry had been only vaguely aware of the rock songs being played on the other side of the heavy fire doors. He had caught snatches of music through his haze of pleasure, brief flashes of Nirvana, Metallica, Whitesnake, and had wondered momentarily if Ash really was playing all those himself — but then Marcus had stood up and spun him around to face the wall, yanking his jeans down to his knees, and Harry had been lost, caught in the biting grip of excitement, and knew no more.

Now he was without distractions, he could see Ash was playing rhythm guitar during his vocal and, during the breaks, was matching the lead guitarist note for note, his supremely confident smile a contrast to the intense focus in his eyes. Harry bit his lip, fighting to ignore the stirring in his gut as the slim, blond figure onstage twisted around to face the mic with a thrust of his hips that raised a wild and distinctly feminine scream from the crowd.

This was wrong. Cataclysmically wrong.

The song was drawing to a close now, both guitarists squaring off against each other for the final chords before leaping skywards and crashing down onto the stage. Ash turned back to the crowd, acknowledging the cheers with a dip of his head, and leaned in to the microphone.

"Thank you," he began.

Another scream rose from the crowd and Ash's mouth twisted into his renowned smirk, leaving Harry grinding his teeth in the darkness of the dance floor.

"We have a special guest for this next song."

The green-haired man had stepped down from the stage. Harry could just make out the untidy mop of his hair as he conversed with someone just out of view, still holding his guitar.

"She's a very experienced guitarist," Ash continued, "and a *very* good friend of mine—"

There was something in that 'very' that made Harry straighten abruptly.

"Give her a warm welcome... Astra Scott, everyone."

Harry's stomach dropped as, from the side of the stage, a familiar figure emerged.

She stepped onto the stage with the cool confidence of one who had done it all her life, dressed in a black sleeveless top, leather skirt and knee-high boots, the stage lights glinting off her mane of dark red hair. As she reached the space the green-haired man had vacated, she lifted her cat-like green eyes to the crowd, smiling at the roar her name had raised from the men in the room, and played one forceful, lingering chord on the blue guitar that hung around her slim body and that Harry recognised as belonging to the lead.

Astra.

It was surprisingly, incredibly, easy.

The first few chords were Astra's alone. She held her body still until the cheering faded, then struck the strings with the plectrum, the deep thrumming notes ringing out, cutting through the hush in the room.

Then the crashing of drums behind her, and the air began to move.

Beyond the dazzling stage lights, the crowd were merely blue-lined shapes in darkness, but their forms could be seen, rising and falling like a great tide. The bass kicked in alongside Astra's guitar, a heavy rumble beneath the two-note hook, then Ash was at the mike, his movements sinuous, keeping the rhythm with a smooth rock of his hips.

Then that dark, dirty voice, undulating through the flow of the melody. Astra watched him, feeling her trance of concentration taking full control, settling over her senses in a haze, and was ready when the chorus kicked in and Ash surged towards the crowd, his vocal rising almost to a scream, and *yes, yes, that's it,* he had them in the palm of his hand.

Adrenaline, passion. Jamie's guitar felt almost exactly like her own, its familiarity sending a welcome thrill through her body. The roar of the music, amplified immensely by the speakers, crashed over her like waves. Out of the corner of her eye she could see Sasha's blonde head sandwiched between two brunettes in black. Bouncing eagerly to the rhythm, she smiled brightly up at Astra, one thumb raised in gleeful acclaim. Astra flashed her a grin before focussing her attention on the task at hand. Ash's vocal gave way to the instrumental, and fire blazed through Astra's veins as all eyes turned to her for the solo.

Yeah!

Fingers moving up and down the fret, lights glinting off the blue body, strings biting. Drums pounding, bass snarling, Ash's voice soaring in the final chorus, the crowd a blur of waving arms and shrieking mouths. One last howling chord —

— and the uncontrollable roar of numberless voices engulfed her.

As she stood, breathless, glowing, Ash reached her side and caught her damp wrist in his equally sweaty hand. He turned to face the room and lifted her arm high, drawing a renewed yell of approbation from the floor.

Astra raised her head to look at him, only to find his eyes already on her. She became strangely aware she was trembling with adrenaline.

"You were great," Ash told her, his voice uneven. Sweat was sparkling on his face, his smile almost blinding.

Then she was being turned towards the audience again for one last ovation, Sasha eagerly waving from her right, face bathed in a golden glow.

At 11:30 the doors opened, unleashing a horde of drunken partygoers into the cool night air.

Stumbling along in the middle of the crowd, Astra and Sasha held hands and slid through the spaces until they reached an alleyway running alongside the bar. Astra pulled Sasha out of the flow of people, leaning back against the wall.

"This is the one, yeah?"

"That's what he said." Sasha glanced towards the far end of the alley. "Meet him in the car park at the back."

"I hope they clean that van. I don't fancy riding in the back otherwise."

"No, I—" Sasha paused, looking over Astra's shoulder, then pulled her farther into the alleyway where they were enveloped in darkness.

"What?"

"Harry."

Astra froze. She turned her head very slowly to her left and watched the figures pass on the dimly-lit street, but saw no-one familiar.

"Where?"

"He must have gone the other way," Sasha whispered. "Unless he's still near the entrance."

"Alone?"

"Didn't see."

Sasha paused and looked away for a moment, consulting with herself.

"You go meet Ash," she said finally. "I'll check if he's gone, then follow you."

"Just follow me now!"

"We'll make too much noise. He'll hear." Sasha eyed Astra for a moment. "Unless you want to talk to —"

"No," Astra cut in firmly, fighting off the cloying cold that threatened at the thought of a long, painful talk with Harry.

"Then go. Quietly."

Sasha made a shooing motion with her hands, hustling Astra into scampering away down the darkened tunnel on tiptoes, still shaking her head.

A beaten-up white van stood in the centre of the brightly-lit car park, its rear doors open while Ash and Jamie loaded their equipment into it. Ash turned round, an amplifier in his arms, as Astra's foot collided with a discarded can.

"Hey, it's the Axe Woman!"

Jamie finished pushing a drum into the van and crossed back towards the stage door, clapping Astra on the shoulder on his way past. Flashing Ash a smile, Astra stepped up to help steady the amplifier.

"Sasha'll be along in a minute."

"Great."

Lifting the amp together, they manoeuvred it into the van and slid it into place alongside the drums. Astra straightened and turned, only to find herself face to face with Ash.

"Ash —"

"Shh," Ash whispered, leaned in and kissed her.

Oh, God.

Astra automatically arched towards him, feeling Ash's hands catch around her waist as her body pressed forcefully against his. He was crushing her, surrounding her, and hard against her stomach, and she moaned into his mouth and heard him chuckle darkly —

Hey!

Tangling the fingers of one hand in his hair, she slowly ran the other along the muscles of his back, sliding lower and lower until she could squeeze the soft curve of his bottom through his jeans. Ash groaned and clutched at her, his hips jerking, then she felt his tongue dart forward, their mouths locking together.

Fuck!

Astra's hand jolted upwards, fingers clenching convulsively in the fabric of his shirt, tugging it higher before slipping underneath, caressing the smooth skin of his back, then dipping lower to brush just beneath the denim waistband.

"Oh *fuck!*" Ash panted, tearing his mouth away and resting his forehead against hers. "You're killing me."

Astra smiled wickedly up at him, opening her mouth to respond, when another sound caught her attention.

A scuffle.

Ash's eyes darted over her shoulder, briefly, before his face took on a strange, unrecognisable expression.

Somehow Astra knew what she would see when she turned, but the knowledge in no way prevented the sickening clutch of her stomach at the image in front of her.

In the glow of the security lights, arms folded and mouth in a sardonic twist, stood Sasha.

Chapter Sixteen

"Oh please," Sasha drawled, raising one eyebrow, "don't stop on my account."

Ash stepped in front of Astra in a movement that was almost protective.

"Get in the van."

"Oh, come *on* –"

"Get in the fucking van. We're not doing this now."

"You're no fun," Sasha pouted.

Astra had the distinct impression she was missing a substantial amount of information here. Sasha's eyes were too hard, too bright, her voice too sharp and brittle for her playful words.

"You know what we're going to do?" Ash continued, impervious to Sasha's protruding lower lip. "We're going back to Omega, and we're going to *sleep*, because I have class in the morning. Then when I've gone to class, you two are going to talk, because I'm getting tired of hiding shit. Now get in the van."

Astra allowed herself to be led round to the front of the van and hoisted into the front seat, remaining still as the other band members, one by one, emerged from the bar and joined Ash in the back, apart from Jamie, who climbed into the driver's seat. Her body felt limp with shock and fatigue.

Jamie's presence prevented any conversation, but Astra was conscious of Sasha's sleep-groggy body alongside her, and felt bizarrely comforted that it radiated an inexplicable lack of rancour.

* * * *

Sasha's bedroom was warm, her bed was comfortable, and Astra was tired enough that she was only barely aware of Ash's movements the following morning. She drifted in and out of sleep as taps ran into the sink, as zips were zipped and laces were tied, and fell completely asleep after the door closed, waking again only when Sasha's alarm went off at nine..

It was suddenly much easier to stare silently at the ceiling.

"Do you have class?" Sasha asked unnecessarily.

"Not till eleven."

The elephant in the room seemed to swell.

"Shall we get dressed first—?" Astra began.

"Good idea."

They managed to stretch out their morning routine for thirty minutes, after which they sat down on the bed, staring at each other awkwardly. Sasha retrieved a plate of sandwiches which had been left on the bedside table, apparently by Ash, and placed it between them.

"Here. He left these."

"Yes."

Astra took the turkey and beetroot sandwich nearest to her, leaving the fluffernutter for Sasha.

Taking the first bite provided an excuse to avoid talking. However, as the silence between them increased, the air of suppressed nerves grew, until Astra's sandwich had been twisted in her fingers so often it was on the verge of falling apart. The mangled bread hit the plate as Astra finally blurted out the question leaping up and down in her throat.

"Why didn't you get mad?"

Sasha paused, the fluffernutter halfway to her mouth. Looking up at Astra, she replaced it on the plate, her steady gaze and calm expression contrasting with the slight tremor running through her hand.

"Because I knew it was going to happen."

Stunned, Astra could only gape.

"You...*knew*?"

"He wants you. And you..." Sasha's eyes drifted for a moment before returning to Astra's own. "Ash and I — we're not in love."

Astra could think of nothing to say.

"I knew he was into you," Sasha continued, lowering her eyes to the duvet, "but I didn't know how much until that night you went out with Harry and came back crying. I thought he was going to break something. So, eventually, I asked him. He wouldn't admit it, but I could tell he really liked you. I don't think he even knew it himself before then."

The brief image of the door slamming in Ash's shocked face flashed in front of Astra's eyes.

"I could have dumped him. I was going to, actually. But...well." She waved a hand idly in Astra's direction. "I couldn't do it."

Astra looked at her sharply, but Sasha kept her face turned away, stiff, awkward.

It was too much to take in. For a moment Astra longed for the casual intimacy that had developed over those weeks in each other's bedrooms, the easy closeness that had allowed them to end awkward conversations in a heated embrace.

The memory was like a blow to the stomach. Sasha had started this, had *known* —

"So that night when you kissed me —"

Sasha laughed without mirth.

"I did that because I wanted to."

"But why would you —?" A thought hit Astra, and she recoiled. "Were you getting back at him?"

"What? No!"

Astra was aware Sasha was trying to look her in the eye, but she kept her face turned away. The memory of Sasha kissing her, now she knew what Sasha had known —

Sasha caught her arm, the grip biting into her flesh.

"Will you look at me?"

"No."

The hand on her arm yanked sharply, causing Astra to snap her head around in pain, hitting Sasha with a fierce glare. Sasha didn't flinch.

"I said I wanted to, and I meant it. If I'd been thinking like that, I'd have told Ash about it straight away. But I *didn't*. You know when he found out."

Astra relaxed her glare slightly, but kept her expression cold.

"Oh, do I?"

"Yes, you do. He saw us together, like I said." Sasha shook her head, the memory of the incident reflected in her face. "He went crazy. I told him I could have some fun if I wanted to, but he insisted on joining in."

I told him I could have some fun if I wanted to. Yeah. Astra could imagine how Sasha would have felt, knowing she was fucking the girl of Ash's dreams.

"How did he know I wouldn't just tell him to go to hell? I nearly did. I thought he wanted to blackmail me."

"I know. I told him that. You were still in love with Harry—"

Astra involuntarily grimaced.

"—but he was too jealous of what we were doing. Then you agreed to it."

"And why did *you* agree to it?"

Sasha flushed, looking away.

"I thought he would dump me. I knew he'd go after you anyway, and I could see you were starting to like him."

"I wouldn't have said yes. Not while he was still with you."

Sasha's mouth twisted sharply and Astra inwardly winced. Coming in the wake of last night's discovery, she could hardly expect Sasha to be convinced.

"I'm sorry."

Sasha darted a glance at her, but her smile was strained. "I know."

Damn it.

"Sash—" She had to try, but the right words wouldn't come. "I didn't want this—"

A raised hand, and her voice faltered to a stop.

"I know you kept knocking him back. I knew this would happen eventually—" Sasha shook her head, blonde hair in a flurry around her face. "I'll be fine. Seriously, I'll be fine."

Astra let her breath out in one long gust. *I can only hope.*

"Just tell me you do want to date him now. You're not going to dump him for Harry next week."

"I—of course not. I like Ash." Astra considered for a moment. "I mean, I really like him."

Sasha paused, her next few words coming out in a rush.

"I'm hoping you more than like him, because Ash is in love with you."

Astra opened her mouth, then closed it again.

There was really nothing to be said.

* * * *

It was a slow day.

Astra spent her Casino Accounting class taking detailed notes. The examination timetables were up on the notice boards. After noting them down, she moved on to the computer laboratory. The final draft of her internship report shone on the screen for a full hour, but Astra was able to type only a few hundred words.

At one o' clock, her concentration finally broken, she returned to Omega Zeta. Rather than face Sasha, however, she found herself unlocking the door to her own room. Astra had returned to her room several times to collect clothes and textbooks, but had never remained longer than a few minutes.

The room had been cleaned, but in the process some possessions had been disarranged—the broken guitar still lay on the floor, surrounded by discarded books, Post-It notes and a pale pink lipstick in a gold tube. Astra moved over to the desk, turning her back on the desecration, leaving it untouched.

Stuck to the wall above the desk was a row of photographs — candid shots taken at parties, herself and Sasha and face after face laughing into the camera. Astra's hand reached out, trailing past frame after frame of goofy drunken shots until it latched onto one in the centre, pulling it free.

Harry.

The photo-Harry was wearing a blue T-shirt emblazoned with a slogan which was obscured by the bottle of beer he was holding. She had taken it at the 'Street Work with the Homeless' after-party early in the first semester. The night had been warm, and Harry's face sparkled with sweat. He was habitually self-conscious in front of a camera, automatically stiffening, his body and smile becoming awkward and gawky, but here, caught off-guard and slightly drunk, his mask had dropped, replaced by the genuine, cheeky grin and vulnerable blue eyes she had loved so much.

That chameleonic quality of his, that range of expression. His innocently widened eyes, his intensity, his sudden moments of seriousness. That darting movement of his body, the way he would weave across a room in a matter of seconds. His willingness to try anything; chocolate sauce, mirrors, ice. That catch in his throat — *oh, God* — the way his hair stirred on the pillow, the taste of his skin.

Nothing.

A photograph behind a veil of glass.

* * * *

Her phone vibrated in her pocket as she left her Casino Operations class at three o' clock.

Sasha's bedroom door seemed to radiate tension. As she approached, the door cracked then opened fully, framing Sasha in polished wood. Their bodies passed in the doorway — the door closed behind her.

Ash was standing beside the bed, next to a depression where he had obviously been sitting. As the door clicked shut, they were already crossing the room to meet in the centre, stopping with desperate breaths just inches apart.

There were too many questions to be asked, but Ash voiced only one.

"Are we doing this?"

"Yes."

Ash's hands shot out, firmly gripping her waist and pulling her against him, moulding their bodies together, and Astra slid her hands along the smooth curves of his arms to meet at the back of his neck, tilting her head back as their mouths met in a kiss.

Ash kissed differently from Harry. Harry was passionate, yet softer, more gentle with the pressure of his mouth and the breaching of his tongue. Ash kissed with absolute confidence in his abilities, the glide of his tongue that of one who had complete certainty of his right to slip and tease and probe wherever he liked.

He also, Astra noted with an arch of her hips, seemed to find kissing far more exciting than Harry had.

Ash tore his mouth away with a gasp, crushing her against him. Remembering his sensitive neck, Astra chose to bury her nose in his shirt collar instead. It was best to let him get his breath back while there was still more to be said.

After a few moments, the second question came.

"Are you going to dump him?"

"Yes," Astra responded immediately.

"When?"

"Tonight, if you like," Astra offered, mentally running through Harry's usual evening schedule. *He doesn't usually go out before eight. I can go over at seven.*

"Want me to meet you after?"

"I'll text you."

Astra rested her head on Ash's shoulder, relaxing, but was unable to repress a body-racking sigh at the thought of the meeting to come. Harry would be hurt, would probably beg and plead with her to reconsider, would demand explanations she no longer had the energy or inclination to give. He would almost certainly be outraged, despite his own behaviour, at being dumped for a jock — and not just any jock, but *Ash*.

"I could," said Ash, his embrace tightening protectively, "wait on the fire escape, and if he starts crying I'll flash you through the window."

Astra thought she ought to disapprove of that, but found herself laughing instead, which she decided must have been Ash's intent.

* * * *

"How could you *not* know he was gay? You really didn't know?"

Astra laughed and shook her head. They were lying side by side on Sasha's bed, their bodies separated by a brief expanse of duvet and an acre of unfamiliarity gradually being worn down by occasional, shy brushes of hands on clothing.

"Please. You only knew because he was boinking guys from Alpha."

"He was *partying* with Larry and Rand. I don't want to know who he boinks."

"No," Astra agreed with feeling. "You don't."

"Why didn't you just dump him that night?"

Astra smiled softly without answering. Now would not be the time to go into the shock of the blow, her desire for revenge, the time spent in front of the mirror holding the plastic strap-on dildo and pondering her own masculinity. Harry was the past, or soon would be, and any navel-gazing would have to wait for a more suitable moment.

Maybe never.

To distract Ash, she raised both arms in an elaborate shrug, allowing one hand to fall casually onto his thigh.

Ash's eyes remained resolutely fixed on the ceiling, but the slight tremor that ran through his body told her all she needed to know.

"I almost kicked his ass that night."

"Sasha said you were pretty mad."

"Yeah, well." Ash made a dismissive movement. "I didn't like seeing you cry."

Astra softly ran her hand along the inside of his thigh, which twitched in response. When Ash continued, his voice was just a little more breathless than before.

"Sasha was mad too. With me. Made me feel like shit." Ash paused and arched an eyebrow. "Course, I didn't know she was going to move in on you herself, but..."

Mouth twisting, Astra struck him teasingly across the hip before Ash's laughter forced her to give way to her own. The ensuing play-fight caused them both to roll inwards, leaving them facing each other, Ash's hand tucked securely around Astra's waist.

For a moment their eyes were locked together. Astra became aware her heart was racing, her body tense with the strain of not touching him. *Damn it, he's too close. I will not lose it first, I won't.* They were almost close enough to kiss —

Ash's eyes darkened, but the tension in his face was suddenly replaced by seriousness.

"I'm sorry if I made you...*do* anything you didn't want."

"What?" Astra's mind had lost track of the conversation.

"When I found out about you two." A worried crease appeared between Ash's eyebrows. "When I asked to —"

—join in.

"Oh! No, I meant it when I said yes."

Ash looked unconvinced. Impulsively Astra slid forward, pulling him against her. Both gasped at the electric jolt as their bodies connected. Astra's head fell back, her fingers biting into Ash's demin-clad buttocks, then Ash had rolled them over and her eyes fluttered closed as his heated kisses trailed down the soft skin of her neck.

"Ash…"

"God, *Astra,*" Ash groaned, and captured her mouth in a kiss.

Aching for the touch of skin on skin, Astra slid her hand under the edge of his T-shirt, feeling the firm body shudder at the light brush of her fingers. But at the movement of her knees as they drew up alongside his hips, Ash stiffened and moaned, clutching her to him in a gesture she was beginning to recognise. Over the blood roaring in her ears, she slowly became aware Ash was whispering into her neck, over and over: "Not yet, not yet, not yet…"

"Not yet?"

"No," came Ash's muffled voice, a thread of determination now cutting through his breathlessness. "Not until you've dumped Harry. I mean—" He shifted and raised his head, looking at Astra with fierce eyes in a flushed face. "You're *mine*. I know you're going to dump him, but I want to make love to you *knowing* you're just mine."

Astra fought it, but failed to prevent a goofy smile spreading across her face. She reached up and mussed his blond hair, delighting in the faintly outraged look Ash's face wore.

"I told you," she murmured, leaning in to touch her nose to his. "I'll dump him tonight. And besides," she added as another thought crossed her mind, "I've been more yours than his for weeks—remember?"

The sudden heat in Ash's eyes told her exactly what he was remembering. However, after a moment, Ash blinked and replied "That was different."

"Oh?"

"Yeah. That wasn't me, that was me and Sasha. I want your first time with me to go right. I don't want *him* in the background."

"It will be right." Astra arched her eyebrows at him. "You were the one who told me how good you were."

"Yeah, but I haven't *shown* you. Not without Sasha helping."

Astra considered arguing this point, but decided against it. If Ash felt Sasha's presence negated all their earlier times together, she was never going to convince him otherwise. And if he wanted to prove himself to be an expert lover, well…she was hardly going to protest.

Ash leant down to whisper in her ear, his breath tickling her skin.

"Dump Harry, and…" His voice dropped seductively "…I'll show you just how good I can be."

Evening could not come quickly enough.

* * * *

Astra stood outside the front door of the Beta Phi house, steeling herself to knock.

It was seven o'clock. The afternoon had been spent whiling away the hours with Ash, after which he had gone back to Alpha Nu Mu while Astra joined Sasha in the kitchen for stir-fried prawns with noodles. Sasha had taken great pleasure in teasing Astra about her new relationship, particularly its unusual origins, and had dropped several dark hints about Ash's staying power until her attention had been forcibly drawn by her inability to handle chopsticks.

But now, standing outside Beta Phi…

Damn it.

It would have been so much easier if she could have simply skipped over this point. Harry was clearly happier with his boyfriends than with her. She was ready to move on and date Ash. Why couldn't they just agree to part amicably, freeing themselves to do what they really wanted?

Because Harry is in denial.

As long as Harry could claim he had a girlfriend, he could deny he was gay.

And he would fight to cling on to that with all his strength.

Damn it.

Astra took a deep breath, marched up the two steps and knocked firmly on the door.

And waited.

Faintly, Astra could hear the sounds of emo music through the nearby window. Astra envisaged a crowd of Harry-esque geeks sitting in a circle in the communal area, pale and sulky, nodding to the beat and ignoring her unwelcome intrusion.

Oh well. There was always the fire escape.

Astra crossed the front lawn and rounded the left-hand corner of the building, where the base of the metal staircase led up to the first floor. Making an effort to walk quietly, she crept up the stairs and began the circuit to Harry's window, which was the furthest one on the right at the rear of the building.

There was a brief flash of a night months earlier, of standing on the fire escape in the dark, undressing, climbing through a window in silky underwear —

Biting her lip, Astra made her way silently along the balcony until she reached the window.

The curtains were shut.

For a moment Astra wanted to turn and run. Harry clearly wasn't in, or didn't want to be disturbed. Or was asleep. Yes, that was it. She should just leave Harry to it.

For fuck's sake, no.

She stepped forward to knock on the glass and only then saw the gap in the curtains, barely two inches across, but affording her a perfect view of what was taking place on Harry's bed.

A strange stillness fell over Astra's body as she stood, gently but irrevocably rooted to the spot, watching the rough yet apparently pleasurable embrace taking form in front of her.

Harry was on all fours, clutching at the duvet as the tall, square-shouldered figure hunched over him, hips thrusting almost violently, flesh quivering with every jolting impact. His face was only visible in profile, but his eyes were open and so was his mouth, stretched in a rictus of ecstasy as his forehead crinkled as if in pain, but it was definitely pleasure racking his body—it was clear in the set of his shoulders, in the curling of his toes, in the sweat glistening on his muscles and the fluid Astra could see *dripping* from his penis, flushed red and jerking and fiercely engorged.

His partner, a much older man, was almost brutal in his movements, but every so often would lean down to mutter something into Harry's ear. *You feel so good, baby,* or maybe *You like that, don't you, bitch?* Or even *I love you.*

Impossible to tell.

As if in a dream, Astra's feet slowly carried her away from the scene, gradually picking up speed as she reached the bottom of the steps, running, running away to an uncertain place.

She had known all along, and yet to see it made things so much simpler.

No matter what was said now, no matter what Harry promised, her feelings had shifted in that one moment. The bond had dissolved.

And she no longer had to feel guilty.

Chapter Seventeen

Astra finished typing the text on her cell phone, selected Harry's number and hit send before reapplying her attention to her meal. Across the table, Jayla was reading over her notes in preparation for their Gaming Regulations class.

Two mouthfuls of chicken risotto later, her phone vibrated.

I'll be in at eight.

"Is that the ex?" Jayla asked, her voice muffled by chilli beef and kidney beans.

"Soon to be."

"What are you going to tell him?"

Astra snapped the phone shut and slid it back into her pocket. Sighing deeply, she met Jayla's concerned eyes.

"I have no idea."

* * * *

Sasha's legs dangled over the plush arm as she sprawled on one of the couches in the Omega lounge. Astra lay on her stomach on the facing sofa, her cell phone discarded on the table in front of them, exerting an invisible traction that irresistibly drew Sasha's gaze.

Eventually the pull grew too much.

"You're going to dump him?"

"Yes," said Astra tonelessly.

"Definitely?"

"After last night, I would even if it wasn't for Ash."

Sasha nodded slowly. For a while they sat in nervous, but companionable, silence.

"Do you think he'll accept it?"

Astra sighed.

"I'm not what he wants. I wish he'd realise that."

"I can't believe he did that." Sasha shook her head in flat disbelief. "I can't believe he fucked that guy. He's, like, old enough to be his *dad*. It's disgusting."

Astra shrugged.

"Do you think it's serious?"

"No," said Astra abruptly, then paused uncertainly.

Is it serious? Was that a one-nighter, or his boyfriend? Was it worth hurting me like he did?

Was it worth hurting Sasha like I did?

"Astra?" Sasha asked, looking around at her, her forehead crinkled in worry. Astra let out a sigh.

"Are we going to be okay?"

Sasha stilled for a moment, then relaxed. "I'll be okay. Will you be?"

The atmosphere thrummed with awkward intensity.

"Sash…I have no idea."

* * * *

As the evening drew in and the house began to fill, Astra and Sasha withdrew to one of the benches that overlooked the grassy quadrangle. Knowing they were in clear view of Alpha Nu Mu, Astra wasn't surprised when Ash slid onto the seat beside her, his arm immediately hooking around her shoulders. She relaxed into the embrace for a moment, not wanting to move.

"Got some news for you," Ash said after a moment.

"Oh?"

"Yeah. That guy you saw? Delfino's been seeing him for weeks."

Astra stared at him, trying to squelch the wave of relief which was already drowning her roiling feeling of shock and humiliation.

"How do you know?"

"Lightoller." Ash's mouth twisted in a half-smirk. "From my frat. Goes out clubbing with him all the time. Said the guy's called Marcus and he's about forty and wears a wig, so no-one can tell what he sees in him."

"Maybe he likes older men."

"No, what *Marcus* sees in *Harry*." Ash caught Astra's hand in mid-punch and grazed the knuckles with an obnoxiously vocal kiss, much to Sasha's visible distaste.

"Okay, okay. Point taken."

"The guy left this morning, anyway. So there's no chance of an ambush."

Astra nodded slowly, feeling her face set into a cold, controlled expression as she straightened her spine and stood.

"I'm going," was all she said, but Ash and Sasha made no comment, instead standing with her and waiting, watching her with expectant faces. "I'll text you after."

"Come over after," Ash commanded, his tone forbidding either procrastination or argument. "I'll be in all night."

It was an attractive invitation and uniquely Ash in its delivery, but Astra found herself raising her eyebrows nonetheless, and while the sweetness of her smile seemed to satisfy Ash's expectations, she spent the solitary walk towards Beta Phi considering ways and means to remind him of the enjoyment he might find by *not* being in charge.

* * * *

Beta Phi was an unremarkable fraternity building, but Astra found herself noting the redness of the walls and the roughness of the carpet as she followed Harry up the stairs, conscious this would probably be the last time she would see them.

Harry was obviously agitated, walking and gesturing in jerky movements, plucking at his clothes. Astra wondered if he knew she'd seen him, if he was going to lie. *Oh God, I have no idea how this is going to go. I just want out of here.*

Entering Harry's room, her eyes were immediately drawn to the bed. That was where Harry had slept with his boyfriends, where he had thrust into an endless array of faceless men, where he had got on his knees and raised his rear end for *fucking* Marcus. Grimacing, she turned away abruptly to meet Harry's wide-eyed, uncertain gaze, and for a moment her gut clenched at the thought of how he might have misinterpreted her—maybe he was expecting her to want sex. *God, no.*

"Look, Harry—"

"Look, Astra—" Harry began at the same time.

They both broke off awkwardly. Astra made a valiant attempt to smile.

"You first."

Harry gave an uncomfortable half-smile and took a swift breath.

"Yeah, I've, um, I've got something to tell you —"

A sudden image of Ash, lying waiting on his bed in Alpha Nu Mu, flashed across Astra's mind, filling her with impatience. *To hell with this.*

"You have a boyfriend. Right?"

Harry gaped.

"I — What?"

"I saw you together last night." Harry was still looking stunned, so Astra elaborated, hearing her voice grow more bitter with every tightly-spoken word. "You and your *boyfriend*. I gather you've been seeing him for ages."

"You — *saw* us?"

Coldly, concisely, Astra recounted the moment at the window, watching the open expression of horror develop on Harry's face with a malevolent feeling of both pleasure and gall.

"Oh, God."

An uncomfortable silence fell between them.

Can I just dump him now, please? Astra pleaded to whatever deity might be listening. She opened her mouth to say something, anything, but was cut off by Harry, who seemed to be having an epiphany.

"He's been chasing me for months. I didn't want to —" He broke off and looked at Astra, guilt radiating from every pore. "I couldn't say no to him."

Oh, that's just pathetic.

"Well, it doesn't matter anymore." Astra drew herself up, taking perverse pleasure in seeing Harry wither at her words. "It's over, Harry."

Harry closed his eyes, flinching as if under a blow.

"I'll break up with him."

"Don't bother."

"Astra—"

"*Harry*," Astra snapped, and Harry's eyes jolted open. "I don't care if you do. It won't change anything."

At this, Harry's eyes closed again and his body stiffened, his hands clenching into fists, before his shoulders dropped and his entire figure seemed to slump, leaving him the picture of defeat.

Finally, Astra thought, turning to leave. *He understands.*

Her hand was on the door handle when his voice arrested her from behind.

"Astra—I'm sorry."

Astra looked back over her shoulder for a moment as she opened the door, leaning her back against it.

"Yeah. Me too."

The door banged shut behind her, the heavy reverberation echoing along the corridor with a dreary, hollow finality.

By contrast, the staircase ahead of her seemed glowing with twilight, her footsteps silenced by the heavy twist-pile as she trotted down to the ground floor. The front door, which had been so heavy on her way in, flew open at the lightest touch, almost as if it was encouraging her to leave.

The lightness of her body was intoxicating.

Alpha Nu Mu was just a few buildings away on Greek Row. Music drifted out from a nearby window and Astra, to her delight, found herself walking to the beat with an airiness of movement that seemed to have been absent for such a long time.

"I want to undress you, I want to caress you..."

A soft breeze rippled through her hair, freeing one errant strand which flicked across her face, sticking to her lower lip. Automatically moving to brush it aside, Astra paused, two fingers still in her mouth, as a memory of Ash was triggered.

That last look on Ash's face, his eyes drawn irresistibly to her smile — no, to her *mouth.*

An unsettlingly wicked smile spread slowly across Astra's face.

Oh, Ash, if you only knew what I can do with my mouth.

Chapter Eighteen

Ash's bedroom window was three-quarters of the way along the Alpha Nu Mu fire escape, a glowing beacon in the fading light.

Astra rested against the wall alongside the window frame, unbuttoning her jeans as she toed off her shoes. Taking a risk, she leaned to her left to dart a glance through the glass. *Is he there?*

He was.

Ash was lying on top of the bed, stretched out flat, eyes staring blankly at the ceiling. Bathed in a soft red light from the lamp, he was barefoot and half-undressed, clad only in a white T-shirt and a pair of red boxer shorts, the silk moulding to the skin of his thighs and rising coyly, tantalisingly over the bulge between.

Catching her breath, Astra slid swiftly out of his line of sight, working her jeans down her legs with more haste than finesse. The summer evening air was warm on her skin, but a light breeze struck her as she pulled her shirt over her head, reminding her she was just a little too exposed on the fire escape.

Especially in nothing more than a blue lace bra and panties.

Bundling up her clothes under one arm, Astra took a deep breath before turning and hooking her fingers under the edge of the sash window, pushing it up and climbing through the space in one smooth movement.

The look on Ash's face was spectacular.

Astra dropped her armful of clothes on the floor and paused, holding herself still as Ash's eyes travelled over her body, slowly rising along the length of her legs, the flare of her hips, the swell of her breasts, until finally they reached her face, locking into her own intense gaze. His mouth had fallen open slightly, his breaths already filling the space between them.

"Astra," Ash choked out, and Astra moved, deliberately swaying her hips as she slowly approached the bed, the mattress dipping under her weight as she placed one knee beside him, then the other. Astride him, she crawled along his body in a panther-like motion until her face was above his.

"Hey."

"Hey," Ash echoed, his voice rough, breathless. He slid his hands along her arms until they rested on her shoulders. "You dumped him?"

"I dumped him."

Lowering her head, Astra brushed her nose against his, smiling as Ash immediately arched beneath her, bringing their lips together for one sweet kiss.

As their mouths parted, both let out a sigh. Astra leant forward, breathing softly against the skin behind Ash's ear.

"So someone told me," she whispered, "that there's something I'm very good at."

A sharp intake of breath, and Ash's fingers clenched convulsively on her shoulders.

"Want me to show you?"

Without waiting for an answer, Astra pressed a soft kiss to Ash's neck and began the slow journey down his supine body.

A light tug at the hem of his T-shirt, a hand sliding underneath to caress his stomach, and Ash was hastily lifting the shirt over his head, flinging it to the floor in a heap of fabric, shadows flickering across his bare chest in the glowing lamplight. Astra felt his moan vibrate as she trailed her tongue over his skin, her mouth closing over one flat nipple and coaxing it to hardness before sliding lower, lower; feeling the muscles in his abdomen contract as one hard lick delved into his navel.

"Oh *fuck...*" Ash moaned from above her, shifting his hips as Astra felt his fingers tangle in her hair. "Please."

Well, since you asked so nicely...

Her tongue glided further, paying special attention to the trail of blond fuzz that led temptingly down under the waistband of his boxers, moving teasingly slowly as Ash whimpered and writhed beneath her, mumbling something incoherent that sounded like 'want'. Something silky and damp nudged the underside of her chin and her stomach sparked, her breath escaping her in a rush of raw heat as her body automatically responded. Astra found herself burying her face in the crease where Ash's thigh met his groin, before she could think, nuzzling deep to inhale his dark scent.

Ash gave a strangled gasp and arched up, twisting his body so as to move her mouth closer to his cock.

Oh, really?

Astra shifted, hooked the tips of her fingers into the waistband and lightly tugged. Ash immediately lifted his hips, bringing his hands to join hers in wrestling his boxers down to mid-thigh and off, leaving his heavy erection laying flat against his stomach, leaking glistening fluid. Wrapping her hand around him, Astra raised her head and caught his eye, holding his gaze for one heated, intense breath.

Then she dived, and Ash's raw cry echoed in the room as she swallowed him down to the root.

It was graceless, breathless, passionate. Ash's hands clutched at the duvet, his feet scrabbling frantically behind her, head thrashing against the pillow as he gasped encouragement. His thighs trembled with tension, his back bowing; teasingly Astra swallowed and hummed around him, pulling back just enough to accommodate the desperate thrust that followed, Ash letting out a groan he only barely managed to muffle with his fist.

Oh, I am good at this.

"Fuck," Ash panted, moving his hand from his face. "You're so good at this."

Astra flashed him a look before lowering her head again, eliciting an excited yelp which was hastily stifled halfway through.

Then Astra was caught up in slick sweat, wild movements and Ash's increasingly unrestrained babbling, swallowing around him again and again. She cupped his testicles in one hand, teasing his skin, before sucking two fingers into her mouth and sliding them down the damp cleft of his —

"*Oh!*" Ash groaned through his hand. "*Fuck!* In me! Please!"

He was wet, his muscles tight, swallowing each finger as they slid inside. As Astra's fingertips found the right spot and pressed, Ash moaned and arched, his hips starting to jerk desperately. Astra kept her mouth in a snug grip around him and let him thrust, massaging that spot inside him with her fingers until Ash's legs began to tremble, his hand falling away from his mouth to clutch at the duvet, and now she could hear him, wordless cries interspersed with sounds of *close* and *fuck* and *now* —

"*Yes!*" Ash gasped, and tensed, and shuddered, and came.

Astra kept her mouth in place and swallowed, her own breathing and his ringing in her ears, and let Ash ride out his pleasure, hoping against hope her own would come next.

"Woah."

Ash's hand closed over her shoulder and tugged lightly, and Astra allowed herself to be coaxed forward, resting her cheek against the slick smoothness of his chest, feeling his heartbeat pounding in her ear.

"That was amazing."

Astra looked up at him, opening her mouth to respond, but Ash seemed to be in the middle of a stream of consciousness.

"That was — I've wanted that for so *long* — I just — "

His body suddenly tensed, and Astra's half-formed question broke off into a surprised squeal as she found herself flipped over and deposited on top of the duvet. Fingers dived under the edge of her bra, pushing it roughly up over her face before disappearing to tug at her panties as she wrestled it down her arms. By the time she had flung the bra onto the floor, her panties had slid over her feet, leaving her completely exposed.

Ash rose over her, looking down at her with a heated expression relieved only by the knowing twist to his mouth.

"That time in the kitchen at that party. What did I say?"

A memory briefly surfaced like a bubble, and Astra bit down on a smile.

"That I was good at giving head."

"And you were. What else did I say?"

"No idea."

An unbearably tormenting grin spread across Ash's face as he leant down, his breath brushing over her mouth.

"I said I'd return the favour."

His face disappeared, but the tantalising motions of mouth and tongue Astra found herself bucking into seconds later were a welcome replacement.

"What time is it?"

"Half past nine. Are you hungry?"

"A bit."

"I'll call for pizza."

Ash rolled to the edge of the bed and reached over the side, surfacing with a pizza menu and his cell phone. Astra folded her hands across her stomach and let herself drift in a dreamy haze until Ash snapped the phone closed, rolled over, and enfolded her in his arms, his mouth finding hers.

It was some time before Ash spoke again.

"Um, I'll be ready again by the time it gets here..."

"It's all right, you know," Astra interrupted, noting the flush starting to spread across his skin. "We have all night."

"Yeah, well, I said I was going to show you—"

"Yeah, and you did. I heard you were good at that."

Ash stilled in her arms. "Oh yeah?"

"Yeah." Astra pulled back to arch a teasing eyebrow at him. "This thing you did with your tongue…"

"Oh, *that*." Ash leaned in to kiss her again and Astra let him, unable to conceal a smile as she felt his tongue twist in a manner evocative of its earlier movements. Conversation could come later.

Some ten or fifteen minutes had passed by the time Ash's phone rang to signal the arrival of the pizza. Throwing on his T-shirt and jeans, Ash withdrew, leaving Astra sprawled in a blissful haze on top of the duvet.

If it comes with plenty of head… I hear you're good at that…

Oh yes, she had made him well aware of that.

He has this thing he does with his tongue…

Oh, didn't he just. Astra let out a sigh, allowing a ridiculously goofy smile to take over her face.

In fact, there was only one more point to cover.

I'll show you just how good I can be.

The night ahead of them stretched out endlessly, filled with tantalisingly shadowed possibilities. Astra allowed herself to drift into hedonistic daydreams about warm tongues and ice cubes until the click of the door lock and a delicious aroma told her Ash had returned with the food.

"Oh man, I need this," Ash muttered as he opened the box on the bed, scooping up a slice with an alacrity that suggested he hadn't eaten in a week. "I am *starving*."

Astra took a slice with studied casualness. It was on the tip of her tongue to mention he would need to eat to keep up his strength, but looking at him, Ash seemed a little too focussed on the food to handle any sexual banter. Smiling inwardly, she took a bite.

And realised that instead of his usual Meat Feast, Ash had ordered a Meat Feast with four cheeses, which was considerably more expensive…and her favourite.

Catching Ash's eye for a moment, Astra swallowed her mouthful of food and licked her lips, deliberately drawing out the sensuality of the movement as Ash's jaw dropped ever so slightly.

Maybe he *could* handle a little playfulness after all.

Ash's eyes were on her as Astra slowly brought her third slice of pizza to her mouth and bit down, allowing some of the juice to trickle down her chin.

Let's see what he does with that, then.

"Uh... You have..."

Ash leant towards her and stroked his thumb below her lip, his hand noticeably trembling. Laying down the slice, Astra caught his wrist, drew his hand up to her face and sucked his thumb into her mouth, flickering her tongue across the tip.

That good?

Eyes widening, Ash let out a gasp before visibly catching himself. His eyes narrowed, and Astra realised she might not have concealed her inner smugness as well as she had hoped.

"What?"

Ash gave her one heated, almost pained look, then his hand flashed and Astra found herself caught in his arms, seized, rolled and sprawled flat on the bed, her head falling back as Ash's mouth met hers with unexpected force.

"*Oh —*"

Ash pulled back for a moment to peel his T-shirt over his head and hastily unfasten his jeans before covering her with his body once again, shifting his hips as Astra drew her knees back and hooked her toes into his waistband to push the denim down his legs.

Suddenly the most important thing in the world was Ash being naked.

The feel of his body sliding against hers, the grip of his embrace and the heat from his skin, were both overwhelming and maddening at the same time. Astra moaned and arched against him, digging her fingers into his shoulders as Ash's mouth trailed and licked along the sensitive skin of her neck, sucking and biting lower until hot kisses were being sprinkled over her breasts.

"Don't stop," Astra heard herself moan, then gasped as Ash's slid his hands up to clasp her bottom, caressing rhythmically until her hips were pressing forcefully against him, urging him further. Abruptly she became aware Ash's mouth had detached itself from her skin and she let out a protesting whine at the loss, tugging at his hair.

"Shh, wait," Ash whispered, sliding up until his face was in line with hers. "Pass me the condom on the table."

Why the hell does he want to use condoms NOW?

"We never used them before! You said you and Sash – "

Her mouth was suddenly covered by Ash's fingers. Looking up, Astra fell silent as she found herself staring straight into his eyes. There was something in their gaze more intimate than anything they had done so far, more than anything they had said. There was feeling, *emotion* there, to a degree that sent silver sparks through her stomach.

A brief image from earlier. Ash's voice. *You're mine.*

"That was a fuck," Ash said in a low voice. "This is…"

He broke off, Astra mentally filling in the words *making love* with the beginnings of a blissful glow. Ash paused, his eyes never leaving hers, until he spoke again.

"We're doing this right," he said firmly. "I'm wearing it."

Not trusting herself to speak, Astra handed him the condom and lay still, waiting as Ash pulled back and made hidden movements, before her attention was drawn abruptly downwards by a delicious pressure just where she wanted it the most.

Ash was looking down at her, a strange light in his eyes, his cock in his hand and *stroking* her with it—

And then it all became too much.

Ash was sliding inside her in one smooth motion, thrusting slowly at first, then harder as Astra hooked her legs over his thighs to pull him deeper. Her head fell back and they were kissing, kissing passionately as Ash's movements became more and more frantic and Astra dug her fingers into his back, moaning into his mouth and it was too *good*, too intense, oh *God*—

With a groan, Ash tore his mouth from hers and buried his face in her neck, gasping for breath as his grip on her body tightened even further, and through a haze of increasing excitement Astra became aware of him murmuring desperately against her skin.

"Oh God, I'm so close—I can't, oh fuck, I *can't*—Oh, baby, please, *please*—"

And she was tensing, clenching down around him, and her body was starting to tremble as her pleasure reached its peak—

—and then Astra was coming and crying out, and Ash let out one choked moan and convulsed, and both were clinging to each other in that final moment of ecstasy.

It was a few minutes before Ash spoke, his voice sounding groggy with sleep.

"I didn't leave you hanging, did I?"

Astra hid a smile in his shoulder. *So we're back at this again.*

"No."

A pause.

"Was that OK?"

Oh, you'll show me how good you can be, will you?

"It was great."

Silence fell for a moment, then Ash's voice came again, this time buoyed with confidence.

"Yeah, I thought it was."

Choking with laughter, Astra gave his bottom a resounding slap. Ash responded with a suggestive growl, arching his back.

"Beat me."

"Kinky fucker."

"You can fucking talk."

Astra opened her mouth to banter back, but was overtaken by a yawn.

"I'll spank you in the morning. Or whatever else you want."

She had expected a suitably suggestive or crude answer from Ash, so it came as a surprise when the body in her arms stilled suddenly and fell silent, the breaths on her neck quickening ever so slightly.

"Ash? What *do* you want?"

There was a long, charged pause.

"Nothing," a little voice mumbled finally, unconvincingly.

"Go on. What do you want me to do? You know I'll do it."

A faint tremor ran through Ash's body, but the silence remained. Astra tilted her pelvis upwards, gauging his reaction, and felt a satisfying tingle when her mound met hardness.

"Tell me."

Ash raised his head and held her gaze for a moment, biting his lip as if considering his words, then thrust sharply. Astra gasped as she felt him sheath himself in her to the hilt.

"I'll tell you in the morning."

And then he lowered his mouth to hers, and Astra was lost again to sensation.

* * * *

Bzzz.

Harry's tousled dark head emerged from under the duvet, one hand rubbing sleep from his reddened eyes, the other fumbling on the bedside table for the source of the noise.

Bzzz.

It was his cell phone. But he hadn't set his alarm for this morning, which meant—

The name on the lit screen became clear, and he groaned. *Marcus.*

It was too early, it was too soon after... The thought of another difficult break-up filled him with dread, and then the word *another* echoed in his head. This was to be his *second* break-up, and the recognition of its truth was cold and heavy.

I can't do this. I can't—

Getting out of bed was impossible. A long, empty day lay ahead of him, a day without Astra, without the chance of seeing her smile or feeling her hand in his—and he had driven her to this point, had taken her for granted over and over, had watched them deteriorate without acting to save what they had.

Surprisingly, there was no pain. Emptiness, yes.

No pain.

The buzzing stopped abruptly before immediately starting again.

Damn it.

Picking up the cell phone, Harry started to press the 'cancel' button before pausing in reluctant thought.

If I do this now, I might still be able to talk her round.

If I don't do this, I have no chance.

He slid his thumb over to 'accept' and pushed, lifting the phone to his ear.

"Hello?"

"About time," that familiar voice growled, sending a shiver over Harry's skin.

He fought to keep his voice calm. "I was in bed."

"That's good." Marcus chuckled darkly. "I'm right outside. I could join you."

Images flashed through Harry's head of dark red hair, green eyes, Astra's fast-retreating back, and his stomach rolled as he answered.

"Come on up."

"You got it, baby." *Click.*

Harry fell backwards onto the bed, the phone dropping from his hand.

He had to do this, and he had to do this right.

Definitively.

Because as long as Marcus remained a possibility, Astra had made it clear she never would be again.

He rolled off the bed and began to dress quickly.

Chapter Nineteen

"Fucking starving."

The morning sunlight was dazzling. Already halfway down the path that led to Alpha Nu Mu, Astra twisted to avoid the rays, shielding her eyes as she looked back at Ash, still in the doorway. Her pocket beeped.

"Hey, Drake!" came another, deeper, voice from inside, cutting off Ash's continued diatribe on the state of his stomach. It was all Astra's fault, apparently, making him burn off all his carbs overnight. "Did you get that message about practice tomorrow?"

"Did I what? Hey, Melville! Wait up!"

Ash bolted after his housemate, letting the door bang shut.

Her cell phone beeped again. Astra dug it out of her pocket and flipped it open.

Are you two up yet?

And then the second: *Guess who I have a date with tonight?*

Astra shook her head in disbelief. Sasha had never had trouble finding dates, but this was fast even for her.

It was a bright day, a Friday. One class ahead of her at eleven, one meeting with her project supervisor at two. Time for breakfast with Ash, *maybe* lunch with Sasha, and then the whole weekend stretched out in front of them. There were at least two parties she knew of on Saturday night. *Ah, decisions.*

Astra sighed happily, sliding her phone back into her jeans—

And froze.

From her left, footsteps.

Running footsteps, getting closer and closer.

* * * *

"You're dumping me."

The expression of disbelief on Marcus's face was almost comical.

"You're dumping me so you can fake being straight."

"I am not—" Harry bit back his automatic response. *I'm not going to give him a chance to win.* "We're not discussing this. It's over."

Marcus shook his head. "Over."

Has he ever been dumped before? Harry wondered. Looking at Marcus, at his heavy build, his jowly face and bald head, it seemed bizarre he should consider himself so untouchable.

And yet there was something about him, something about that gravelly voice and supreme self-confidence that drew men to him, had drawn *Harry* to him, expecting no experience, yet promising delights.

Marcus *radiated* sex.

The stunned, slack-jawed expression had now given way to a scowl, and Harry steeled himself for another verbal assault. When it came, it was with devastating force.

"So you're going crawling back to that little firecrotch. I knew it."

You bastard. To think I lost her for you.

Marcus was smirking, and something flashed before Harry's eyes—a row of stitches, his cell phone lying dead on the carpet alongside Marcus's tanned knees, and fury blazed forth.

"Don't you *ever* say that about her again, you fucking arsehole!"

Marcus opened his mouth again, sneering, and Harry clenched his fist, fingernails gripping the last edges of his control.

"Astra is worth ten of you."

The sneer was still in place, but Marcus had gone very still, the look in his eyes and the set of his shoulders hardening like metal.

"Oh really?"

"Yeah, really." Harry had the advantage now, and he rushed ahead. "So get the hell out of my life...old man."

That last epithet did it.

Marcus twisted around abruptly and wrenched open the door. He turned briefly to spit one last rejoinder over his shoulder.

"Then I may as well have some fun...*bitch*."

As the door slammed, Harry felt his heart grow cold.

How had Marcus known Astra had red hair?

* * * *

Something crashed into Astra's back with stunning force, pitching her forward onto her knees, the ground looming threateningly before her. Astra broke her sudden fall with her hands, but a hand was in her hair, gripping it tightly, forcing her head down to the concrete path.

"You *whore*—" a voice snarled in her ear before pain, blinding pain, as a fist slammed into her cheekbone with a sickening crack.

It was a male voice, rough, dark, but not one she knew, and she caught a brief glimpse of olive skin and dark stubble before the face withdrew.

Another blow to her head, this time to her left temple, and the world grew blurred, spinning though she was pinned to the ground by his heavy weight, and she was screaming wildly and over the roaring in her ears she could hear him growling foul words, *bitch* and *cunt* and *fucking whore* and the pain was building, mounting, and blood was trickling into her eye—

And then she was rolling over onto her back, the weight suddenly gone, and Ash was there, the back of the man's shirt clenched in his fist, and he was so tall, so much stronger as he threw him down to the ground like a sack of cement, so much *faster* as he knocked the struggling man back down with a sharp kick to his ribs before dropping down onto him and punching him over and over again.

"I'll fucking kill you, you worthless cunt!" Another punch to the face, and her attacker's nose made a satisfyingly bloody sound that seemed only to encourage Ash to hit it again. "I'll break your fucking neck, you son of a bitch! You filthy—fucking—piece of *shit!*"

"*Astra!*"

Harry appeared in her field of vision, panting and sweating as if he had been running. He fell to his knees beside her, brushing blood-drenched hair out of her face and touching his finger to her temple, making Astra jolt away.

"Oh God, sorry! I've called the police — they should be here in a minute," Harry babbled, brushing his knuckles against her cheek and causing another stab of pain. "I dumped him and Marcus just went mad. I don't know how he knew who you were. I was so afraid you'd be alone when he found you — thank *God* — "

He paused and looked across at where Ash was still beating an increasingly bloodied and bruised Marcus. Astra watched him as his eyes narrowed, clouded by something intangible, and for a moment they both fell still, the silence between them broken only by the sounds of flesh pounding on flesh, of pained grunts and angry curses.

Then, in the distance, came the welcome sound of the sirens.

"I broke up with him."

Astra gave a mute shrug. They were sitting on the steps of the fraternity house, Harry holding an ice-pack to her left temple, which was covered in bloodied gauze.

"You're dating *him*. Aren't you." It wasn't a question.

"Yeah. I am."

They both looked towards the police car, still parked in the road, where Ash was being interviewed by a uniformed officer. One of his hands was bandaged — his knuckles had been badly skinned. The ambulance had already left, taking Marcus in the custody of two police officers and three paramedics. Astra had deliberately turned her face away from his medical examination. To her mind, he had deserved every minute of it.

"Why?" Harry's voice was barely a breath.

Astra turned her head slowly, to give him the benefit of her cool, emotionless stare. Harry flushed, dropping his eyes.

They sat in silence for a moment before he spoke again.

"I don't know what I'm going to do without you."

His voice was so tired, so defeated, that Astra found herself reaching to take his hand. It would have been so easy. But the barrier between them remained, awkward and uncomfortable, and she paused with her fingers in mid-air for a moment before returning to toy with the pocket of her jeans.

"Harry..."

She took a deep breath.

"You'll be fine. Really."

Harry didn't reply, but a tense, shuddering sigh stirred her hair.

"We both know it's not me you want." The memory of Marcus rose, prompting Astra to continue. "So you had bad luck with the last one. There'll be other guys. There really will. And you know you can always talk to me."

It was tempting to add something more, something along the lines of, *We should have ended things a long time ago.*

But there had been enough misery between them already, Astra thought. It was better this way.

Harry stood abruptly to leave. Retrieving the ice pack, Astra looked up to see Ash approaching, his long strides eating up the space between them. For a brief, stiff moment the two men eyed each other steadily. Ash's expression was inscrutable, while Harry's was thoughtful.

Astra, watching him, thought she could see resignation in his face, but there was something else — distress, nerves, and what almost looked like a touch of yearning in the set of his body, in the steadfastness of his eyes...

Harry lowered his gaze, breaking the tension, and made eye contact with the police officer, still waiting beside the car at the kerb. Passing Ash, he lightly punched his biceps.

"Take care of her."

Ash returned the gesture to Harry's shoulder. "I will."

The police officer was waiting impatiently. Harry walked away from them, walked away from Astra, shoulders set and head aloft, facing his interrogation. The movement had a finality to it that made Astra's chest ache.

"It's five to ten." Ash sat down beside her, taking the ice pack out of her hand and holding it in place. "Do you want me to skip class? I don't mind."

Astra contemplated it for a moment. She had already given her statement, and class for her wasn't until eleven. The prospect of a glorious hour with Ash was tempting.

But it was nearly time for finals, and whatever Ash said, he needed the class time. The image of the computer lab, some report revision or an hour's web-surfing, offered itself as a comforting, numbing prospect — mind-clearing and blissfully dull.

"No, it's fine. Go to class. I need to —" she waved her hand aimlessly in the air. " — you know."

Ash nodded and stood, Astra following.

"I'll see you later," he said.

"Later," Astra said.

And they parted, bandaged but not broken.

* * * *

It was a productive day.

Sasha had been free for lunch and, over a bowl of chilli and rice, had been very forthcoming about her date that evening. Astra had been amused, but not surprised, to hear she was being taken to a bar by one of Ash's bandmates — the drummer, Finn. So far Sasha's knowledge of him apparently only covered three points, the first two being 'music student' and 'lives off campus', but any concerns about this were negated by the third point, which was 'great ass'.

Her professor had returned the final draft of her internship report with positive feedback, and the relief at the thought of completing it was immense. Finals were looming, but beyond lay management training, her life running the casino, and the unseen future that teased just past the horizon.

With Ash? Maybe.

You want that, said a knowing voice in her head.

"Shut up," Astra told the voice.

You're in love with him, was the mocking response.

The word sent a shudder through her body.

She had loved Harry, loved him far longer than necessary. Longer than he deserved, because whatever he felt — whatever he had *claimed* to feel — the pull towards men would always be too strong. With the best will in the world, Astra couldn't begrudge him that. It was a pull she understood, well enough to know it was better to follow than to fight.

Desire was straightforward.

Love was terrifying.

Ash, however, seemed to have no expectations beyond an entertaining evening. As they sat on his bed, sharing a Chinese takeaway, he had taken the news of Sasha's new boyfriend with a lack of surprise that suggested Sasha had probably asked him to give Finn her phone number in the first place.

"She'll like Finn," Ash said with certainty through a mouthful of stir-fried beef. "He has this thing about feet. And you know what she's like for getting her toes sucked."

"Mmm," Astra agreed, choosing to focus on her sweet-and-sour prawns rather than elaborate on that point. There was something rather *wrong* about knowing her friend's—*best* friend's?—fetishes, even if Ash was a co-conspirator.

From the slight smirk on his face, Ash could tell exactly what she was thinking, but his only comment was, "Can you get me another beer?"

"Sure." Supporting herself on her hand, Astra ducked down to the six-pack beside the bed and hooked one out. The movement unbalanced her and, with a startled yelp, she half-fell onto the floor, her feet still on the mattress as her head landed on the carpet, giving her a sudden and surprising view of a very familiar shape lying under the bed.

"Hey, is that—?"

Ash caught her arm and pulled her upright, but Astra was too swift for him—she had already reached under the bed, and surfaced holding the object at head height.

It was her strap-on dildo.

Ash's eyes widened, but his jaw and shoulders immediately set in a pose of forced casualness which was directly at odds with the almost scarlet flush creeping over his skin.

"And where, exactly—" Astra began, deliberately adopting a mocking tone to conceal her genuine question, " —did you get this? I know I didn't leave it here."

If possible, Ash seemed to flush even deeper, although his squared shoulders and lowered brow defied any suggestion he might be affected.

"I might've—like—asked Sasha to borrow it. It was in her room," he added defensively as Astra raised her eyebrows.

Now this is interesting.

Astra was about to ask the obvious question when her own words from the previous night came back to her.

I'll spank you in the morning. Or whatever else you want...

An image of Ash appeared, so clear it almost hurt— Ash's curved buttocks slipping out of his jeans, her holding a slim vibrator against the tight pink pucker of his hole, Ash begging, pleading, and then coming with force at the first thrust.

Dipping her head, she lowered her eyelashes and cast Ash a kittenish glance through them, hoping to show him she knew what he wanted, and he could ask.

Admittedly the thought was a little strange, but not for the reasons he thought—she had been prepared to do this for Harry, prepared to show him a woman could do the same as a man, and she would have been wrong. For Harry it wasn't about the act, it was about the man performing it, and while his taste left something to be desired, she had no doubt he would find another man capable of making him happy.

But for Ash, it was all about the act. He wanted a woman, wanted *her*, but the discovery of his prostate and his secret submissive side meant he still had that desire, that *need*, and if he wanted it that badly, she would do it for him, because it was Ash, and because it was her he wanted at the business end of the toy.

She ignored the kick her stomach gave at the memory of Sasha writhing beneath her as the dildo slid in and out of her, of the sense of control and power she had felt which had rendered the vibrating bullet in the device almost redundant, the excitement of topping enough to send her over the edge.

Ash was looking more and more uncomfortable, and Astra spoke without thinking.

"Tell me what you want."

For the first time, understanding seemed to strike Ash, and his breathing quickened, the fingers of one hand digging convulsively into the duvet.

Oh, God. The surge of power, of lust, that flooded through her at the sight of Ash's desire was overwhelming, and Astra's hand trembled as she held the strap-on out towards him.

"Ask me," she commanded, and her gut clenched. "Ask me, and I'll do it."

Ash swallowed visibly, gripping the quilt more tightly, and Astra tensed, expecting to find herself knocked flat upon the bed at any moment. Slowly, carefully, she shifted position to allow the manoeuvre easily, but instead Ash drew himself up stiffly, his mouth set in a firm line.

"I want you to… "

He paused, licked his lips, and began again. Astra held herself still and waited.

Say it. Say it. Say it.

"I want you to wear that and fuck me."

Oh, yes.

It had been some time since Astra had worn the device, and that had been for Sasha, but, as she stripped and stepped out of her underwear to step into the rubber panties, feeling the familiar heavy drag of the dildo and the intimate nudge of the bullet, it felt as though she was returning to a role she should never have stopped performing.

And as Ash's eyes widened further, his face transforming into the deeply vulnerable cast she remembered from his most submissive moments, it felt as though *this* was what the toy should have been used for all along.

It needed to be slow.

Ash lay face down on the bed in front of her, a pillow tucked under his hips which lifted his bottom temptingly, his thighs falling open on either side to accommodate Astra as she knelt between them.

One finger.

His face was buried in his folded arms, a dishevelled mop of blond hair the only thing visible, but Astra could see it in the responses of his body, the excitement hidden in the taut arch of his back and the occasional tremors running through his frame.

Two fingers.

Ash's body clenched involuntarily around the intrusion, quivering like a moist glove, and Astra reached down to stroke his back soothingly. This would be the last point of familiarity, she knew—even the vibrator was no bigger than this, and she felt him shudder as she withdrew her hand, either with nerves or with anticipation.

Three fingers.

A gasp, and Ash's hips jerked, almost in shock. Twisting her hand, Astra felt for his prostate and pressed, unable to restrain her smile as Ash squirmed, groaning into the protective shield of his arms.

"Ready?" she purred.

Ash's body trembled, but his voice was strident with determination. "I'm ready."

Go slowly, Astra reminded herself as she rose up on her knees, quickly slicking the toy with lubricant before positioning it at his entrance.

It was a cautious manoeuvre. The pressure was intense; Ash was still so tight, and for a few moments his body fought the intrusion before giving way with a sudden jolt, a good three inches of the toy sliding inside him in one abrupt movement. Ash let out a startled yelp and Astra stopped short, steadying herself by clasping his thigh.

"Are you okay?"

"Yeah, I'm okay. I'm okay." Ash was panting, clutching at the duvet like a lifeline. "Just give me a minute, yeah?"

Astra waited, leaning her weight on his hips and stroking his leg distractedly, torn between soothing his nerves and hiding the fact her entire body was trembling with anticipation.

"Okay," Ash said finally, his voice breathless and strained. "You can move."

Astra slid a hand higher to cup his balls as she pressed forward, listening carefully for any gasps or whimpers from Ash that might have signalled pain, but though Ash's breathing was nervous and rapid, he made no sound until Astra's thighs were resting flush against the backs of his legs.

"Want me to stop? Or wait?"

"No." Ash took several deep breaths. "Could you lean forward a bit?"

Right. Prostate.

Astra stretched upwards, raising herself slightly on her toes, and angled her body forward and down, aiming for that spot—

—and suddenly Ash gave a shocked gasp and shifted, the line of his body abruptly melting from panic and pain into pleasure, and Astra knew.

"Ready?"

Sweat-slick thighs pressed back against her, and Ash groaned. "Oh God, yeah. Move!"

Astra picked up the remote for the bullet vibrator, flicked the switch, drew back and then slammed her hips forward.

It was different, familiar and yet unfamiliar in all the ways that were most welcome. Ash's body was firmer, lacking Sasha's soft curves, and his voice was deeper; instead of letting out high-pitched cries, Ash *groaned*, ragged and harsh with every breath, swearing almost violently every time a thrust was angled just right.

Astra's fingers dug into Ash's warm skin, her knees burning with the force of each hard push, and the bullet was buzzing wildly, pressing exactly where it was needed, and the pleasure centred in her groin was already beginning to swell and tighten, making her clench down on empty air, and she heard herself moan with the need to come—

Ash groaned in response and pushed backwards, and their bodies crashed together, the headboard slamming hard against the wall.

"Touch me," Ash panted. "God, fucking touch me—"

And as Astra leant forward to wrap her hand around him, shifting the angle of penetration, the bullet slipped a little lower and the delicious tingling sharpened abruptly; barely aware of her hand tugging at Ash's cock, Astra threw her head back and cried out as her body tightened and shuddered, bliss rippling along every nerve.

Ash let out one final yell and jerked hard, falling forward onto his elbows as her hand became slippery.

"Oh God, I love you, I love you, I love you—" and then his head dropped, his voice muffled by the duvet. Astra slumped forward, still firmly attached to him, and laid her cheek on his back.

"I love you," she mumbled, wondering if he had heard her, and part of her not caring.

There was time, endless time, to say it again.

Chapter Twenty

Two suitcases lay on the bed, packed and zipped closed.

Three full boxes stood on the wooden desk alongside a fourth, still half-empty. Reaching up to the shelf above, Astra brought down a handful of framed photographs and placed them on the chair. Those could go on top.

Moving out of the Omega Zeta house was proving to be more difficult than she had imagined. She and Sasha had signed a rental agreement on an apartment two weeks earlier; a surprisingly attractive place with wood flooring, a good-sized kitchen and two bedrooms with a bathroom between them. Astra had taken the room nearest the front door, hoping this would ensure she didn't wake Sasha coming in late at night.

A knocking, and then Tori poked her head around the door. Astra had introduced her to Ash's bandmate, the luridly green-haired lead guitarist Jamie, and the two had been dating for two weeks, much to the chagrin of Sasha, who had bet Astra twenty dollars Tori would take one look at him and run screaming. It was always satisfying for Astra to receive proof, yet again, that when it came to gambling she was the queen.

"Astra? Harry's downstairs."

Harry? Oh fuck.

She had known this would happen; Harry had made it clear the last time she had seen him, and she had viewed it with the dread she felt for an upcoming root canal.

Fuck.

* * * *

The morning of May 8th had dawned bright and clear.

Drifting like leaves, black cloth floating on the breeze, the caps and gowns of graduating students peppered the campus, the dark herds broken only by the bright summer colours worn by fussing, proud parents as they swarmed their young like bees.

It was a day long-awaited, a day to be fixed in the memory for all time.

Astra had seen Sasha, flanked by her parents and twin sister, three blonde and bubbly women corralled by a tall, distinguished-looking man who wore his dark suit like an undertaker might. She had seen Ash, taller than both his pretty, delicate-featured mother and his muscular, broad-shouldered father, feigning modest embarrassment while his pride radiated from every angle.

She had not seen Harry. Not, in fact, since the day of the attack.

The weeks had passed like a beautiful dream; an expression Astra would never have expected to use for revision and finals, and yet accurate, for things had developed better than she could have hoped.

Her career was decided.

Sasha had forgiven her.

And Harry had left her to it at last.

Her parents had flown down the previous evening. Astra had left them in their seats ten minutes earlier before going to join the other students. Her mother had insisted on pushing her hair aside to check on the scarring at her temple, which Astra had submitted to meekly; it had been difficult enough to keep them from flying down after the accident, and even now her mother's fussing had been curtailed only by the casual mention of "my new boyfriend, Ash", thereby attracting maternal attention.

"Ash? Wasn't that the name of your friend Sarah's boyfriend?"

"Yes. They broke up."

This had been enough to set her mother off on a tangent, and the ensuing barrage of questions — occasionally punctuated by one from her father about what Ash intended to do for a career — had ensured the subjects of scarring and Harry remained undercover.

Waiting at the back of the hall, Astra had taken a deep breath and relaxed, letting all the stresses of the day — of the many, many preceding days — float away with the dust on the air.

Harry was out of the picture.

Ash was very much *in* the picture.

And with her degree came the promise of a career, of low-running excitement and dazzling lights and control, controlling her patrons' loss of money and the influx of her own.

As the crowds of parents began to settle into their seats, a dark-haired figure had pushed past her, and the familiar voice of Harry had whispered in her ear.

"I need to talk to you."

Astra had turned, but he was already gone.

* * * *

Harry had been conspicuously absent at the Omega Zeta party that evening.

Sasha had spent the evening alternating between dancing with the other sisters and snuggling on the sofa with Finn, who had drunk his way through almost an entire crate of French bottled beer. Astra had suppressed a shudder at the thought of the breath that would result from such an overindulgence, and had casually turned away when Finn had leapt from his seat to play air guitar in the middle of the room before falling over his feet and landing in the fireplace. It was Sasha, and if Finn made her happy — or even provided some entertainment in the interim — she wasn't about to pass judgement. Although if Finn decided to vomit or urinate all over the floor in their new apartment, she would have to put her foot down.

After two hours of dancing, Astra had just been wandering out of the kitchen with a drink when a familiar voice drifted out of the lounge. Ash was standing just inside the doorway, bottle in hand, holding forth in conversation with a group of fellow football players.

"You know Ackerley's signed to the Bengals now," someone had said.

"Fuck Cincinnati," was Ash's response. "Too damn cold."

"Oh yeah?" came another voice, sharp and sarcastic. "You've entered the supplemental draft, right? You might end up in Minnesota."

"I might." Ash's voice was cool.

"Hey, I'd take Minnesota," said the first voice, laughing. "You hoping for the coast, Drake?"

"Mm-hmm." A swallow of beer. "Oakland or San Francisco."

"And we all know why, don't we?" There was a thud that sounded like a light punch. "So let's hear it. Is she good?"

Astra had stiffened, clenching the bottle in her hand with white fingers.

"Is she really that good at blow jobs?"

"Does she take—?"

Ash's voice cut across the overlapping questions, leaving Astra to complete the last in her head, her anger manifesting in a deep flush.

"Guys, shut up. No—" He paused; Astra envisaged him holding up a hand in the face of some indignant interrupter. "No. Drop it."

"Aw, come on, Ash," the first voice urged. "You've never been shy before—"

"Those were one-nighters. They talked more than I did." Someone else had started to protest, but Ash's voice cut them off abruptly. "*No*, okay? Astra's my girl, and I'm not sharing, so find someone else to jerk off to."

There was a brief, startled silence. Astra had bitten her lip, imagining Ash encircled by sagging jaws on bemused faces. She had heard them all bragging about girls at parties before, lurid details about breasts and bottoms and acts, and to find Ash suddenly changing the rules— because she knew full well he had been no exception— well, *that* would floor them completely.

But it hadn't.

Instead, a raucous cheer had risen up, followed by a barrage of teasing comments about how "Drake's fallen in love!", and Astra had slipped away quietly, smiling to herself.

Drake's fallen in love.

It had been an enlightening few weeks.

Ash was still Ash, still arrogant, still occasionally obnoxious, still firmly convinced of his own good looks and his sporting prowess. He was still inclined to respond to everything physically rather than intellectually, still fiercely protective of his own sexual identity, still irresistible.

Still so much to discover.

For Ash was deeper than she had believed, smarter and far more thoughtful; a better conversationalist than she had expected, and after spending so much time in the company of over-emotional men, Ash's blunt speech and filthy mouth were a welcome contrast.

He was a generous lover, more tender than she could have hoped, yet just as passionate as she had imagined.

He had an unerring sense for when she felt the urge to slip into the strap-on panties, and could arch his back and take harder and deeper and breathlessly faster thrusts than Astra had ever dreamed possible.

And when Ash had appeared behind her later that evening and whispered promises in her ear of tongues, toys and glistening ice, the urge to submit and be submitted to—and that blissful throb in her chest she spoke of to no-one but him—was stronger, more insistent, than ever.

* * * *

Harry was waiting for her at the bottom of the stairs. His hair was dishevelled, as usual; he was looking up at her with those same sweet eyes, so heavy with emotion, only now they seemed restrained — an emotion unrelated to her, perhaps, or one he was choosing not to impose.

He had never been so beautiful, yet so easy to resist.

Astra had thought she would feel nothing for him, but somehow she felt the urge to hug him to her and never let go. He was leaving, as was she; he would go on with his life and she with hers, and all they had shared would evaporate into dust.

It had been painful, all those times, to forget and know what she was forgetting.

Though the tug of desire had long since been lost, the pull of affection remained. "Hi, Harry."

"Hi, Astra."

Astra rounded the end of the banister and stood directly in front of him, scanning his face. The last time she had seen him, he had looked distressed, beaten down by the final realisation of the consequences of his obsession, and by his ultimate loss.

I don't know what I'm going to do without you, he had said.

Now he was different. Harry was facing her with the stance of one who was wavering under pressure but determined to withstand it, his eyes painfully sharp in a face which was relaxed in resignation. The firm line of his mouth gave him a newly purposeful air.

I need to talk to you, he had said.

"You said you needed to talk to me."

Harry gave a brief nod, lowering his eyes for a moment before raising them again to meet her gaze.

"I thought you might like to know I—" His voice caught, forcing him to clear his throat before speaking again. "I came out to my parents."

"Harry, that's great!" In a sudden, glad rush of feeling Astra reached to clasp his hand in hers, but she recoiled immediately upon brushing against his fingers.

Wrong. Wrong.

Before Harry could comment, Astra pressed onwards, hoping to keep his mind on the topic. "How did they take it?"

"Fine," Harry answered after a pause, but Astra noticed him slide his hand back into his pocket. "That wasn't the hardest part."

He trailed off, and Astra nodded sympathetically. For Harry the hardest part would have been admitting it to himself, when he had denied what his body and actions had been telling him for so long. After her own behaviour with Ash, she could hardly criticise him for that. She could only commend him for finally understanding.

"I'm sorry your first experience went so badly."

If Harry held any doubts about her meaning, he hid them well. He straightened up, sticking his jaw out in a gesture that was unfamiliar and yet so uniquely Harry that a strange warmth filled Astra's stomach.

"Yeah, well. I'm sorry about what he did to you." A pause. "He followed you home one night. That's how he knew who you were."

Astra blinked.

"Apparently he—" Harry took a deep breath. "—tried to get into your room one night, but the room was empty, so I guess he got it wrong."

The open window. Astra opened her mouth to answer, but Harry had taken another breath and was steadying himself to speak, and the words died on her tongue.

"I don't think about him anymore." He bit his lip awkwardly, and Astra felt a sudden premonition. "I've actually met someone else."

Somewhere in Astra's mind, a chain seemed to break. The thought of Harry with someone else, happy with someone else, filled her with almost unimaginable relief.

"That's wonderful, Harry. It really is."

Harry lowered his eyes shyly, and through his fringe Astra noticed a light rose glow suffuse his face.

"Are you *blushing*?"

Though Harry turned his head away, he couldn't conceal the goofy smile that was struggling to surface, and Astra laughed delightedly. It was just too adorable.

"What's his name?"

"Bryan."

"Tell him 'hi'."

The words were out too late to retract them, and both fell silent, feeling the unbending distinction between friends and exes spring forth again like a force field.

"I—"

"Are you staying in Nevada?" Harry blurted out. Astra heard the desperate edge to the question and winced.

"Yes. I've got an apartment with Sasha. She's been offered a research position."

"And you? Did you get that job?"

"Yeah." It was impossible to stifle the wave of pleasure at the memory of her last shift at the casino, when Brad had called the team together and announced her as one of the three newest management trainees. The congratulations from her fellow team members had been sweeter than she had expected.

And the absence of Ally had been a welcome bonus. Apparently she had been offered a job at a place on the Strip. Astra wasn't convinced, but was happy to fake it.

"What about Ash?"

"We don't know yet. We'll work it out."

At the repeated 'we' Harry visibly deflated.

"Are you staying?" Astra finally asked, after an uncomfortable pause.

The normality of the question seemed to rally him.

"Yeah, I've got an IT job. Entry-level, but hey."

An uneasy shrug, and the silence spread again between them; Astra, skin crawling with discomfort, was considering a trite remark about the weather when the hallway rang with a series of strident knocks on the door.

It was Ash, and if he noticed the slightly frantic expression on Astra's face he made no comment, nor did he complain about the enthusiasm of the kiss Astra found herself giving him.

"Ash! I'm nearly packed. Just got a few more boxes." *Oh God, get me out of here.*

"I'll come up and help you—oh, hi, Delfino." Ash glanced ostentatiously over Astra's shoulder, making it clear he was perfectly aware of the situation already. "Tell me when you're done. I'll just wait in the lounge."

"Okay."

Astra turned back to face Harry before jolting under a sudden slap to her bottom.

"Don't be long, Starlight." The door to the lounge closed.

Astra was conscious of his final word—*Starlight? That's new!*—hanging in the air, the look on Harry's face now somewhere between fight and flight. Unsure of what to say, she was glad when Harry took the baton.

"I'll leave you to it."

"I'm glad you're happy," Astra said without thinking.

"You too." Harry took a breath, as if in preparation. "I'm sorry I didn't—"

"I know you are."

"I'll go now."

"Yes."

They collided in the doorway, Harry's urgency to leave impeding Astra's haste to open the door, and froze almost nose to nose.

"Can I call you?" Harry jerked out.

"Yes." *No.* "If you like."

Astra was vaguely aware of a male figure outside the door as Harry left, her attention already drawn by a drawling voice to her right.

"He's *too* precious."

"Oh, stop it." Astra half-turned, slipping easily into Ash's embrace as she fixed him with a steely look. "You're such a jock."

"I only say it 'cause it pisses you off. He can fuck who he likes." Ash arched an eyebrow, deliberately tugging her closer. "And I fuck who I *love*."

Astra had heard many professions of love from Harry, none of which meant anything anymore, but Ash's bald statement somehow did *something* to her brain. There was clearly something to be said for jocks and inarticulacy.

"Ash," she murmured, tilting her head up in a way she knew he could never resist.

"Starlight," Ash whispered back, capturing her mouth with his.

Halfway down the path, Harry turned back.

Astra was still in the hallway, but enfolded in Ash's arms. Standing there, half in the doorway, they looked almost statuesque, bathed in the May sunlight; Ash's hair luminescent, Astra's sparkling with amber and ruby lights.

She had been uncertain, unenthusiastic, about the prospect of him calling, and Harry knew, somehow, this could be the last time he saw her.

"Is that her?"

Bryan was standing beside him, his chiselled face concerned, and Harry managed a smile.

"Yeah. That's her."

"Fast mover," Bryan commented, watching the two figures in the doorway.

Harry smiled.

"That's Astra. I've never known anyone like her for playing the hand she's dealt."

His expression turned wistful, and the bump to his shoulder took him by surprise. Glancing round, he found Bryan's eyes on him, coolly understanding.

"You said goodbye?"

"Yeah. I said goodbye."

"Then let's go." Bryan's hand landed on his shoulder, comforting yet urging him onward. "Let's go, baby."

Harry looked up at him, paused, before giving a determined nod.

"Let's go."

About the Author

Tanith Davenport has been writing for ten years and first got into erotic romance through the Romantic Novelists' Association New Writer's Scheme. Besides writing, her first loves are rock music and travel. She lives in Yorkshire with her long-suffering husband and cat.

Tanith Davenport loves to hear from readers.

You can find her contact information, website details and author profile page at http://www.total-e-bound.com

Total-E-Bound Publishing

www.total-e-bound.com

Take a look at our exciting range of literagasmic™
erotic romance titles and discover pure quality
at Total-E-Bound.